E.T.A. Hoffmann

THE TALES
OF HOFFMANN

57622

*Newly selected and translated
from the German by*
MICHAEL BULLOCK

FREDERICK UNGAR PUBLISHING CO.
NEW YORK

THE TALES OF HOFFMANN

CONTENTS

THE SANDMAN

Nathanael to Lothar

You must all be very worried because I haven't written for so long. I expect Mother is angry with me and Klara may imagine I am spending my time in riotous living and have entirely forgotten my lovely angel, whose image is so deeply imprinted in my heart. But it isn't like that; I think of you all every day and every hour, and my pretty Klärchen is ever-present to my inward eye, smiling radiantly as she always did. But how could I write to you in the distracted frame of mind that has been throwing all my thoughts into disorder? Horror has entered my life. Dark premonitions of an atrocious fate loom over me like the shadows of black clouds, impervious to every ray of sunshine. I shall tell you what has happened to me. I must tell you, I can see that; but the mere thought of it sets me laughing insanely. Oh, my dearest Lothar, how can I begin to make you feel that what befell me a few days ago is capable of reducing my life to ruins? If only you were here you could judge for yourself; but as it is, I'm sure you will think that I am mad and seeing ghosts. In a word, the frightful thing which happened to me, the mortal effects of which I am trying in vain to shake off, was merely that a few days ago, on 20 October at twelve o'clock noon, a barometer-seller came into my room and offered me his wares. I bought nothing and threatened to throw him down the stairs, whereupon he left of his own accord.

You will guess that only events from my own past that deeply affected my life could have made this incident seem important and the person of this unfortunate pedlar appear to be a threat. Such is, in fact, the case. I shall do all I can to get a grip on myself and tell you calmly about my early youth so that everything appears clearly and vividly to your lively mind. As I try to begin, I can hear you laugh and Klara say: 'This is all childish nonsense!' Laugh, by all means, laugh as loud as you like. My hair is standing on end and I feel like imploring you to laugh me out of my terror. Here is my story.

Apart from the midday meal, my sisters and I saw little of our father. He must have been kept very busy by his work. After supper, which was served at seven in the old-fashioned way, we all, including Mother, used to go into Father's study and sit at a round table. Father used to smoke tobacco and drink a large glass of beer. He often used to tell us marvellous stories, getting so carried away that his pipe kept going out and I had to relight it for him by holding a piece of burning paper to it, in which I took great pleasure. There were other times, however, when he put picture books in our hands and sat mute and stiff in his armchair blowing out clouds of smoke, till we were all enveloped in a thick fog. On such evenings my mother was very dejected, and no sooner had the clock struck nine than she would say: 'Now, children, off you go to bed. The Sandman is coming, I can hear him already.'

At such times I really did hear someone clumping up the stairs with a rather heavy, slow step. 'That must be the Sandman,' I thought. One day this muffled clumping and bumping sounded particularly horrible. I asked my mother, as she led us away: 'I say, Mama, who is this naughty Sandman who always drives us away from Papa? What does he look like?'

'There isn't any Sandman, my dear child,' replied my mother. 'When I say the Sandman is coming, it only means you are sleepy and can't keep your eyes open, as though someone had thrown sand into them.'

Mother's answer didn't satisfy me, because in my childish mind I was convinced that she was only denying the existence of the Sandman to save us from being frightened—after all, I could hear him coming up the stairs. Full of curiosity to know more about this Sandman and his connexion with us children, I finally asked the old woman who looked after my youngest sister what kind of man the Sandman was.

'Oh, Thanelchen,' she replied, 'don't you know that yet? He is a wicked man who comes to children when they won't go to bed and throws handfuls of sand in their eyes, so that they pop all bloody out of their heads; then he throws them into a sack and carries them to the half-moon as food for his children; the children sit there in a nest and have crooked beaks like owls with which they gobble up the eyes of human children who have been naughty.'

A hideous picture of the cruel Sandman now formed within me; when he came clumping up the stairs in the evening I trembled with fear and horror. My mother could get nothing from me but the stammered, tearful cry: 'The Sandman! The Sandman!' Then I ran into my bedroom and was tormented all night long by visions of the atrocious Sandman.

A time came when I was old enough to know that the story of the Sandman and his children's nest in the half-moon told by my sister's nurse couldn't be entirely true; but the Sandman was still a frightful phantom to me, and I was seized with terror and horror when I heard him not merely mounting the stairs, but tearing the door of my father's room violently open and going in. He frequently stayed away for long periods; then he would come on several nights in succession. This went on for years, and I couldn't get used to the eerie spectre; my mental image of the cruel Sandman grew no paler. His dealings with my father began to exercise my imagination more and more. An insurmountable reluctance prevented me from asking my father about it; but with the passing of the years the desire to probe the mystery myself, to see the fabulous Sandman with my own eyes, was born and continually grew. The Sandman had directed my interest towards the supernatural and fantastic, which so easily takes root in the mind of a child. I liked nothing better than to hear or read gruesome tales of hob-goblins, witches, Tom Thumbs, and the like; but over

3

everything loomed the Sandman, of whom I kept drawing strange, repulsive pictures all over the place—on tables, cupboards, and walls—in charcoal and chalk.

When I was ten my mother moved me from the nursery into a little bedroom in the corridor close to my father's room. We still had to hurry away on the stroke of nine, when the footsteps of the unknown man echoed through the house. From my room I could hear him go into my father's, and it seemed to me that soon afterwards a thin, strange-smelling vapour spread through the house. As my curiosity about the Sandman grew, so did my courage. I often used to creep quickly out of my room into the corridor after my mother had passed; but I could never see anything, for the Sandman had always gone in through the door by the time I reached the spot from which he would have been visible. Finally, impelled by an irresistible urge, I resolved to hide inside my father's room and there lie in wait for the Sandman.

One evening I observed from my father's silence and my mother's dejection that the Sandman was coming. I therefore pretended to be very tired, left the room before nine o'clock, and hid in a corner close to the door. The front door grated; slow, heavy, creaking footsteps crossed the hall to the stairs. My mother hurried past me with my sisters. As quietly as I could, I opened the door of my father's room. He was sitting, as usual, silent and stiff with his back to the door; he didn't notice me; in an instant I was inside and hiding behind the curtain drawn across an open cupboard by the door, in which my father's clothes hung. Closer, ever closer creaked the footsteps; there was a strange coughing, scraping, and growling outside. My heart was pounding with fear and expectancy. There was a sharp step just outside the door; a violent blow on the latch; the door clattered open. Summoning all my courage, I peeped out. The Sandman was standing in the middle of my father's room, the bright light from the lamp full on his face. The Sandman, the terrible Sandman, was the old lawyer Coppelius, who often used to have lunch with us!

But the most hideous figure could not have inspired greater horror in me than this Coppelius. Picture to yourself a big, broad-shouldered man with a fat, shapeless head, earthy-yellow face, bushy grey eyebrows beneath which a pair of greenish cat's eyes flashed piercingly, and a large nose that curved down over the upper lip. The crooked mouth was often twisted in malicious laughter; at such moments two red patches appeared on his cheeks and a strange hissing sound came out through his clenched teeth. Coppelius always used to appear in an ash-grey coat of old-fashioned cut and a waistcoat and trousers to match, but accompanied by black stockings and shoes with small buckles set with ornamental stones. His little wig hardly reached beyond the crown of his head, his pomaded curls stood high over his big red ears, and a broad bag-wig stood out stiffly from the back of his neck, disclosing the silver buckle that joined his folded cravat. His whole appearance was odious and repulsive; but we children were repelled above all by his big, gnarled, hairy hands, which left us with a lasting aversion to anything they had touched. He noticed this, and thereafter he delighted in touching, under some pretext or other, any piece of cake or sweet fruit which our mother had slipped on to our plates, so that our eyes filled with tears, and disgust and loathing prevented us from enjoying the titbit put there for our enjoyment. It was the same when our father poured out a small glass of sweet wine for us on feast days. Coppelius would quickly pass his hand over it or even bring the glass to his blue lips, and he laughed demoniacally at the low sobs that were the only expression we could give to our anger. He always called us the little beasts; when he was present we were not allowed to make a sound, and we execrated the hateful man who went out of his way to spoil our slightest pleasure. My mother seemed to detest him just as much as we did; for the moment he appeared her natural gaiety and light-heartedness gave way to dejected brooding. My father treated him like a superior being whose boorishness had to be endured and who must at all costs be humoured. He had

5

only to drop a hint and his favourite dishes were cooked and rare wines served.

Seeing Coppelius now, the horrible conviction shot through me that he, and he alone, was the Sandman; but the Sandman was no longer the bogy of the nurse's tale, the monster who fetched children's eyes to feed his brood in the owl's nest in the half-moon; no, he was a horrible, spectral monster who spread grief and misery, temporal and eternal perdition wherever he set foot.

I was spellbound with horror. At the risk of being discovered and severely punished, as I clearly anticipated, I stayed where I was with my head stretched out through the curtains, watching. My father received Coppelius ceremoniously. 'To work!' cried the latter in a hoarse, grating voice, throwing off his coat. My father gloomily removed his dressing-gown and both of them put on black overalls. I didn't see where they got them from. My father opened the folding-door of what I had always believed to be a cupboard, but which proved to be a dark recess housing a stove. Coppelius approached the stove and a blue flame flickered up. There were all sorts of strange utensils standing round. God above!—as my old father now bent down to the fire he looked quite different. His gentle, honest features seemed to have been twisted into an ugly, repulsive grimace by some griping agony. He looked like Coppelius. The latter was wielding a pair of red-hot tongs and drawing masses of sparkling metal out of the thick smoke, which he then hammered industriously. It seemed to me that human faces were appearing on all sides, but without eyes—instead they had horrible, deep black cavities.

'Eyes, we must have eyes!' cried Coppelius in a deep, booming voice.

Overcome by uncontrollable horror, I screamed and fell out of my hiding-place on to the floor.

Coppelius seized hold of me. 'Little beast, little beast!' he screeched, grinding his teeth, dragged me to my feet and threw me on to the stove, so that the flame began to scorch my hair. 'Now we have eyes,' he whispered, 'a fine pair of child's eyes.' And he pulled glowing coal dust out of the fire with his bare hands and made as though to sprinkle it in my eyes.

At this my father raised his hands beseechingly and cried: 'Master, master, leave my Nathanael his eyes, leave him his eyes!'

Coppelius laughed shrilly and exclaimed: 'All right, let the boy keep his eyes and weep his way through the world; but now we will carefully observe the mechanism of the hands and feet.' With this, he gripped me so that my joints cracked, unscrewed my hands and feet and put them back on again now in one place, now in another. 'They're not right anywhere else! It's best the way they were! The Old Man knew what he was doing!' hissed Coppelius. But everything around me went black, a sudden convulsion ran through my nerves and bones—and I felt no more.

A warm, gentle breath passed across my face; I woke as though from death; my mother was bending over me. 'Is the Sandman still there?' I stammered. 'No, my dear child, he went long ago, he will do you no harm,' said my mother, kissing and cuddling her darling whom she had now won back.

I don't want to bore you, my dearest Lothar. There is no point in my going into details, when so much must in any case remain unsaid. Suffice it to say that I had been caught eavesdropping and manhandled by Coppelius. Terror had put me into a high fever, from which I lay ill for many weeks. 'Is the Sandman still there?' This was my first sentence spoken in health, the first sign of my recovery, my salvation.

There only remains for me to tell you of the most terrible moment in the years of my youth; then you will be convinced that my eyes do not deceive me when everything seems drained of colour, you will agree that a sombre destiny really has hung a murky veil over my life, a veil which I shall perhaps not tear apart until I die.

Nothing more was seen of Coppelius, he was said to have left the town.

One evening, about a year later, we were all sitting at the round table as we always used to. Father was very gay and was telling us all sorts of amusing tales about his youthful travels. Then suddenly, as the clock struck nine, we heard the front door creak on its hinges and slow, leaden footsteps stumped across the hall and up the stairs.

'It's Coppelius,' said my mother, turning pale.

'Yes, it's Coppelius,' repeated my father in a dull, broken voice.

The tears started from my mother's eyes. 'But Father, Father,' she cried, 'must it be like this?'

'He is coming to see me for the last time,' replied my father. 'I promise you that. Now go, and take the children with you. Go to bed, all of you. Good night.'

I felt as though I were being crushed between two heavy, cold masses of stone. I had difficulty in breathing. As I stood motionless, Mother took me by the arm. 'Come, Nathanael, come along!' I let myself be dragged away. 'Calm yourself, calm yourself, go to bed! Sleep, sleep!' my mother cried to me; but I was tortured by indescribable anxiety and couldn't close my eyes. The detestable, repulsive Coppelius stood before me with glittering eyes, laughing at me malevolently; in vain I tried to rid myself of this vision. It must have been around midnight when there was a terrible bang, like the firing of a gun. The detonation echoed through the whole house and the blast whistled past my room; doors throughout the house were slammed shut with a clatter.

'That's Coppelius!' I cried in horror, jumping out of bed. Then the air was rent by a series of despairing wails and screams. I rushed to my father's room; the door was open, suffocating smoke billowed out at me; the servant girl screamed: 'Oh, the master, oh, the master!' On the floor in front of the reeking stove, my father lay dead, his face burnt black and horribly contorted; my sisters were howling and whimpering around him and my mother lay unconscious beside him.

'Coppelius, abominable Satan, you have murdered my father!' I cried, then fell senseless to the ground.

8

Two days later, when he was put into his coffin, my father's features had become mild and gentle again, as they had been in life. I was consoled by the sudden conviction that his pact with the devilish Coppelius could not have thrust him into everlasting perdition.

The explosion had woken the neighbours; the incident was talked about and came to the ears of the authorities, who wished to proceed against Coppelius. But he had vanished from the town without a trace.

When I now tell you, my dearest friend, that the barometer-seller was the villainous Coppelius, you will not blame me for interpreting this apparition as heralding some terrible disaster. He was differently dressed, but Coppelius's face and figure are too deeply imprinted upon my mind for any mistake to be possible. Moreover, Coppelius has barely changed his name. I am told that he is passing himself off as a Piedmontese mechanic called Giuseppe Coppola.

I am resolved to have it out with him and to avenge my father's death, come what may.

Don't tell Mother anything about the arrival of the loathsome monster.

Give my love to my dear, sweet Klara. I shall write to her when I am in a calmer frame of mind.

Best wishes, etc., etc.

Klara to Nathanael

It is true that you haven't written for a long time, but nevertheless I believe that I am in your thoughts. You must have been thinking of me very vividly when you addressed your last letter to Lothar, because you wrote my name on the envelope instead of his. I joyfully opened the letter and didn't realize my mistake until I came to the words 'Oh, my dearest Lothar'. I ought to have stopped there and immediately given the letter to my brother. But even though in your childhood you used to tease me by saying that I was so calm and reflective that if the house were about to collapse and I saw a crease in the curtain, I should quickly smooth it out before fleeing the doomed building, nevertheless I need hardly assure you that the beginning of your letter distressed me profoundly. I could scarcely breathe, and everything swam before my eyes. 'Oh, my beloved Nathanael,' I thought, 'what terrible thing can have entered your life? Are we perhaps to part and never see one another again?' The thought pierced my breast like a stab with a red-hot dagger. I read on and on. From your description Coppelius sounds horrible. I never knew before that your good old father died such a dreadful death. When I passed the letter on to its rightful owner my brother Lothar tried to pacify me, but he wasn't very successful. The baleful barometer-seller Giuseppe Coppola dogged my every step, and I am almost ashamed to confess that he succeeded in disturbing my normally sound and peaceful sleep with all kinds of fantastic dream images. But by next morning I saw everything differently. Don't be angry with me, my dearly beloved, if Lothar tells you that, in spite of your strange presentiment that Coppelius will do you some harm, I am still just as gay and light-hearted as ever.

I will admit straight out that in my opinion all the terrible things you speak of happened only within your own mind and that the outer world had very little part in them. Old Coppelius may well have been a repulsive character, but it was because he hated children that you children developed such an aversion towards him.

Of course the dreadful Sandman of the nurse's tale became linked in your child's mind with old Coppelius, whom, even when you no longer believed in the Sandman, you still regarded as a monster especially dangerous to children. The sinister nocturnal activities in which he had your father engaged were nothing but clandestine alchemistic experiments, which were bound to displease your mother because they are sure to have resulted in a great deal of money being wasted; moreover, as always happens in such cases, your father's mind must have become filled with the illusory desire to acquire higher wisdom and thereby diverted from his family. Your father's death was undoubtedly due to his own carelessness and not Coppelius's fault. Yesterday I asked the experienced apothecary who lives next door whether such instantly lethal explosions could occur during chemical experiments. He replied, 'Most certainly,' and went on to explain at length and in detail how this might happen, mentioning so many strange-sounding names that I can't remember any of them.

Now you will probably be annoyed with your Klara, you will say: 'No ray of the mysterious forces that often clasp men in their invisible arms can penetrate that cold spirit; she sees only the colourful surface of life and rejoices over it, like the thoughtless child over the bright and shining fruit within which poison lurks.'

Oh, my dearly beloved Nathanael, don't you believe that gay, light-hearted, care-free spirits may also sense the presence of dark powers within ourselves that are bent upon our destruction? But forgive me if, simple girl that I am, I try to show you what I really think about such inner conflicts. In the end, I shan't be able to find the right words and you will laugh not at what I say, but at the clumsy way in which I say it.

If there is a malignant power that treacherously introduces a thread into our hearts, by means of which it then drags us along a dangerous, a ruinous path which we should never have trodden of our own accord, then it must become part of us, part of our own self; for only thus shall we believe it and give it the freedom of action it needs in order to carry out its secret purpose. But if our minds are firm enough and sufficiently strengthened by a happy life always to recognize alien, hostile influences and to proceed with calm steps along the path chosen by our own inclinations, the sinister power perishes in the vain attempt to create the shape that is to serve as a reflection of ourselves.

'There can also be no doubt,' adds Lothar to this, 'that once we have surrendered ourselves to the dark physical power, it frequently draws inside us external figures thrown in our path by the world; then it is we ourselves who endow these figures with the life with which, in wild delusion, we credit them.'

You see, my dearly beloved Nathanael, that my brother Lothar and I have discussed the question of malignant powers at length, and now that I have, not without difficulty, written down the main points in our argument it all seems very profound. I don't entirely understand Lothar's last words, I have only an inkling of what he means, and yet it all seems to me very true. Cast the horrible lawyer Coppelius and the barometer man Giuseppe Coppola entirely out of your mind, I beg of you. Be sure that these external figures cannot harm you; only your belief in their baneful power can make them baneful to you in reality. If the profound agitation of your mind was not apparent from every line of your letter, if your suffering did not cut me to the quick, I assure you I could laugh about the lawyer, Sandman, and barometer-seller Coppelius. Be cheerful, cheerful! I have made up my mind to come to you like a guardian angel, and, if he lets me near him, to scare nasty old Coppola away with loud laughter. I'm not in the very least afraid of him and his horrid hands; he isn't going to spoil my titbits as a lawyer nor my eyes as the Sandman.

For ever, my best beloved Nathanael, etc., etc., etc.

Nathanael to Lothar

I'm very sorry that, as a result of my slip, Klara accidentally opened and read my recent letter to you. She wrote me a very profound and philosophical letter in reply, in which she sets out to prove that Coppelius and Coppola exist only within me and are phantoms of my own ego, which would instantly fall to dust if I recognized them as such. It is hard to believe that the mind which shines forth from her bright and smiling child's eyes, that are like a vision in a dream, is capable of such a sagacious and masterly interpretation. She quotes you. The two of you have been talking about me. You must have been lecturing her, teaching her to see and analyse things clearly. Stop it! Anyhow, it is now quite certain that the barometer-seller Giuseppe Coppola is not the old lawyer Coppelius. I am attending lectures by the new professor of physics, who, like the famous natural philosopher, is called Spallanzani and is of Italian origin. He has known Coppola for many years, and apart from this you can tell that Coppola really is a Piedmontese from his accent. Coppelius was a German, though, I suspect, not a true German. I am not entirely reassured. You and Klara may continue to think me a gloomy dreamer, but I cannot get Coppelius's accursed face out of my mind. I'm glad he has left the city, as Spallanzani tells me.

This professor is an extraordinary fellow. A tubby little man with protruding cheek-bones, a slender nose, thick lips, and small, piercing eyes. But if you look at an engraving of Cagliostro by Chodowiecki in some Berlin calendar it will give you a far more accurate idea of his appearance than any description of mine. That's what Spallanzani looks like. As I went up the stairs in his house the other day I noticed a narrow gap on one side of the curtain that is generally drawn across a particular glass door. I don't know myself how I came to do such a thing, but I inquisitively peeped through. There was a tall, very slim, beautifully proportioned, magnificently dressed woman sitting in the room at a small table, on which both arms were resting with folded hands. She was facing the door, so that I could see the whole of her angelically lovely face. She didn't seem to notice me, and there was a curiously fixed look in her eyes, almost as though they lacked the power of vision, as though she were asleep with her eyes open. It gave me an uncanny sensation and I quickly slipped away into the lecture-room, which is next door. Later I learnt that the figure I had seen was Spallanzani's daughter Olympia, whom for some strange reason he wickedly keeps shut up, never allowing anyone near her. Perhaps there is something the matter with her; perhaps she is a half-wit or something.

I don't know why I am writing you all this: I could have told you everything better and at greater length by word of mouth. The fact is, I am coming to stay with you for a fortnight. I must see my sweet angel, my Klara, again. That will blow away all the ill-humour which, I must admit, took possession of me after her terribly sensible letter. That's why I'm not writing to her as well today.

A thousand greetings, etc., etc.

Here I must add a word about the background to the extraordinary events which befell the student Nathanael, and which are introduced by the foregoing letters. Soon after his father died, Klara and Lothar, the children of a distant relative who had likewise died and left them orphans, were taken in by Nathanael's mother. Klara and Nathanael quickly conceived a passionate affection for one another, to which no one in the world had any objection to raise. They therefore became engaged when Nathanael left the town to pursue his studies at G———. His letters were written from G———, where he was attending lectures by the famous professor of physics, Spallanzani.

Klara was considered by many people cold, unfeeling, prosaic, because of her clarity of vision and impatience with hocus-pocus; but others, better able to distinguish the true from the false, dearly loved the spirited, sympathetic, and unsophisticated girl; none loved her so deeply as Nathanael, a man well versed in the arts and sciences. Klara was whole-heartedly devoted to her beloved, and the first shadow fell across her life the day he parted from her. With what delight she flew into his arms when now, as he had announced in his last letter to Lothar, he returned to his native town and entered his mother's room. As Nathanael had foreseen, the moment he saw Klara he thought neither of the lawyer Coppelius nor of Klara's over-sensible letter; all his ill humour vanished.

Yet Nathanael was quite right when he wrote to his friend Lothar that the entry of the repulsive barometer-seller Coppola into his life had been fraught with disastrous consequences. This was evident to everyone in the first few days of his visit, for Nathanael's whole nature had changed. He sank into gloomy brooding and behaved in an extraordinary way quite unlike his normal self. Life seemed to have become for him nothing but dream and foreboding; he kept on saying that everyone who imagined himself free was really the plaything of dark and cruel powers; it was useless to rebel, we all had to bow humbly to our destiny. He went so far as to assert that it was foolish to suppose that man's creative activities in the fields of art and science were the outcome of free will, claiming that the inspiration which enables us to create does not come from within us, but is imposed upon us by some higher power outside ourselves.

The clear-headed Klara found all this mystical nonsense in the highest degree objectionable, but it seemed pointless to contradict. She said nothing until Nathanael stated that Coppelius was an evil spirit, as he had realized when he eavesdropped upon him from behind the curtain, and that this abominable demon would wreak havoc with their happiness. Then Klara replied very seriously: 'Yes, Nathanael, you are right: Coppelius is an evil, malignant spirit; he can exercise the terrible powers of a demon incarnate; but only if you do not banish him from your mind. So long as you believe in him, he will exist and interfere with you; it is only your belief that gives him power.'

Angered by Klara's refusal to credit the demon's existence outside his own mind, Nathanael was about to launch into a disquisition on the whole mystical doctrine of devils and sinister powers, when to his annoyance Klara brought the conversation to a close with some casual interruption. He thought to himself that people with cold, insensitive natures render themselves inaccessible to profound mysteries of this kind. But since he was not fully aware of numbering Klara among people of inferior sensibility, he continued his efforts to initiate her into these mysteries. While Klara was getting breakfast in the morning, he stood beside her, reading aloud from all sorts of mystical books, till Klara commented: 'You know, you are the evil spirit that is threatening to spoil my coffee. If I were to drop everything, as you want me to, and look into your eyes while you read, the coffee would boil over and none of you would get any breakfast.' Nathanael slammed the book shut and made off to his room, much put out.

In the ordinary way, he had a notable gift for making up delightful and amusing stories, to which Klara listened with the greatest pleasure; now his tales were gloomy, unintelligible, formless, and although Klara refrained from saying so to spare his feelings, he could feel how little she liked them. Klara found nothing more deadly than boredom, and her uncontrollable drowsiness was expressed in her eyes and voice. Nathanael's tales were indeed very tedious. His resentment at Klara's cold, prosaic mind increased; Klara could not overcome her dislike of Nathanael's dark, gloomy, dreary mysticism; and so the two of them drifted farther and farther apart without realizing it. Nathanael himself had to admit that the image of the atrocious Coppelius had paled within him, and it often cost him an effort to give life to this figure when he introduced him into his writings in the role of a sinister bogy-man. Eventually he made a poem out of his dark foreboding that Coppelius would destroy his happiness in love. He portrayed himself and Klara as bound in true love but plagued by a black hand that thrust itself between them and snatched away their joy. In the end, when they were already at the altar, the abominable Coppelius appeared and touched Klara's lovely eyes, which sprang into Nathanael's breast, searing him like blood-red sparks. Coppelius seized hold of him and flung him into a circle of flames that spun round and round with the speed and noise of a whirlwind and dragged him away. There was a roaring sound like a hurricane whipping up the waves of the sea so that they reared up in revolt like black giants with heads of white foam. But through this fierce roaring he heard Klara's voice: 'Can't you see me? Coppelius has tricked you. Those weren't my eyes that burnt into your breast, they were red-hot drops of your own heart's blood. I still have my eyes—just look at me!' Nathanael thought: 'That is Klara, I am hers for ever.' Then it was as though this thought had taken a grip upon the circle of flame, which came to a stop, while the roaring sound died away in the black abyss. Nathanael gazed into Klara's eyes; but it was death that looked at him with Klara's friendly eyes.

While Nathanael was composing this poem he was very calm and serene; he worked and polished each line, and since he had assumed the yoke of metre he did not rest until the whole poem was flawless and euphonious. But when at last he had finished and read it aloud to himself, he was seized with horror and cried out: 'Whose hideous voice is that?' Soon, however, the whole thing once more seemed nothing but a very successful poem, and he felt convinced that Klara's cold temperament would be set afire by it; though he had no very clear idea why Klara should be set afire or what purpose would be served by frightening her with these horrifying visions which predicted a terrible fate and the destruction of their love.

Nathanael and Klara were sitting in his mother's little garden; Klara was very cheerful because during the three days he had spent writing the poem Nathanael had ceased bothering her with his dreams and premonitions. Instead he talked gaily of things that amused her, as in the past, which led Klara to remark: 'Now I've really got you back entirely. You see how we have driven out old Coppelius?'

At this, Nathanael remembered that he was carrying in his pocket the poem he had intended to read aloud. He immediately pulled out the sheets of paper and started reading. Klara, expecting something boring as usual and making the best of the situation, quietly started knitting. But as the threatening cloud of the poem grew blacker and blacker, she let the stocking she was knitting sink down and gazed fixedly into Nathanael's eyes. The latter was carried away by his own poem; emotion had coloured his cheeks bright red; tears poured from his eyes. Finally, he came to a stop, gave a groan of utter exhaustion, took Klara's hand, and sighed as though dissolving in hopeless grief: 'Oh—Klara— Klara!'

Klara pressed him tenderly to her bosom and said in a low voice, but very slowly and gravely: 'Nathanael, my

17

dearly beloved Nathanael, throw the mad, senseless, insane fairy tale into the fire.'

Thereupon, Nathanael sprang to his feet indignantly, pushed Klara away from him and cried: 'You lifeless damned automaton!' Then he hurried away.

Deeply hurt, Klara wept bitterly and sobbed loudly: 'He can never have loved me, since he doesn't understand me.'

Lothar came into the arbour and made Klara tell him what had happened. He loved his sister with all his soul, and every word of her complaint fell into his heart like a spark, so that the hostility he had long felt for the visionary Nathanael flared up into furious rage. He ran to Nathanael and reproached him for his senseless behaviour towards his beloved sister in harsh words, which the irascible Nathanael answered in kind. 'Crazy addle-brained dreamer' was answered by 'Miserable dull-witted oaf'. A duel was inevitable. They agreed to fight next morning outside the garden with sharpened rapiers, in accordance with the custom at the local university. They stalked about mute and scowling; Klara had heard the violent argument and saw the fencing master bring the rapiers after dusk. She guessed what was afoot.

Having arrived at the duelling ground and cast off their coats in grim silence, blood-thirsty battle-lust in their blazing eyes, Lothar and Nathanael were on the point of falling upon one another when Klara rushed out of the garden gate. Sobbing, she cried out: 'You ferocious beasts! Strike me down before you set upon each other; for how can I go on living if my lover has murdered my brother, or my brother my lover?'

Lothar lowered his weapon and stared in silence at the ground; but in Nathanael's heart all the love he had felt for sweet Klara in the finest days of his youth came to life again accompanied by an agonizing nostalgia. The murderous weapon fell from his hand and he flung himself at Klara's feet. 'Can you ever forgive me, my one and only, my beloved Klara? Can you forgive me, my dearest brother Lothar?'

Lothar was moved by his friend's profound anguish; all three embraced in tearful reconciliation and swore ever-lasting love and friendship.

Nathanael felt as though a heavy burden had been lifted from him, as if, by resisting the dark power that had held him in thrall, he had saved his whole being from annihilation. He spent another three days with his dear friends and then went back to G——, where he had to remain for another year before returning home for good.

Not a word about Coppelius was said to Nathanael's mother; they all knew she could not think of him without horror, since, like Nathanael, she blamed him for her husband's death.

On returning to his lodgings Nathanael was astounded to find that the whole house had been burnt down, leaving nothing standing but the bare chimney shafts. The fire had broken out in the apothecary's laboratory on the ground floor and spread upwards; consequently there had been time for Nathanael's courageous and active friends to force their way into his room on the top floor and save his books, manuscripts, and instruments. They had transported everything undamaged to a room they had rented for him in another house, into which he at once moved. He did not pay any particular attention to the fact that he was now living opposite Professor Spallanzani; nor did he attach any special significance to the discovery that he could see out of his window straight into the room in which Olympia often sat alone, so that he could clearly distinguish her figure even though her features remained blurred. It did finally strike him that Olympia frequently sat for hours on end at a small table in the same position in which he had seen her when he looked through the glass door, doing nothing and staring across at him with an unwavering gaze. He had to admit that he had never seen a lovelier figure; at the same time, with Klara in his heart, he remained totally indifferent to the stiff and rigid Olympia, and only every now and then did he glance up from his textbook at the beautiful statue for a fleeting instant.

He was just writing to Klara when there was a soft knock at the door. It opened at his invitation and Coppola's repulsive face looked in. Nathanael quivered inwardly; but after what Spallanzani had told him about his countryman Coppola, and what he had solemnly promised his sweetheart regarding the Sandman Coppelius, he felt ashamed of his childish fear of ghosts, forcibly pulled himself together, and said as gently and calmly as he could: 'I don't want a barometer, go away, please.'

At this, however, Coppola came right into the room and exclaimed in a hoarse voice, his wide mouth twisted in a horrible laugh and his small eyes gleaming piercingly under their long, grey lashes: 'All righta, no barometer! But I've gotta lovely eyes, lovely eyes!'

Horrified, Nathanael cried: 'Eyes, you madman? How can you have eyes.'

Coppola instantly put away his barometers, thrust his hand into his capacious coat pockets, took out lorgnettes and spectacles and laid them down on the table. 'See—see—spectacles to put ona your nose, those are my eyes, my lovely eyes!'

So saying, he pulled out more and more spectacles, till the whole table began to glitter and sparkle. A myriad eyes glanced and winked and stared up at Nathanael; he could not look away from the table; Coppola laid down more and more spectacles, and the blood-red beams of their intersecting gaze flared in ever-wilder confusion and pierced Nathanael's breast. Overcome by uncontrollable horror, he seized Coppola's arm and cried out: 'Stop, stop, you terrible man!'

Coppola, who had just been reaching into his pocket for more spectacles, although the table was already covered, gently freed himself with the words: 'Nothing there you lika? Well, here are fina glasses.' So saying, he swept up the spectacles, put them back in his pocket, and drew a number of binoculars of all sizes from the side pocket of his coat. As soon as the spectacles had gone Nathanael became quite calm and, thinking of Klara, he could see that the terrifying spectre was solely the product of his own mind and that Coppola was a perfectly honest mechanic and optician and could not possibly be the double or ghost of the accursed Coppelius. Moreover, there was nothing out of the way about the binoculars which Coppola now put on the table, certainly nothing weird and ghostly as there had been about the spectacles. To make up for his previous behaviour, Nathanael decided to buy something. He picked up a small, very neatly made pair of pocket binoculars and looked out of the window to test them. Never in his life had he come across binoculars which brought objects so clear and close before his eyes. Involuntarily, he looked into Spallanzani's room; Olympia was sitting at the small table as usual, her arms resting on it and her hands folded.

Now, for the first time, Nathanael caught sight of Olympia's beautifully formed face. Only her eyes appeared to him curiously fixed and dead. But as he stared more and more intently through the glasses it seemed as though humid moonbeams were beginning to shine in Olympia's eyes. It was as though the power of sight were only now awaking, the flame of life flickering more and more brightly. Nathanael leaned out of the window as though bound to the spot by a spell, staring unceasingly at Olympia's heavenly beauty.

The sound of a throat being cleared woke him as though out of a deep sleep. Coppola was standing behind him. '*Tre zechini*—three ducats,' he said. Nathanael, who had completely forgotten the optician, quickly paid him what he asked. 'A fine pair of glasses, eh?' asked Coppola with his repulsive hoarse voice and malevolent laugh.

'Yes, yes,' replied Nathanael irritably. 'Goodbye, my friend.'

Coppola left the room, but not without casting many strange sidelong glances at Nathanael. He heard the optician laughing loudly as he went down the stairs. 'Aha,' thought Nathanael, 'I suppose he is laughing at me because I paid too dearly for the binoculars—I paid too dearly!' As he muttered these words softly to himself, he seemed to hear a deep sigh, like a dying man's, echo terrifyingly round the room, and fear stopped his breath. But it was he himself who had sighed, he realized that. 'Klara is quite right to consider me a preposterous ghost-seer,' he told himself; 'it is stupid, more than stupid to be so strangely frightened by the foolish thought that I paid too dearly for Coppola's binoculars; I can see absolutely no reason for it.'

Then he sat down to finish his letter to Klara; but a glance out of the window showed him that Olympia was still sitting where she had been, and instantly, as though impelled by an irresistible force, he jumped up, seized Coppola's glasses, and could not tear himself away from the seductive vision of Olympia until his friend Siegmund called him to Professor Spallanzani's lecture. The curtain was pulled right across the fateful door and he could catch no glimpse of Olympia. Nor did he see her during the next two days, although he hardly left his window and kept on looking across through Coppola's binoculars. On the third day her window was actually covered with a curtain. In utter despair and driven by longing and hot desire, he hurried out beyond the city gates. Olympia's figure floated before him in the air, emerged from the undergrowth, and stared at him with big, shining eyes out of the sparkling stream. Klara's image had completely faded from his mind; he thought of nothing but Olympia and lamented in a loud and tearful voice: 'O my lofty, noble star of love, did you rise only to vanish again and leave me in a gloomy, hopeless darkness?'

On his return home, he became aware of a great deal of noise and activity in Spallanzani's house. The doors were open, all sorts of gear was being carried in, the first-floor windows had been taken off their hinges, maids were busily sweeping and dusting, running to and fro with big hair-brooms, while inside the house carpenters and upholsterers were banging and hammering. Nathanael stood stock still in the street with amazement. Siegmund came up to him and asked with a laugh: 'Well, what do you say about old

Spallanzani?' Nathanael replied that he couldn't say anything, because he knew absolutely nothing about the Professor; on the contrary, he observed to his astonishment that the silent, gloomy house had become the scene of feverish activity. Siegmund told him that tomorrow Spallanzani was giving a big party, concert, and ball, to which half the university was invited. Rumour had it that Spallanzani was going to show his daughter in public for the first time, after for so long anxiously concealing her from human eyes.

Nathanael received an invitation card and went to the Professor's house at the appointed hour, when carriages were already driving up and lights shining in the decorated rooms. The gathering was large and brilliant. Olympia made her appearance very richly and tastefully dressed. Everyone admired her beautifully modelled face and figure. Her rather strange hollow back and wasp waist seemed the result of excessively tight clothing. There was something measured and stiff about her gait and posture that struck many people as unpleasant, but it was attributed to a feeling of constraint due to the social occasion. The concert began. Olympia played the harpsichord with great proficiency and also sang a *bravura aria* in a high-pitched, almost shrill, bell-like voice. Nathanael was quite enchanted; he was standing in the back row and could not fully distinguish Olympia's features in the dazzling candlelight. Surreptitiously, therefore, he pulled out Coppola's binoculars and looked at her.

He discovered to his astonishment that she was gazing at him full of longing, that every note she sang was reflected in the amorous glances which pierced and set fire to his heart. Her skilful roulades seemed to Nathanael the heavenly exultations of a spirit transfigured by love, and when finally the *cadenza* of the long trill echoed shrilly through the room, he felt as though he were being clasped by her hot arms and, unable to restrain his anguish and delight, he shouted loudly: 'Olympia.' Everyone looked round at him and many laughed. The organist from the cathedral merely pulled an even sourer face than before, however, and said: 'Now, now!' The concert was at an end, the ball began.

'Now to dance—with her!' This was Nathanael's one wish and purpose; but how was he to find the courage to ask the queen of the festivities to dance with him? And yet, after the dance had started, he found himself to his own surprise standing close by Olympia, who had not yet been asked to dance. Barely able to stammer a few words, he seized her hand. It was like ice; a cold shudder passed through him; he gazed into Olympia's eyes, which beamed back at him full of love and longing; and at the same instant a pulse seemed to start beating in the cold hand and the warm life-blood started flowing. Simultaneously the fires of love in Nathanael's breast began to burn more brightly; he put his arm round the lovely Olympia and whirled with her through the lines of dancers.

He imagined that he had been dancing in very good time to the music, but he soon observed from the peculiar, fixed rhythm in which Olympia danced and which often confused him, that he was badly out of step. Nevertheless, he did not want to dance with any other woman and would have felt like murdering anyone else who asked Olympia to dance. To his astonishment this happened only twice, however; thereafter Olympia was left sitting at every dance and he partnered her again and again. Had Nathanael had eyes for anything but the lovely Olympia, any number of unpleasant quarrels would have been inevitable; for the half-suppressed laughter that broke out in this corner or in that among the young men was obviously directed towards the lovely Olympia, whom for some unknown reason the students continually watched.

Heated by the dancing and the plentiful wine he had drunk, Nathanael had cast aside all his usual shyness. He sat beside Olympia, her hand in his, and spoke with burning fervour of his love in words that no one understood, neither he nor Olympia. But perhaps the latter did, for she gazed steadfastly into his eyes and sighed time after time: 'Oh—oh—oh!' Whereupon Nathanael exclaimed: 'O magnificent, heavenly woman—ray shining from love's land of promise beyond this earthly realm—deep soul in which my whole being is mirrored,' and more of the same kind; but Olympia merely went on sighing: 'Oh, oh!'

Professor Spallanzani walked past the happy couple and gave them a curiously satisfied smile. It seemed to Nathanael that, although he himself was in a totally different and higher world, it was getting noticeably dark down here in Professor Spallanzani's house; he looked round and saw with no little dismay that the last two lights in the room were burning low and on the point of going out. Music and dancing had long since come to an end. 'We must part, we must part,' he shouted in wild despair; he kissed Olympia's hand, then he bent down to her mouth; ice-cold lips met his burning hot ones! Just as when he touched Olympia's cold hand, he felt a shudder run through him; the legend of the dead bride flashed across his mind; but Olympia had pressed him to her, and in the kiss her lips seemed to warm to life.

Professor Spallanzani walked slowly through the empty room; his steps echoed hollowly and his figure looked sinister and ghostly as the shadows cast by the guttering candles played over it.

'Do you love me? Do you love me, Olympia? Just say one word! Do you love me?' Nathanael whispered, but all Olympia sighed as she stood up was, 'Oh, oh, oh!'

'My lovely, splendid star of love,' said Nathanael, 'now that you have appeared to me you will illumine my soul for evermore!'

'Oh, oh!' replied Olympia as she strode away.

Nathanael followed her; they came to a stop in front of the Professor. 'You had an extraordinarily animated conversation with my daughter,' said the latter with a smile. 'If you like talking to the stupid girl, my dear Nathanael, you are welcome to visit us at any time.'

Nathanael left with all heaven ablaze in his breast. Spallanzani's party was the talk of the town for the next few days. Despite the fact that the Professor had done everything to create an impression of magnificence, wits found plenty of *gaucheries* and oddities to comment upon. A particular target of criticism was the rigid, mute Olympia, who, notwithstanding her beautiful outward appearance, was credited with total idiocy, which was assumed to be the reason why Spallanzani had kept her hidden for so long. Nathanael felt inwardly enraged as he listened to all this, but he said nothing. 'What would be the use of pointing out to these fellows that it is their own idiocy that prevents them from recognizing Olympia's profound and splendid mind?' he thought to himself.

'Will you please tell me, friend,' Siegmund said to him one day, 'how an intelligent fellow like you can possibly have fallen for that waxen-faced wooden doll across the road?'

Nathanael was about to fly into a rage, but he quickly gained control of himself and answered: 'Tell me, Siegmund, how Olympia's heavenly charms have escaped your eye, normally so quick to discern beauty, and your alert mind? And yet on that account, thanks be to fate, I do not have you as a rival; for if we were rivals one of us would die a violent death.'

Siegmund saw how things stood with his friend, adroitly gave way, and after stating that there was never any point in arguing about the object of a person's love, added: 'But it is strange that many of us are of very much the same opinion about Olympia. She seems to us—forgive me for saying so, friend—curiously stiff and inert. Her figure is symmetrical and so is her face, that's true. She might be considered beautiful, if her eyes were not so completely devoid of life, I would almost say of vision. Her walk is strangely measured, every movement seems to be controlled by clockwork. She plays and sings with the unpleasantly accurate but lifeless rhythm of a singing machine, and her dancing is the same. We found Olympia thoroughly un-canny, we didn't want to have anything to do with her, we felt she was only acting the part of a living being and that there was something odd about her.'

Nathanael did not yield to the feeling of bitterness that assailed him as he listened to Siegmund's words; mastering his resentment, he merely said very gravely: 'Olympia may well appear uncanny to you cold, prosaic people. A poetic nature is accessible only to the poet. Her loving gaze reached me alone and irradiated my thoughts and feelings; only in Olympia's love do I find myself. You may not like the fact that she does not chatter away and make dull conversation like most shallow-minded people. She utters few words, it's true; but those few words are true hieroglyphs that express the inner world filled with love and higher knowledge of the spiritual life as seen from the viewpoint of the world beyond. But you have no understanding for all this and I am wasting my words.'

'May God preserve you, friend,' said Siegmund very gently, almost sadly. 'It seems to me that you are on an evil path. You can rely on me if everything—no, I will say no more!'

Nathanael suddenly had the feeling that the cold, prosaic Siegmund meant very well by him; he therefore shook the proffered hand with great warmth.

Nathanael had totally forgotten that there was in the world a girl called Klara, whom he used to love. His mother . . . Lothar . . . they had all vanished from his memory; he lived only for Olympia, with whom he sat for hours on end every day talking wildly of love, sympathy, and the affinity of souls, to all of which Olympia listened with great reverence. From the depths of his desk, Nathanael dug up everything he had ever written. There were poems, fantasies, novels, stories, and the number was increasing daily by a multitude of high-flown sonnets, stanzas, canzonets. All this he read to Olympia for hours at a time without tiring. Never had he found such a wonderful listener. She didn't embroider or knit, she didn't stare out of the window, she didn't play with a lap-dog or cat, she didn't twist scraps of paper or anything else between her fingers, she had no need to force a cough to cover up a yawn; she gazed stead-fastly into her lover's eyes for hours on end without moving,

27

and her own eyes became continually more ardent, more alive. Only when Nathanael stood up and kissed her hand and her lips, did she murmur, 'Oh, oh!' and then, 'Good night, dearest!'

'O glorious, profound soul,' cried Nathanael when he was back in his room, 'you, and you alone, understand me utterly.' He trembled with inward delight when he thought of the wonderful harmony that was growing daily between his mind and Olympia's; it seemed to him that Olympia had spoken about his works, about his whole poetic talent, from the depths of his own soul, as though the voice had come from within himself. This must indeed have been the case, for Olympia never uttered a word more than those already recorded, but even at moments of lucidity, for example on first waking up in the morning, when Nathanael became aware of Olympia's passivity and taciturnity, he said to himself: 'What are mere words? A single look from her heavenly eyes expresses more than any earthly language. Can a child of heaven confine herself within the narrow circle drawn by wretched earthly needs?'

Professor Spallanzani seemed highly delighted over his daughter's relations with Nathanael, giving the latter all sorts of unequivocal signs of his benevolence; and when Nathanael ventured to drop a few oblique hints about a possible union with his daughter, the Professor smiled all over his face and commented that he would leave his daughter a completely free choice.

Encouraged by these words, and with burning desire in his heart, Nathanael resolved to beseech Olympia the very next day to put clearly into words what her loving glances had long since told him: that she wished to be his for evermore. He looked for the ring his mother had given him when he left, intending to bestow it upon Olympia as a symbol of his devotion and of the new life upon which they were about to embark together. As he looked he came across the letters from Klara and Lothar; he cast them indifferently aside, found the ring, put it in his pocket, and hurried across to Olympia.

While still on the stairs and landing he heard an extra-ordinary hubbub that seemed to be coming from Spallan-zani's study: stamping, clattering, thudding, banging on the door, interspersed with curses and imprecations. 'Let go, let go, you rogue, you villain! . . . Did I give everything I had for that? . . . Ha ha ha ha, that wasn't our wager. . . . I made the eyes. . . . And I the clockwork. . . . To hell with you and your wretched clockwork, you paltry mechanic! . . . Satan. . . . stop. . . . Miserable wise-twister. . . . Fiendish beast! . . . Stop. . . . Get out. . . . Let go!' The voices that thus raved in indistinguishable confusion were those of Spallanzani and the abominable Coppelius.

Nathanael rushed in, seized by a nameless fear. The Pro-fessor was holding a female figure by the shoulders, Coppola the Italian had her by the feet, and they were twisting and tugging her this way and that, fighting for her with un-bridled rage. Nathanael recoiled in horror when he recog-nized the figure as Ólympia. Bursting with fury, he was about to tear his beloved away from the frantic pair when Coppola, twisting the figure with a giant's strength, wrenched it from the Professor's hands and struck him such a blow with it that he toppled backwards over the table—on which stood phials, retorts, bottles, and glass cylinders—staggered and fell; all the vessels crashed to the ground in fragments. Then Coppola threw the figure over his shoulder and ran down the stairs with a terrible, screeching laugh, the figure's dangling feet bumping and rapping woodenly on the stairs as he ran.

Nathanael stood transfixed—he had seen all too clearly that Olympia's deathly pale waxen face had no eyes, but only black cavities: she was a lifeless doll. Spallanzani was writhing on the floor; his head, chest, and arm had been cut by broken glass, and the blood was pouring out like water from a spring. But he summoned his strength and cried: 'After him, after him, what are you waiting for? Coppelius has stolen my best automaton. I worked on it for twenty years, I put everything into it. The mechanism, the walk, the power of speech are mine; the eyes he stole from you. The villain, the rogue, after him, bring back my Olympia. There are your eyes!'

Now Nathanael saw a pair of blood-flecked eyes staring up at him from the floor; Spallanzani seized them in his uninjured hand and flung them at his breast. Then madness gripped him with red-hot claws and entered into him, disrupting his mind and senses. 'Hoa—hoa—hoa! Circle of flames, circle of flames, spin circle of flames—merrily— merrily! Wooden doll—hoa—spin, wooden doll. . . .' With these words he hurled himself upon the Professor and squeezed his throat. He would have throttled him, but the din had attracted a number of people, who forced their way in and pulled off the frenzied Nathanael, thus saving the life of the Professor, whose wounds were then bandaged. Strong as he was, Siegmund was unable to hold his raging friend, who kept screaming, 'Wooden doll, spin,' at the top of his voice and striking about him with his fists. He was finally overcome by the united efforts of several men, who threw him to the ground and tied him up. His words degenerated into a hideous animal bellowing. Frenziedly struggling, he was taken away to the madhouse.

Before continuing my account of what happened to the unfortunate Nathanael I should like to assure any reader who may feel some sympathy with the skilful mechanic and automata-maker Spallanzani that he completely recovered from his wounds. He had to leave the university, however, because Nathanael's story had attracted a great deal of attention, and people considered it unpardonable deceit to have smuggled a wooden doll into well-conducted tea parties (which Olympia had, in fact, successfully attended) in the guise of a living person. Jurists called it a fraudulent imposture and considered it worthy of all the more severe punishment because it was directed against the public and undetected by anyone (apart from a few highly intelligent students)—although everyone, wise after the event, now pointed to all sorts of facts which they claimed had struck them as suspicious. There was very little sense in these claims, however. Why, for example, should anyone's suspicions have been aroused by the fact that, according to an elegant gentleman given to attending tea parties, Olympia had contradicted the normal custom by sneezing more often than she yawned? This gentleman claimed that the sneezing automatically wound up Olympia's hidden mechanism, which had audibly creaked as she sneezed, and so on. The professor of poetry and rhetoric took a pinch of snuff, snapped his snuff-box shut, cleared his throat, and solemnly declared: 'Ladies and gentlemen, do you not see the point of it all? The whole thing is an allegory— an extended metaphor! You understand what I mean! *Sapienti sat!'*

But many gentlemen were not reassured; the story of the automaton had made a deep impression, and a horrible distrust of human figures insinuated itself into people's minds. To make sure they were not in love with a wooden doll, many lovers insisted upon their mistresses singing and dancing out of time, embroidering, knitting, or playing with a lap-dog while being read to, and, above all, not merely listening but also speaking from time to time in such a way as to prove that they really thought and felt. Many lovers became more firmly and joyfully allied than ever, but others gradually drifted apart. 'You really can't be sure,' commented a few. At tea parties people yawned with tremendous frequency and never sneezed, to avert all possible suspicion.

Spallanzani, as I have said, had to leave the city to escape criminal proceedings for fraudulently introducing an automaton into human society. Coppola had also disappeared.

Nathanael awoke as though out of a frightful dream, opened his eyes, and felt an indescribable bliss permeate him with a gentle, heavenly warmth. He was lying on the bed in his room at home; Klara was bending over him, and his mother and Lothar were standing close by.

'At last, at last, my dearly beloved Nathanael. Now you are cured of your terrible illness, now you are mine again!' cried Klara from the depths of her heart, taking Nathanael into her arms.

31

Bright, hot tears of longing and delight welled from his eyes, and he groaned: 'Klara, my Klara!'

Siegmund, who had stood loyally by his friend in his hour of need, came in. Nathanael held out his hand to him, saying: 'Faithful friend, you did not forsake me.'

All trace of madness had vanished, and Nathanael soon regained his strength in the loving care of his mother, sweetheart, and friends. Good fortune had meanwhile entered the house; a miserly old uncle, of whom no one had had any hopes, had died and left Nathanael's mother not merely a tidy fortune but also a small farm in a pleasant district not far from the town. Nathanael, his mother, Klara, whom he now intended to marry, and Lothar planned to move into the farm. Nathanael had grown gentler and more childlike than ever before, and now fully appreciated the heavenly purity of Klara's noble spirit. Only as Siegmund was saying goodbye to him did he remark: 'By God, friend, I was on an evil road, but an angel led me to the path of sanity in time! It was Klara! . . .' Siegmund would let him say no more for fear that deeply wounding memories might return to him too vividly.

The time came for the four happy people to move into the little farm. They were walking at midday through the streets of the town, where they had made a number of purchases. The high tower of the Town Hall cast its gigantic shadow over the market-place. 'Oh, let us climb it once more and look across at the distant mountains,' suggested Klara. No sooner said than done. Nathanael and Klara ascended the tower; Nathanael's mother went home with the servant; while Lothar, feeling disinclined to mount so many steps, stayed down below. The two lovers were standing arm in arm on the topmost gallery of the tower, looking down into the fragrant woods beyond which the blue mountains rose like a giant city.

'Just look at that strange little grey bush that really seems to be striding out towards us,' exclaimed Klara. Nathanael automatically put his hand in his side pocket, found Coppola's binoculars, and looked slightly to one side. Klara was standing in the way of the glasses. There was a convulsive twitching in his pulses and arteries. He stared at Klara, his face deathly pale; but soon streams of fire glowed and spurted from his eyes, he began to roar horribly like a hunted beast; then he bounded into the air and, interspersing his words with ghastly laughter, yelled: 'Wooden doll, spin! Wooden doll, spin!' He seized Klara with tremendous force and tried to hurl her down from the tower; but Klara, with the strength of desperation, clung to the parapet. Lothar heard the madman raving, he heard Klara's cry of terror; a terrible foreboding took possession of him, he raced up the stairs; the door to the second flight was shut. Klara's cries of distress were growing louder. Frantic with rage and fear, Lothar hurled himself against the door, which finally gave way. Klara's cries were now becoming fainter and fainter. 'Help—save me—save me. . . .' Her voice died away. 'She is dead, murdered by the madman,' cried Lothar. The door to the gallery was also shut. Despair gave him the strength of a giant; he burst the door from its hinges. Merciful God—Klara, in the grip of the raving Nathanael, was hanging from the gallery in mid air; only one hand still clung to the iron railing. Quick as lightning, Lothar seized his sister, pulled her back and smashed his fist into the face of the madman, who stumbled backwards and let go of his prey.

Lothar raced down the stairs with his unconscious sister in his arms. She was saved. Nathanael was now rampaging round the gallery, bounding into the air and shouting: 'Circle of flames, spin—circle of flames, spin!' Attracted by his yelling, a crowd gathered; in the midst of it was the gigantic figure of the lawyer Coppelius, who had just arrived in the town and had come straight to the market-place. People wanted to go up and overpower the madman. Coppelius laughed and said: 'Just wait, he'll come down of his own accord.' Then he stared aloft with the rest. Nathanael suddenly stopped in his tracks, leaned forward, caught sight of Coppelius and with an ear-splitting shriek of 'Ha, lovely eyes, lovely eyes,' leapt over the parapet.

By the time Nathanael lay on the pavement with his skull smashed, Coppelius had vanished.

Many years later, Klara was reported to have been seen in a place far from her home town, sitting hand-in-hand with a friendly looking man outside the door of a beautiful country house, with two merry little boys playing in front of her. From this we may infer that Klara eventually found the calm domestic bliss which her serene and cheerful nature demanded and which Nathanael with his perpetual inner strife could never have given her.

MADEMOISELLE DE SCUDÉRY

A TALE FROM THE TIME OF LOUIS QUATORZE

THE little house occupied by Madeleine de Scudéry, who was known for her charming verses and novels, and for the favour shown her by Louis XIV and the Marquise de Maintenon, stood in the Rue Saint-Honoré.

At midnight one night—it must have been in the autumn of 1680—a loud knocking at the door of this house echoed through the entrance hall. Baptiste, who filled the posts of cook, footman, and door-keeper in this little household, had been given permission by his employer to go to the country for his sister's wedding; consequently Martinière, Mademoiselle's chambermaid, was the only person awake in the house. She heard the repeated knocking and remembered that Baptiste was away and that she and Mademoiselle were alone and unprotected in the house; she called to mind all the robberies and murders ever committed in Paris and felt sure that some pack of ruffians, aware that the house was unprotected, were furiously seeking admittance and, once inside, would assault her mistress; she therefore stayed in her room, shaking with fright and cursing Baptiste and his sister's wedding.

Meanwhile, the blows continued to thunder on the door and it seemed to her as though they were interspersed by a voice crying: 'Open the door, in the name of Christ, open the door!'

Finally, in rising terror, Martinière took the lighted candlestick and hurried out into the hall. There she clearly heard the voice of the man who was knocking, crying: 'In the name of Christ, open the door!'

'No robber would speak so,' thought Martinière. 'Who knows whether it is not some fugitive seeking refuge with my mistress, who is always disposed to acts of mercy. But let us be cautious.'

She opened a window and asked in a loud voice, which she made as deep and masculine as she could, who was down there knocking so wildly at the door and waking everybody from their sleep. In the glimmer of the moonlight, which just then broke through the dark clouds, she discerned a tall figure wrapped in a pale-grey cloak and with his broad-brimmed hat pulled down over his eyes. She then shouted loudly, so that the man below could hear: 'Baptiste, Claude, Pierre, get up and see what good-for-nothing is trying to batter down our door!'

Then a soft, almost plaintive voice spoke from below: 'Oh, Martinière, I know it is you, dear lady, however much you try to disguise your voice, and I know that Baptiste has gone to the country and that you and your mistress are alone in the house. Let me in, you have nothing to fear. I must speak to your mistress without delay.'

'What makes you think my mistress will talk to you in the middle of the night?' replied Martinière. 'Don't you know that she has been asleep for a long time and that nothing would induce me to wake her from the first and sweetest sleep, which at her age she certainly needs.'

'I know,' said the man below, 'that your mistress has just put aside the manuscript of her novel *Clélie*, on which she has been tirelessly working, and is now copying out some verses which she intends to lay before the Marquise de Maintenon tomorrow. I beg you, Martinière, have mercy and let me in. It is a question of saving an unfortunate from perdition; my honour and freedom, indeed my very life, depend upon my speaking to your mistress immediately. I assure you that your mistress's anger will rest upon you eternally if she learns that it was you who hard-heartedly turned away the unfortunate man who came to beseech her aid.'

'But why do you appeal to my lady's pity at this unusual hour? Come back early tomorrow morning,' said Martinière to the man below.

The latter answered: 'Does fate respect the time of day when it strikes like deadly lightning? Can help be delayed when only a moment is left in which to save? Open the door and let me in; you have nothing to fear from a poor, defenceless wretch abandoned by the world, hunted down by a monstrous fate, who wishes to beseech your lady to save him from the awful danger that threatens him!'

Martinière heard the man below groan and sob in anguish as he uttered these words; his voice sounded young, gentle, and full of deep feeling. Her heart was touched, and without further reflection she fetched the key.

No sooner was the door open than the cloaked figure burst in, strode past Martinière into the hall, and cried wildly: 'Take me to your mistress!'

Martinière, terrified, raised the candlestick; the light of the candle fell upon the deathly pale, fearfully contorted face of a young man. Martinière could have sunk to the floor with terror when the man tore open his cloak to reveal the gleaming handle of a stiletto at his breast. He looked at her with flashing eyes and cried even more wildly than before: 'Take me to your mistress, I tell you!'

Seeing her mistress in imminent danger, all Martinière's love for her kindly employer, who was at the same time an affectionate mother to her, blazed up in her heart and aroused a courage of which she would not have believed herself capable. She slammed the door of her room, which had remained open, stood in front of it, and said in a firm, strong voice: 'Your frenzied behaviour now that you are in the house does not tally with the lamentations you uttered while you were still outside, which, as I now see, I wrongly allowed to stir my pity. My mistress must not and will not speak to you now. If you have no evil intentions you will not fear daylight: come back tomorrow and make your request then. Now leave the house!'

The man uttered a deep sigh, stared at Martinière with a terrifying expression, and reached for his stiletto. Martinière silently commended her soul to God; but she stood firm and looked the intruder boldly in the eye, pressing herself more firmly against the door through which he would have to pass to reach Mademoiselle.

'Let me go to your mistress,' cried the intruder again.

'Do what you will,' replied Martinière. 'I will not move from this spot. Complete the evil deed you have begun. You too will die an ignominious death in the Place de Grève, like your villainous accomplices.'

'Ha,' shouted the intruder, 'you are right, La Martinière, I look and am armed like a villainous robber and murderer, but my accomplices have not been executed, they have not been executed!' So saying, he cast a venomous glance at the terrified woman and drew his stiletto.

'Jesus!' she screamed, awaiting the death blow; but at this moment the rattle of weapons and the clatter of horses' hooves could be heard from outside. '*La Maréchaussée—la Maréchaussée.* Help, help!' cried Martinière.

'Abominable woman, you are determined to ruin me— now I'm done for, done for! Take this, give it to your mistress tonight—or tomorrow, if you wish.' Murmuring this in a low voice, the stranger tore the candlestick from Martinière, put out the candles, and pressed a small casket into her hands. 'As you wish for salvation, give your mistress this casket,' he cried and raced towards the door.

Martinière had sunk to the floor; with an effort, she stood up and groped her way through the darkness back to her room, where she dropped into an armchair in a state of prostration and incapable of uttering a sound. Then she heard someone turning the key she had left in the front-door keyhole. The door had been unlocked and soft, uncertain footsteps approached her room. Frozen to the spot with fear, she waited for the worst. Imagine her relief when the door opened and by the glimmer of the nightlight she recognized honest Baptiste! He looked deathly pale and greatly upset.

'In the name of all the saints,' he began, 'in the name of all the saints, tell me, Madame Martinière, what has happened? Some terrible fear, I do not know of what, drove me away from the wedding yesterday evening. When I came into the street I thought to myself: "Madame Martinière is a light sleeper, she will hear and let me in if I knock softly

38

on the front door." But I was met by a powerful police patrol, on horseback and on foot, all armed to the teeth; they stopped me and refused to let me go. But as luck would have it, Desgrais, the lieutenant in the Maréchaussée, was with them, and he knows me very well. As they held their lantern under my nose, he said: "Why, Baptiste, what are you doing, coming back in the middle of the night? You should stay at home like a good lad and look after the house. It isn't safe round here, we're expecting to make a catch tonight." You can imagine, Madame Martinière, how these words pierced my heart. Then I stepped on to the threshold and a cloaked man clutching a stiletto rushed out of the house and knocked me down. . . . The house was open, the keys in the door—tell me, what does it all mean?'

Martinière, freed from her terror, told him all that had happened. She and Baptiste then went into the hall; they found the candlestick on the floor, where the stranger had thrown it as he fled. 'There can be no doubt that our mistress was to have been robbed and probably murdered. As you told me, the man knew that you were alone with Mademoiselle and even that she was still sitting up over her writing; he was undoubtedly one of those accursed rogues who break into houses, spy out the lie of the land, and note everything that may assist them in their evil designs. And I think, Madame Martinière, we should throw the little casket into the deepest part of the Seine. What guarantee have we that some villainous monster is not seeking to take our mistress's life and that, when she opens the casket, she will not fall dead on the spot, like the old Marquis de Tournai, when he opened a letter received from an unknown hand!'

After a long discussion, the two faithful servants finally decided that next morning they would tell their mistress everything and give her the mysterious casket, which could be opened with appropriate caution. Both of them, when they considered all the circumstances of the suspicious stranger's visit, came to the conclusion that there might be some secret involved which they could not deal with themselves but must leave it to their mistress to uncover.

. . . . .

Baptiste's fears were well founded. At just this period Paris was the scene of dastardly atrocities, made easy by a hellish invention.

Glaser, a German apothecary and the best chemist of his day, occupied himself, like most followers of his science, with alchemistic experiments. His aim was to discover the philosopher's stone. He was joined by an Italian named Exili. But for the latter alchemy was only a subterfuge. All he wanted was to learn the art of mixing, boiling, and sublimating the poisons in which Glaser hoped to find salvation, and finally, he succeeded in producing a poison so subtle that it was odourless and yet capable of killing a man, either instantaneously or slowly; since it left no trace in the human body, it deceived all the art and science of the physicians, who had no reason to suspect poisoning and unquestioningly diagnosed death from natural causes. Despite all his precautions, Exili came under the suspicion of selling poisons and was taken to the Bastille. Soon afterwards he was joined in the same cell by Captain Godin de Sainte-Croix. The latter had long been living with the Marquise de Brinvilliers in a liaison that had brought disgrace to the whole family; finally, since the Marquis remained indifferent to his wife's misconduct, her father, Dreux d'Aubray, civil lieutenant of Paris, was compelled to part the criminal pair by ordering the Captain's arrest. Nothing could be more welcome to the Captain—a man who was passionate, unprincipled, hypocritically pious, given to vice from his youth on, jealous and furiously vengeful—than Exili's devilish secret, which gave him the power to destroy all his enemies. He became Exili's eager pupil and soon his equal, so that when he left the Bastille he was able to continue working on his own.

Brinvilliers was a dissolute woman, through Sainte-Croix she became a monster. He induced her to poison, one after the other, her own father, with whom she was living under the hypocritical pretext of caring for him in his old age, then her two brothers, and finally her sister—her father for revenge, the others for the sake of the rich inheritance. This story of multiple poisoning is a horrible example of the way in which such crimes develop into an irresistible passion. For no other reason than pleasure—as the chemist carries out experiments for his own enjoyment—poisoners have frequently murdered people whose life or death was a matter of complete indifference to them. The sudden death of several paupers in the Hôtel Dieu later gave rise to the suspicion that the loaves of bread which Brinvilliers, posing as a paragon of charity, distributed there every week were poisoned. In any case it is certain that she set poisoned pigeon-pies before her invited guests. The Chevalier du Guet and several other persons fell victim to these infernal meals. Sainte-Croix, his assistant La Chaussée, and Brinvilliers were able for a long time to conceal their atrocious crimes behind an impenetrable veil; but no matter how great the unscrupulous cunning of abandoned evil-doers, the eternal power of heaven resolutely brings them to justice here on earth.

The poison Sainte-Croix prepared was so subtle that if the powder (*poudre de succession*, the Parisians called it) lay open during preparation, a single inhalation was sufficient to produce instantaneous death. During his operations, therefore, Sainte-Croix wore a mask of thin glass. One day this mask fell from his face just as he was shaking the finished powder into a phial; he inhaled the poisonous powder and dropped dead on the spot. Since he died without heirs, the Court hastened to place its seal on his possessions. In his home they found locked in a box the whole hellish arsenal of poisons that had been at the villainous Sainte-Croix's command; but they also found Brinvilliers's letters, which left no doubt about their evil deeds. She took refuge in a convent at Liége. Desgrais, an officer of the Maréchaussée, was sent in pursuit. He appeared in the convent disguised as a priest and succeeded in entering into an amorous intrigue with the abominable woman and decoying her to an assignation in a lonely garden outside the city. No sooner had she arrived at the rendezvous than she was surrounded by Desgrais's policemen. The priestly lover suddenly changed into an officer of the Maréchaussée and forced her to enter the carriage that was standing ready outside the garden and was driven straight to Paris, surrounded by policemen. La Chaussée had already been beheaded; Brinvilliers met the same death; after execution her body was burnt and the ashes scattered in the air.

The Parisians breathed a sigh of relief, thinking that the world had been rid of the monster who had turned this deadly secret weapon against friend and foe. But it soon transpired that Sainte-Croix's atrocious art had been inherited. Like an invisible, malignant ghost, murder insinuated itself into the most intimate circles formed by kinship, love, or friendship, and swiftly and surely seized the unhappy victim. The man who today was a picture of health tomorrow tottered about sick and ailing, and all the physicians' skill was powerless to save him from death. Wealth— a profitable post—a beautiful, perhaps too youthful wife— any of these were enough to bring death. The most sacred bonds were sundered by horrible suspicion. The husband trembled before his wife—the father before his son—the sister before her brother. Food and wine were left untouched at the meal to which a man invited his friends; and where there had once been gaiety and jest, savage glances now sought out the hidden murderer. Fathers of families were to be seen nervously buying provisions in remote districts and preparing the food themselves in some filthy cookshop, fearing devilish treachery in their own homes. And yet the greatest precautions were sometimes in vain.

In order to halt this evil, which was continually gaining ground, the King set up a special court for the exclusive purpose of investigating and punishing these furtive crimes. This was the so-called Chambre Ardente, which sat near the Bastille and was presided over by La Régnie. For some time La Régnie's efforts, zealous as they were, remained fruitless, and it was left to the crafty Desgrais to uncover the most secret hideout of crime.

In the Faubourg Saint-Germain there lived an old woman, La Voisin by name, who practised fortune-telling and necromancy and, with the aid of her accomplices Le Sage and Le Vigoureux, was able to strike terror and stupefaction even in people not normally considered weak and credulous. But this was not all. A pupil of Exili's like La Croix, she too prepared the subtle poison that left no trace and thereby assisted unscrupulous sons to an early inheritance and dissolute wives to a new and younger husband. Desgrais penetrated her secret; she confessed everything; the Chambre Ardente condemned her to be burnt at the stake, and the execution was carried out in the Place de la Grève. A list was found in her house of everyone who had enlisted her aid; as a result not only did execution follow execution but grave suspicion fell even upon persons standing in high esteem. Thus Cardinal Bonzy was believed to have obtained from La Voisin the means of bringing about the early death of all those to whom, as Archbishop of Narbonne, he had to pay a pension. Thus the Duchesse de Bouillon and the Comtesse de Soissons, whose names were found on the list, were accused of dealings with the evil hag, and even François Henri de Montmorency-Bouteville, Duke of Luxembourg, Peer and Marshal of the Realm, was not spared. He too was prosecuted by the frightful Chambre Ardente and imprisoned in the Bastille, where the hatred of Louvois and La Régnie caused him to be immured in a hole six feet long. Months passed before it was conclusively proved that the Duke's only crime was to have had his horoscope cast by Le Sage.

There can be no doubt that the blind zeal of President La Régnie led to acts of violence and brutality. The tribunal acquired all the character of the Inquisition; the faintest suspicion was enough to bring harsh imprisonment, and it was often left to chance to prove the innocence of the man accused of a capital crime. At the same time La Régnie, who was repulsive in appearance and malignant by nature, quickly earned the hatred of those very people whose avenger or protector he was called upon to be. The Duchesse de Bouillon, asked in the course of an interrogation whether she had seen the devil, replied: 'I think I see him at this moment!'

While the blood of the guilty and the suspect flowed in streams in the Place de Grève, and murder by poisoning grew rarer and rarer, an evil of another kind made its appearance, and spread fresh alarm and despondency. It seemed as though a band of thieves was determined to get possession of all the jewels in Paris. Rich ornaments un-accountably disappeared as soon as they were bought, how-ever carefully they were guarded. Even worse, anyone who ventured to carry jewellery in the evening was robbed, and even murdered in the open street or in the dark passages of houses. Those who escaped with their lives reported that a fist had struck them on the head like a thunderbolt and on regaining consciousness they had found themselves robbed and in quite a different place from where they had been struck. The victims of murder were to be found almost every morning lying in the street or inside houses, and all had the same fatal wound. They had all been stabbed in the heart with a dagger so swiftly and surely, according to the doctors, that they must have sunk to the ground without uttering a sound. Who, at the lascivious Court of Louis XIV, was not involved in an amorous intrigue and did not creep off to his mistress late at night, often carrying a costly gift? As though in league with spirits, the robber band knew exactly when anything of this sort was taking place. Very often the unfortunate man never reached the house in which he hoped to enjoy the delights of love, very often he fell upon the threshold, or even outside the room of his mistress, who had the horrifying experience of finding his bloodstained corpse.

In vain did Argenson, the minister of police, have every-one arrested against whom there was the least suspicion; in vain La Régnie raged and tried to extort confessions; in vain were watches and patrols strengthened; no trace of the wrong-doers was to be found. Only the precaution of going armed to the teeth and preceded by a torchbearer helped to some extent; but even then it sometimes happened that the servant was scared off by a hail of stones and the master murdered and robbed.

Curiously enough, searches at all the places where jewellery might possibly be disposed of failed to bring any of the stolen valuables to light, so that here too investigations drew a blank.

Desgrais frothed at the mouth with rage at the way the rogues eluded his cunning. The district of the city in which he happened to be was always spared, while murder with robbery reaped a rich harvest in some other part where no crime had been anticipated.

Desgrais hit upon the device of using a number of doubles, all so alike in gait, posture, speech, figure, and face that even the police did not know where the real Desgrais was. Meanwhile, at the risk of his life, he eavesdropped in the most secret hideouts and followed at a distance this man or that who, at his instigation, was carrying expensive jewellery. The man he was watching always went unscathed; so the thieves were informed about *this* measure too. Desgrais lapsed into despair.

One morning Desgrais came to President La Régnie in a state of agitation, his face pale and contorted.

'What news have you?' cried the President of the Court. 'Are you on their tracks?'

'Ha, Monsieur,' began Desgrais, stammering with rage, 'last night—not far from the Louvre—the Marquis de la Fare was attacked in my presence.'

'Heaven be praised,' exulted La Régnie, 'we have them!'

'Just wait till I tell you the whole story,' interrupted Desgrais with a bitter smile. 'I was standing by the Louvre, with all hell in my breast, watching out for the devils who mock me. Then a figure passed with faltering step and continually looking over his shoulder. He did not see me, but in the moonlight I recognized the Marquis de la Fare. I had expected him, I knew where he was going. He was a bare

45

ten or twelve paces from me when a figure sprang up as though from the earth, struck him down, and fell upon him Without stopping to think, caught unawares by this moment that might deliver the murderer into my hands, I let out a yell and sprang from my hiding-place to assail him; but in my haste I tripped over my cloak and fell headlong. I saw the man racing away as though on the wings of the wind; I jumped to my feet and ran after him—blowing my horn as I ran—the policemen's whistles answered me from the distance—turmoil broke out—weapons rattled and horses' hooves clattered on all sides. "Here—here—Desgrais— Desgrais!" I cried, so that it echoed through the streets. I could still see the man in front of me in the bright moonlight as he dodged up side streets to throw me off his track; we came to the Rue Niçaise, his strength seemed to be failing, I strained my own to the utmost—he was no more than fifteen paces ahead of me. . . .'

'You caught up with him, you seized him, the police arrived,' cried La Régnie with flashing eyes, grasping Desgrais by the arm, as though he were the fleeing murderer himself.

'Fifteen paces in front of me,' continued Desgrais in a dull voice and breathing laboriously, 'the man jumped into the shadow at the side of the street and vanished through the wall.'

'Vanished? Through the wall! Are you mad?' cried La Régnie, taking two steps back and clapping his hands together.

'Call me mad, if you like, Monsieur,' replied Desgrais, rubbing his forehead like a man plagued by evil thoughts. 'Tell me I suffer from hallucinations, but it was as I say. I was standing dumbfounded in front of the wall, when several policemen came panting up, accompanied by the Marquis de la Fare, who had recovered from the assault and was brandishing a naked dagger. We lit torches and tapped up and down the wall; not a sign of a door, a window, or any opening. It was a solid stone wall enclosing a courtyard, and inside it was a house occupied by people entirely above suspicion. I made a careful examination of the place again today. It is the devil himself who is making fools of us.'

Desgrais's story spread through Paris. Heads were filled with tales of magic, necromancy, and pacts with the devil entered into by La Voisin, Le Vigoureur, and the villainous priest Le Sage. Unchanging human nature is such that belief in the miraculous and supernatural always outweighs reason; consequently people soon came to believe as a fact what Desgrais had merely exclaimed in his exasperation, namely that the devil himself was protecting the villains who had sold him their souls. As may be imagined, Desgrais's story was much embroidered upon. An account of it, topped by a woodcut depicting a ghastly looking devil vanishing into the ground in front of the horrified Desgrais, was printed and sold on every street corner. It was enough to intimidate the populace and to rob even the police of their courage, so that they now wandered about the streets at night in fear and trembling, hung with amulets and consecrated with holy water.

Argenson saw the efforts of the Chambre Ardente coming to nothing and petitioned the King to set up a court for the new crimes possessed of even wider powers to track down and punish the evil-doers. The King, convinced that he had already given too much power to the Chambre Ardente and horrified by the countless executions imposed by La Régnie, dismissed the suggestion out of hand.

Another means of stimulating the King to act in the matter was hit upon.

In Maintenon's apartment, where the King was accustomed to spend the afternoons and doubtless also to work late into the night with his ministers, a poem was delivered to him in the name of endangered lovers, complaining that while gallantry demanded that they should take their mistress a costly present, this now meant risking their life. While it was a joy and an honour to shed their blood for their beloved in knightly combat, it was quite a different matter to face the treacherous assault of a murderer, against

47

which there was no defence. They called upon Louis, the shining pole star of all love and gallantry, to blaze forth and dissipate the darkness of night, uncovering the black mystery concealed within it. Let the divine hero, who had crushed all his enemies, now draw his victoriously flashing sword again and strike down—as Hercules struck down the Lernean hydra and Theseus the Minotaur—the fearful monster that was undermining all the pleasures of love and turning all joy into deep grief and unconsolable mourning.

Serious as the matter was, this poem was not lacking in witty twists, particularly in the passages describing how lovers now trembled on their furtive way to the beloved and how their fear nipped in the bud all the pleasures of love and every gallant adventure. Since, moreover, the poem ended with a grandiloquent panegyric to Louis XIV, the King read it with visible satisfaction. Having finished it, he turned to Maintenon, keeping his eyes on the sheet of paper, read the poem through again, this time out loud, and then asked with a charming smile what she thought of the endangered lovers' plea. Maintenon, true to her grave cast of mind and a certain tinge of piety, replied that secret and forbidden journeys did not deserve any special protection, but that the loathsome criminals certainly merited special measures for their extirpation. The King, dissatisfied with this undecided answer, folded the sheet of paper and was about to return to the Secretary of State, who was working in the other room, when his eyes happened to meet those of Mlle de Scudéry, who had just sat down in a small armchair close to the Marquise de Maintenon. He walked towards her; the charming smile that had played about his mouth and cheeks and then disappeared now regained the upper hand. Standing directly in front of Mademoiselle and unfolding the poem again, he said gently: 'The Marquise doesn't want to know about the gallantries of our enamoured gentlemen and their perfectly legitimate activities and evades my question. But you, Mademoiselle, what do you think of this poetic petition?'

Mlle de Scudéry rose respectfully from her armchair; a fleeting blush like the red of sunset passed across the dignified old lady's cheeks; curtseying slightly and with downcast eyes, she said:

A lover, afraid of thieves,
Is unworthy of love.

The King, astonished by the chivalrous spirit of these few words, which made mincemeat of the whole poem with its endless tirades, cried with flashing eyes: 'By St Denis, you are right, Mademoiselle! Cowardice shall not be protected by any blind measures that fall upon the innocent along with the guilty! Let Argenson and La Régnie do what they can!'

Martinière depicted all the horrors of the period in the liveliest colours when she told her mistress next morning what had happened the night before and handed her the mysterious casket with fear and trembling. Both she and Baptiste, who stood in the corner white-faced, nervously twisting his night-cap in his hand and almost speechless with dread, implored Mademoiselle by all the saints to exercise every possible care in opening the casket. Mlle de Scudéry, balancing and testing the closed enigma in her hand, said with a smile: 'You are both seeing ghosts! The villainous assassins, who, as you told me yourselves, spy out the innermost secrets of houses, know as well as you or I that I am not rich and that there is no treasure here worth murdering for. You think my life is in danger? Who can have any interest in the death of a woman of seventy-three who has never persecuted anyone but the miscreants and ruffians in the novels she wrote herself; who produces mediocre verse that can arouse no one's envy; who will leave nothing behind but the finery of an old spinster who occasionally went to Court, and a few dozen well-bound books with gilded edges. However terrible the description you give of the stranger, Martinière, I cannot believe that he intended evil. So what have we to fear?'

Martinière recoiled three paces, Baptiste sank half to his

knees with a hollow groan, as Mademoiselle now pressed a projecting steel knob, causing the lid of the casket to spring up with a click.

How astonished Mademoiselle was to see a pair of gold bracelets set with jewels and a matching necklet sparkling up at her from the casket. She took the jewellery out and praised the wonderful workmanship of the necklet, while Martinière eyed the costly bracelets, exclaiming over and over again that not even the vain Montespan possessed such jewellery.

'But what is this?' said Mlle Scudéry. She had just noticed a folded sheet of paper at the bottom of the casket. She rightly hoped to find in it the clue to the mystery. Hardly had she read it, than the note fell from her trembling hands. She turned eloquent eyes to heaven and sank back in her armchair as though half swooning. Greatly frightened, Martinière and Baptiste sprang to her side. 'Oh,' she cried in a voice half choked with tears, 'oh, the insult, oh, the shame! Must I suffer such a thing at my time of life? Have I been guilty of a foolish, wanton act, like a thoughtless young girl? Oh, God, are words uttered without reflection and half in jest capable of such a horrifying interpretation? Are criminals to accuse me, who remained blameless and true to virtue and piety from my childhood on, are criminals to accuse me of being in league with the devil?'

Mademoiselle held her handkerchief to her eyes and wept and sobbed bitterly, so that Martinière and Baptiste, completely bewildered and deeply distressed, did not know how to aid their good mistress in her great affliction.

Martinière had picked up the fateful message from the floor. It read:

> *A lover, afraid of thieves,*
> *Is unworthy of love.*

'Your ready wit, Mademoiselle, has saved us—who exercise the right of the stronger upon the weak and cowardly and acquire valuables that would have been unworthily squandered—from great persecution. Please accept this jewellery as proof of our gratitude. It is the most costly we have been able to lay hands on for a long time, although you, worthy lady, should be adorned with far finer jewellery than this. We beg you not to withdraw from us your friendship and your gracious remembrance.

'The Invisibles Ones.'

'Is it possible,' cried Mlle de Scudéry, when she had to some extent recovered, 'for shameless impudence and wicked mockery to be carried so far?'

The sun was shining brightly through the curtains of brilliant red silk, so that the gems lying on the table beside the casket flashed with a reddish gleam. Mlle de Scudéry looked across at them, then covered her face with her hands in horror and ordered Martinière immediately to remove the frightful jewellery spattered with the blood of murdered men. After shutting the bracelets and necklet in the casket, Martinière suggested that the most advisable thing would be to hand the jewels over to the Minister of Police and tell him all about the terrifying visit from the young man who had delivered the casket.

Mlle de Scudéry rose from her chair and strode silently up and down the room, as though reflecting upon the best course of action. Then she ordered Baptiste to fetch a sedan chair and Martinière to dress her, because she was going at once to the Marquise de Maintenon.

Mlle de Scudéry had herself borne to the Marquise at precisely the hour when, as she knew, the latter would be alone in her apartment. She took the casket of jewellery with her.

The Marquise was greatly surprised to see Mlle de Scudéry, generally the embodiment of dignity—indeed, despite her age, of amiability and charm—enter pale, with drawn face and tottering steps. 'What in heaven's name has happened to you?' she cried to the poor frightened lady, who, quite distraught and barely able to stand upright, made as fast as she could for the armchair which the Marquise pushed towards her. Finally regaining the power of speech, Mademoiselle told of the deep and rankling insult brought upon her by the thoughtless jest with which she had answered the petition of the endangered lovers. After hearing the whole story, the Marquise expressed the opinion that Mlle de Scudéry was taking the strange occurrence far too much to heart and that the mockery of villainous rabble could never touch a pious, noble mind. Then she asked to see the jewellery.

Mlle de Scudéry handed her the open casket, and as she caught sight of the costly ornaments the Marquise could not restrain a loud exclamation of wonder. She took out the necklet and went with it to the window, where she at one moment let the gems play in the sun, at the next held the delicate gold work close to her eyes in order to study the miraculous skill with which every little link in the intricate chain was worked.

All of a sudden the Marquise turned to Mademoiselle and cried: 'Do you know, Mademoiselle, these bracelets and this necklet cannot have been made by anyone but René Cardillac?'

René Cardillac was at that time the most skilful goldsmith in Paris, and one of the most ingenious and also the most singular men of his day. Rather below medium height, but broad-shouldered and of powerful, muscular build, Cardillac, though well into his fifties, still possessed the strength and agility of a young man. This strength, which was exceptional, was also borne out by his thick, curly red hair and compact, shiny face. If Cardillac had not been known throughout Paris as the most upright man of honour, unselfish, frank, without guile, and always ready to help, the strange expression in his small, deep-set, flashing green eyes might have led to his being suspected of secret cunning and malignity.

As we have said, Cardillac was the most skilful master of his craft not only in Paris but perhaps anywhere at that time. Intimately familiar with the nature of gems, he knew how to treat and set them in such a way that the ornament which had previously seemed quite insignificant left Cardillac's workshop in shining glory. He accepted every commission with burning eagerness and fixed a price so small as to appear out of all proportion to the labour. Then the work would leave him no peace, he could be heard hammering away in his workshop day and night; and frequently, when the work was almost complete, he would take a sudden dislike to the shape or begin to doubt whether one of the settings of the gems, or some little link, was sufficiently delicate —reason enough to throw the whole ornament back into the melting pot and start afresh. As a result, everything he undertook emerged as a pure and unsurpassable masterpiece that astonished his customer. But then it was almost impossible to obtain the finished work from him. With a thousand excuses, he would keep the customer waiting week after week, month after month. In vain the customer offered him double the fee, he would not take a louis more than the sum agreed. If, finally, he had to yield to the customer's pressure and hand over the jewellery, he could not conceal all the signs of profound chagrin and inward rage. If he had to deliver a piece of work of exceptional importance and value, perhaps worth several thousand louis by virtue of the costliness of the gems and the supreme delicacy of the goldsmith's work, he would often rampage as though distracted, cursing his work and everything around him.

But as soon as a new customer ran after him, crying loudly, 'René Cardillac, wouldn't you like to make a fine necklace for my betrothed—bracelets for my girl,' or whatever it might be, he would stop in his tracks, look at the client with his little, glittering eyes, rub his hands, and say: 'What have you got?' The customer would then take out a casket and reply: 'Here are some gems, nothing special, commonplace stuff, but in your hands . . .' Cardillac wouldn't let him finish, he would snatch the casket from his hands, take out the gems, which were really not up to much, hold them up to the light, and exclaim delightedly: 'Ho, ho—commonplace stuff? Not a bit of it! They're pretty stones, magnificent stones, let me get to work on them ! And if you're not worried about a handful of louis I'll add a few little stones that will sparkle in your eyes like the sun itself. . . .' To which the customer would reply: 'I leave it to you, Master René, and I'll pay whatever you ask.' Regardless of whether he was a rich burgher or a fine gentleman from the Court, Cardillac would then fling his arms round his neck, hug and kiss him, and declare that he was now perfectly happy and that the work would be finished in a week. He would race back home at breakneck speed, rush into his workshop, and start hammering away, and in a week he would have produced a masterpiece.

But as soon as the customer joyfully came to pay the small sum demanded and take away the completed piece of jewellery, Cardillac would become morose, rude, obstinate. 'But Master Cardillac, remember, my wedding is tomorrow.' 'What do I care about your wedding? Come back in a fortnight.' 'The jewellery is ready, here's the money, I must have it.' 'And I tell you I still have to make a lot of alterations to it and I shan't give it to you today.' 'And I tell you that I will pay you double what you asked, but that if you don't give me the jewellery at once I shall be back in no time with Argenson's faithful halberdiers.' 'May Satan torment you with a hundred red-hot pincers and hang three hundredweights on the necklace so that it strangles your bride!' So saying, Cardillac would thrust the jewellery into his customer's breast pocket, seize him by the arm, and throw him out of the door so that he tumbled all the way down the stairs; then he would lean out of the window and laugh like the devil to see the poor young man limp out of the house with a handkerchief to his bloody nose.

For some inexplicable reason, too, it sometimes happened that Cardillac, after accepting a commission with enthusiasm, would suddenly beseech the customer with every sign of outward agitation, with heart-rending protestations, tears and sobs, and appeals to the Holy Virgin and all the saints, to release him from the task he had undertaken. Many people highly esteemed by the King and the populace had vainly offered large sums for even the smallest piece of work by Cardillac. He threw himself at the King's feet and implored the favour of being excused from working for him. He likewise refused to accept any commission from the Marquise de Maintenon; indeed, he rejected with every appearance of repugnance and horror her request to manufacture a small ring decorated with emblems of the arts, which she wished to present to Racine.

For this reason, the Marquise now exclaimed: 'I wager that if I send for Cardillac to find out for whom he made these pieces of jewellery he will refuse to come, because he fears that I may wish to order something from him and is determined not to work for me. Although he seems to have grown somewhat less eccentric lately, for according to what I hear he is now working more industriously than ever and delivering his work on time, though still reluctantly and with averted face.'

Mlle de Scudéry, who was most anxious to return the jewellery to its rightful owner, if this was in any way possible, suggested that the temperamental maestro might consent to come if they made it clear from the outset that they did not wish to commission work from him, but merely to consult him regarding certain gems. The Marquise agreed to this. Cardillac was sent for, and as the messenger found him already out and about, it was not long before he entered the room.

When he caught sight of Mlle de Scudéry he seemed disconcerted, and as though forgetting the demands of etiquette in his surprise at this unexpected meeting he first bowed deeply and reverently to the venerable lady and only then turned to the Marquise. Pointing to the jewellery that was sparkling on the dark-green tablecloth, she quickly inquired if it were his work. Cardillac scarcely glanced at it; looking the Marquise straight in the face, he hurriedly packed the necklet and bracelets in the casket that was standing beside them and thrust it violently away from him.

Then, an ugly smile spreading over his red face, he said: 'Indeed, Madame la Marquise, you must be ill acquainted with my work if you can believe for a moment that any other goldsmith in the world could produce such articles. Of course it's my work.'

"Well, then,' went on the Marquise, 'tell us for whom you made it.'

'For no one but myself,' replied Cardillac. 'Yes,' he continued, as the Marquise and Mlle de Scudéry looked at him in astonishment, the former full of mistrust, the latter of trepidation and eagerness to know what was coming now. 'Yes, you may think it strange, Madame la Marquise, but that's how it is. For no other reason than to produce something really first class, I gathered together my finest gems and for the sheer joy of it worked on them more carefully and diligently than ever before. A short while ago, the pieces inexplicably disappeared from my workshop.'

'Heaven be praised,' cried Mlle de Scudéry, her eyes sparkling for joy, and as quickly and nimbly as a young girl she jumped up from her armchair, strode across to Cardillac, and placed both hands on his shoulders. 'Master Cardillac,' she said, 'take back the property of which the rascally thieves robbed you.' Then she related how the jewellery had come into her possession.

Cardillac listened to it all unspeaking and with downcast eyes. Every now and then he uttered an almost inaudible 'H'm! So! Ah! Oho!', clapped his hands on his knees or ran them over his chin and cheeks. When Mlle de Scudéry had finished her story Cardillac appeared to be struggling with some new idea which had just struck him and which placed him before a difficult decision. He rubbed his forehead and ran his hand over his eyes, apparently to restrain his tears. Finally, he seized the casket Mlle Scudéry was holding out to him and said: 'Destiny intended these jewels for you, noble and worthy lady. Yes, I now realize for the first time that I was thinking of you while I was engaged upon them. Do not scorn to accept and wear this jewellery, the best I have made for a long time.'

'Oh, oh,' replied Mlle de Scudéry, merrily jesting, 'what are you thinking of, Master René? Would it be fitting at my age, to deck myself out with sparkling gems? And why should you bestow such immensely costly gifts upon me? Come, come, Master René, if I were as beautiful as the Marquise de Fontange and rich, indeed I should not let these ornaments slip through my fingers; but what place is there for this vain splendour on these shrivelled arms, for this glittering adornment round this wrinkled neck?'

Cardillac had meanwhile risen and spoke as though distracted, with wild eyes, still holding out the casket to Mlle de Scudéry: 'Have pity on me, Mademoiselle, and take the jewellery. You have no idea what veneration for your virtue and your high merits I carry in my heart! Regard my meagre gift as simply an attempt to prove to you my most heartfelt admiration!'

As Mlle de Scudéry still hesitated, the Marquise de Maintenon took the casket from Cardillac's hand, saying: 'Heavens above, Mademoiselle, you keep talking about your age—what have you and I to do with age and its burdens? And are you not acting like a bashful young thing who longs for the sweet fruit that is offered her, if only she could take it without a hand and without fingers? Do not reject honest Master René, who is offering you as a present what thousands of others cannot get for all their gold and all their entreaties.'

The Marquise de Maintenon had meanwhile forced the casket upon Mlle de Scudéry, and now Cardillac fell to his knees—kissed Mlle de Scudéry's skirt—her hands—groaned —sighed—wept—sobbed—jumped up and ran madly from the room, knocking over chairs and tables in his blind haste, so that china and glasses fell tinkling to the ground.

Greatly startled, Mlle de Scudéry cried: 'By all the saints, what's the matter with the man?'

But the Marquise, gay to the point of exhibiting an unaccustomed exuberance, laughed loudly and said: 'Now we know, Mademoiselle, Master René is desperately in love with you and is beginning, according to the proper and ancient customs of true gallantry, to assail your heart with costly gifts.' Maintenon carried this jest further, admonishing Mlle de Scudéry not to be too cruel towards her despairing lover, and Mademoiselle, giving free rein to her innate high spirits, was carried away by a rushing torrent of witty fancies. She commented that, if things were really like that and she were once conquered, she would present to the world the unique picture of a goldsmith's bride seventy-three years old and of unimpeachable nobility. Maintenon offered to weave the bridal wreath and to instruct her in the duties of a good housewife, which naturally such a chit of a girl could know nothing about.

Despite all their laughter and jesting, Mlle de Scudéry once more became very serious as she finally rose to leave the Marquise and picked up the jewel casket. 'Madame la Marquise,' she said, 'I shall never be able to use this jewellery. However that may have come about, it was once in the hands of those hellish ruffians who rob and murder with the impudence of the devil and probably in accursed alliance with him. I shudder to think of the blood that seems to adhere to this sparkling jewellery. And now even Cardillac's behaviour, I must confess, appears to me strangely sinister and frightening. I cannot escape a dark foreboding that there is some hideous, horrifying secret behind all this, but if I clearly visualize the whole affair in every detail, I have not the slightest inkling of what this secret may be or how the honest, upright Master René, the model of a good and pious citizen, can be mixed up in anything evil and damnable. But one thing is certain: I shall never dare to put the jewellery on.'

The Marquise protested that this was carrying scruples too far; but when Mlle de Scudéry asked her on her conscience what she would do in her place, the Marquise replied gravely and firmly: 'I would far rather throw the jewellery into the Seine than ever wear it.'

Her encounter with Master René led Mlle de Scudéry to compose some delightful verses, which she read out to the King next evening in Maintenon's apartment.

Overcoming her ominous foreboding, she succeeded in painting in vivid colours the amusing picture of the seventy-three-year-old goldsmith's bride of unimpeachable nobility. The King laughed heartily and declared that Boileau-Despréaux had met his master, which led to Mlle de Scudéry's poem being regarded as the wittiest ever written.

Several months had passed when Mlle de Scudéry happened to be driving over the Pont-Neuf in the Duchesse de Montausier's glass coach. These delicate glass coaches were such a recent invention that the populace crowded round to look whenever a vehicle of this kind appeared in the street. Thus the gaping rabble on the Pont-Neuf crowded round Montausier's coach, almost bringing the horses to a halt. All of a sudden Mlle de Scudéry heard cursing and swearing and perceived a man forcing his way through the densest mass with fists and elbows. As he came nearer, her eyes met the piercing gaze of a deathly pale and anguished young man. He kept his eyes fixed upon her as he battled his way to the door of the coach, which he tore open in desperate haste; then he threw a note into Mlle de Scudéry's lap and vanished as he had come, giving and receiving punches and jabs with the elbows. As soon as the man appeared at the coach door Martinière, who was sitting beside Mlle de Scudéry, uttered a cry of horror and fell back senseless against the cushions. In vain did Mlle de Scudéry tug the cord and call out to the coachman; as though impelled by an evil spirit, the latter whipped up the horses, which reared and struck out with their hooves with foam flying from their mouths, and finally thundered off across the bridge at a brisk trot. Mlle de Scudéry poured the contents of her smelling bottle over the unconscious woman, who finally opened horror-struck eyes and, shaking and trembling and clinging convulsively to her mistress, groaned with an effort: 'In the name of the Blessed Virgin, what did the terrible man want? It was he, yes, he, who brought you the casket on that dreadful night!'

Mlle de Scudéry calmed the poor woman, telling her that nothing untoward had happened and that the only sensible thing to do was to find out what was in the note. She unfolded the sheet of paper and read:

59

'An evil fate, which you can avert, is thrusting me into the abyss!—I beseech you, as a son addressing a mother to whom he is attached with all the ardour of childish love, return the necklet and bracelets you received from me to Master René Cardillac on some pretext or other—in order to have some improvement or alteration made or something of that sort. Your welfare, your very life depends upon it. If you do not do so by the day after tomorrow I shall force my way into your house and kill myself before your eyes!'

'Now it is certain,' said Mlle de Scudéry, when she had read this, 'that even if the mysterious young man does belong to the band of villainous thieves and murderers, he has no evil intentions towards me. If he had managed to speak to me that night, who knows what strange events, what occult facts, might have been revealed to me, for the slightest inkling of which I now rack my brains in vain? But however that may be, I shall do what I am bid in this note, if only to rid myself of the accursed jewellery, which seems to me like an unlucky charm that puts the possessor under a curse. True to his old habits, Cardillac will not so easily let it out of his possession again.'

Mlle Scudéry intended to take the jewellery to the goldsmith the next day. But it seemed as though all the *beaux esprits* of Paris had made an appointment to assail Mademoiselle with verses, plays, and anecdotes that morning. Scarcely had La Chapelle finished a scene from a tragedy and slyly assured his listener that it was his intention to outdo Racine, when the latter entered in person and crushed him with the dramatic speech of some king or other; after which Boileau sent up his meteor into the black sky of tragedy, to escape from an unending tirade on the colonnade of the Louvre which Dr Perrault, the architect and physician, was inflicting upon him.

By now it was high noon, and Mlle de Scudéry was due to visit the Duchesse de Montausier; as a result the visit to Master René Cardillac had to be postponed till next morning.

Mlle de Scudéry was plagued by an odd restlessness. The young man was continually before her eyes, and some dim recollection strove to rise from deep within her, as if she had seen this face, these features before. Her light doze was disturbed by frightening dreams in which it seemed that she had thoughtlessly, criminally failed to grasp the hand which the unhappy young man had stretched out to her as he sank into the abyss, in fact as though it had lain with her to avert some terrible disaster, some hideous crime! As soon as the sun was up she had herself dressed and set out in her carriage for the goldsmith, carrying the casket.

The populace were streaming towards the Rue Niçaise, where Cardillac lived, and gathering outside the door of his house. Here they yelled, clamoured, raged, and tried to break in, but were held back by the Maréchaussée, who had the house surrounded. In the wild, confused hubbub angry voices shouted: 'Tear the accursed murderer limb from limb, crush him!' Finally Desgrais appeared with a considerable number of his men, who formed a passage through the thick of the crowd. The door of the house sprang open, a man weighed down by chains was brought out and dragged off to the accompaniment of hideous curses from the mob. No sooner had Mlle de Scudéry, almost swooning with shock and terrible foreboding, perceived this than a shrill cry of distress reached her ears.

'Forward! Farther forward!' she cried distractedly to the coachman, who parted the dense mass with a quick, adroit turn and came to a stop just outside Cardillac's front door. Here Mlle de Scudéry saw Desgrais and, at his feet, a young girl as lovely as day with hair hanging loose, half naked, an expression of wild fear and hopeless despair on her face, who had flung her arms round his knees and was crying in tones of heart-rending anguish: 'He is innocent—he is innocent!' In vain did Desgrais and his men strive to pull her away and lift her up from the ground. At last an uncouth, muscular fellow took hold of her arms with his great fists and dragged her away from Desgrais by force; after which he stumbled clumsily and dropped the girl, who bumped down the stone steps and lay in the street without a sound, as if dead.

Mlle de Scudéry could restrain herself no longer. 'In the name of Christ, what has happened, what is going on?' she cried, quickly opened the coach door, and stepped out. The crowd made way for the worthy lady, who, seeing that a few compassionate women had picked up the girl and placed her on the steps and were rubbing her forehead with spirits, approached Desgrais and emphatically repeated her question.

'Something terrible has happened,' replied Desgrais. 'René Cardillac was found today stabbed to death. His journeyman, Olivier Brusson, is the murderer. He has just been taken off to prison.'

'And the girl?' cried Mlle de Scudéry.

'Is Madelon, Cardillac's daughter,' answered Desgrais. 'The murderer was her lover. Now she weeps and wails and cries over and over again that he is innocent. In the end I shall find that she knew about the deed and have to have her taken to the Conciergerie as well.' As he said this, Desgrais gave the girl a sly, malicious glance that made Mlle de Scudéry tremble.

The girl was just beginning to breathe, but she was incapable of uttering a sound or making a movement; she lay there with her eyes closed, and no one knew what to do, whether to carry her into the house or stay with her till she regained consciousness. Mlle de Scudéry looked at the innocent angel with tears of emotion in her eyes; she felt a horror of Desgrais and his men. Then a series of dull thuds could be heard on the stairs—they were bringing down Cardillac's corpse. Quickly making up her mind, Mlle de Scudéry cried in a loud voice: 'I shall take the girl with me, you can see to the rest, Desgrais!' A low murmur of approval ran through the crowd. The women lifted the girl up, everyone pressed towards her, a hundred hands came to her aid, and she was borne to the coach as though floating through the air, while blessings on the worthy lady who had snatched an innocent from the bloody tribunal streamed from all lips.

The efforts of Séron, the most famous doctor in Paris, were finally successful in bringing Madelon back to her senses after she had lain for hours rigid and unconscious. Mlle de Scudéry completed what the doctor had begun by lighting gentle rays of hope in Madelon's soul, until a violent outburst of tears poured from her eyes and cleared the air. Then, although from time to time her poignant grief overcame her and choked her words in sobs, she was able to relate all that had happened.

She had been awakened around midnight by a low knocking at the door of her room and had heard Olivier's voice beseeching her to get up at once, because her father was dying. She had jumped from her bed in horror and opened the door. Olivier, his face pale and contorted, dripping with sweat, and carrying a light, had made his way with tottering steps to the workshop, and she had followed him. There she found her father lying with staring eyes and rattling in his throat as he struggled with death. She rushed towards him with a wail, and only then perceived that his shirt was stained with blood. Olivier drew her gently away and then tended a wound in the left side of her father's chest, washing it with balm and bandaging it. Meanwhile her father recovered his senses, the rattling in his throat ceased, he gave Madelon a look full of deep feeling, took her hand, placed it in Olivier's, and pressed their two hands fervidly. Both Olivier and she fell to their knees at her father's bedside, he sat up with a piercing cry, but immediately sank back and, with a deep sigh, passed away. Then they both wept and wailed loudly. Olivier told her that at his master's request he had been for a walk with him in the night, that he had been murdered in Olivier's presence and that, with the greatest difficulty, he had carried the big, heavy man home, not believing him to be mortally wounded. At daybreak the other occupants of the house, who had been struck by the thudding and the weeping and wailing in the night, came upstairs and found them kneeling in despair beside her father's corpse.

Then uproar had broken out, the Maréchaussée had

forced their way in and dragged Olivier off to prison as his master's murderer. Madelon now added the most moving description of the virtue, piety, and fidelity of her beloved Olivier. How he had honoured his master as if he had been his own father, how the latter had returned his love to the full, how despite his poverty he had chosen him as his son-in-law, because his skill was equal to his honesty and nobility of mind.

Madelon recounted all this with the deepest sincerity, finally declaring that if Olivier had thrust the dagger into her father's breast in her presence she would more readily have taken it for a satanic hallucination than have believed Olivier capable of such a hideous, atrocious crime.

Mlle de Scudéry, profoundly moved by Madelon's unspeakable suffering and fully prepared to believe poor Olivier guiltless, made inquiries and found all Madelon's statements regarding the domestic relations between the master and his journeyman confirmed. The other occupants of the house unanimously praised Olivier as a model of virtuous, devout, true, and industrious behaviour; no one had a bad word to say against him; when the abominable deed came to be spoken of, they shrugged their shoulders and commented that there was some mystery here.

When brought before the Chambre Ardente, Olivier, as Mlle de Scudéry heard, denied the deed imputed to him with the greatest steadfastness and candour, asserting that his master had been attacked in his presence in the street and struck down, and that he had carried him still living to his home, where he had quickly passed away. This, too, tallied with Madelon's account.

Again and again Mlle de Scudéry had the smallest details of the terrible event repeated to her. She inquired closely whether there had been any quarrel between master and journeyman, whether perhaps Olivier occasionally suffered from those sudden accesses of rage that may come over the most good-natured people like a blind madness and cause them to commit deeds that suggest a total absence of free will. But the more often she listened to Madelon's enthusiastic descriptions of the calm domestic happiness in which the three people had lived, bound together by the sincerest love, the paler grew all shadow of suspicion against Olivier, who was now on trial for his life. After investigating all the circumstances on the assumption that, in spite of everything that spoke so loudly for his innocence, Olivier nevertheless was Cardillac's murderer, Mlle de Scudéry was unable to find any possible motive for the terrible deed, which could do nothing but destroy Olivier's happiness.

'He is poor, but skilful. He succeeded in gaining the affection of the most famous of all master goldsmiths, he loves the daughter, the master approved of his love, life-long happiness and prosperity awaited him! But if, exasperated for heaven knows what reason and overcome by rage, Olivier actually had made a murderous assault upon his benefactor, his father, what demonic hypocrisy it would have required to act as in fact he did act!' Firmly convinced of Olivier's innocence, Mlle de Scudéry resolved to save the innocent youth, cost what it might.

She felt that, before a possible appeal to the clemency of the King himself, it would be best to approach President La Régnie, draw his attention to all the facts that spoke in Olivier's favour, and perhaps arouse in him an inner conviction of the latter's innocence, which he might communicate to the judges.

La Régnie received Mademoiselle de Scudéry with the great deference which the worthy lady, who was held in high honour by the King himself, had a right to expect. He listened quietly to everything she had to say about the horrible deed and about Olivier's life and character. A subtle, almost malicious smile was, however, the only sign that her protestations and her admonitions that, like every judge, he should not be the prisoner's enemy, but also consider everything which spoke in his favour—admonitions accompanied by burning tears—had not fallen on totally deaf ears.

When Mademoiselle, now completely exhausted, wiped the tears from her eyes and fell silent, La Régnie began:

'It does credit to your kind heart, Mademoiselle, that, moved by the tears of a young girl in love, you believe all she tells you, in fact that you find the horrifying crime altogether inconceivable; but it is different for the judge, who is used to tearing the mask from impudent hypocrisy. It is not my place to divulge the course of a criminal trial to anyone who asks. Mademoiselle, I do my duty and care little for the judgement of the world. Let evil-doers tremble before the Chambre Ardente, which knows no other punishment than blood and fire. But I do not wish to be considered a monster of harshness and cruelty by you, Mademoiselle; therefore let me conclusively prove to you in a few words the blood-guilt of the young scoundrel who, heaven be praised, has been delivered up to vengeance. Your own quick intelligence will then repudiate the good nature which does you honour, but would not be fitting in me. Well, then: In the morning René Cardillac was found stabbed to death. Nobody was with him but the journeyman Olivier Brusson and his daughter. In Olivier's room there was found, among other things, a dagger smeared with fresh blood that exactly fitted the wound. "Cardillac," said Olivier, "was struck down before my eyes during the night." "Did the murderer intend to rob him?" "I do not know." "You were walking with him, couldn't you have warded off the murderer, have caught hold of him, have called for help?" "The master was walking fifteen, probably twenty paces in front of me, I was following him." "Why were you so far from him?" "The master wished it so." "What was Master Cardillac doing out in the street so late at night at all?" "I cannot say." "But in the ordinary way he never went out of the house after nine in the evening, did he?" At this point Olivier hesitated, he was perplexed, he sighed, he shed tears, he protested by everything holy that Cardillac really did go out that night and met his death in the street. But now take careful note, Mademoiselle. It has been proved with absolute certainty that Cardillac never left the house that night, hence Olivier's assertion that he went out with him is an impudent lie. The front door of the house is fitted with a heavy lock that makes a piercing noise when it is opened and shut; also the door makes a terrible grinding and screeching as it moves on its hinges, a din which, as experiments have proved, reaches even to the top of the house. Now on the ground floor, that is to say next to the door, old Master Claude Patru lives with his housekeeper, a woman close on eighty, but still bright and nimble. These two people heard Cardillac come downstairs as usual that evening on the stroke of nine, lock and bolt the door, then mount the stairs again, read out the evening prayer aloud, and then, as could be heard from the banging of the doors, go into his bedroom. Like many old people, Master Claude suffers from insomnia. That night, once again, he never closed his eyes. At about ten o'clock, therefore, the housekeeper crossed the entrance hall into the kitchen, put on the light, and sat down with Master Claude at the table and read an ancient chronicle, while the old man mused, now in the armchair, now walking slowly to and fro in search of fatigue and sleep. Everything was quiet till after midnight. Then they heard vigorous footsteps overhead, a hard bump, as though a heavy object were falling to the floor, and immediately afterwards a muffled groaning. Both were filled with a strange fear and dread. The horror of the atrocious deed that had just been committed passed over them. When day broke, the light revealed what had been done in the dark.'

'But in the name of all the saints,' Mlle de Scudéry broke in, 'after all I have told you, can you imagine any motive for this hellish deed?'

'H'm,' replied La Régnie, 'Cardillac was not poor—he possessed some splendid gems.'

'But was it not all going to the daughter?' Mlle de Scudéry continued. 'You forget that Olivier was to become Cardillac's son-in-law.'

'Perhaps he had to share, or even to murder for others,' said La Régnie.

'Share, murder for others?' Mlle de Scudéry asked in astonishment.

'You must know, Mademoiselle, that Olivier would long ago have bled in the Place de Grève if his deed were not connected with the thickly veiled mystery that has hitherto lain so threateningly over the whole of Paris. Olivier is evidently a member of that villainous band that has carried out its misdeeds with impunity in contempt of all the watchfulness, all the efforts, all the investigations of the courts of law. Through him everything will, everything must, be cleared up. Cardillac's wound is identical with the wounds borne by all those who were murdered and robbed in the streets and in the houses. There is also the decisive fact that since the day of Olivier Brusson's arrest all murders and robberies have ceased. The streets are as safe at night as they are during the day—strong evidence that Olivier was perhaps at the head of the band of murderers. As yet he refuses to confess, but there are means of forcing him to speak against his will.'

'And what about Madelon,' cried Mlle de Scudéry, 'what about Madelon, the true, innocent dove?'

'As to her,' said La Régnie with a venomous smile, 'who will guarantee that she was not in the plot? What does she care about her father? All her tears are for the assassin.'

'What are you saying?' cried Mlle de Scudéry. 'It is impossible! Her father—that girl!'

'Oh,' continued La Régnie, 'just remember Brinvilliers. You must forgive me if soon I find myself compelled to tear your protégée away from you and have her thrown into the Conciergerie.'

A shudder ran through Mlle de Scudéry at this abominable suspicion. It seemed to her as though there could be no honesty, nor virtue, for this terrible man, as though he espied murder and blood-guilt in everyone's deepest and most secret thoughts. She stood up. 'Be humane!'—this was all she could bring out as she left, breathing with difficulty because she was oppressed by anxiety. She was about to descend the stairs, to which the President had conducted her with ceremonious courtesy, when a strange idea came to her, she herself did not know how. 'Should I be allowed to see the unhappy Olivier Brusson?' she asked the President, quickly turning round.

The latter looked at her thoughtfully, then his face twisted into the repellent smile characteristic of him. 'No doubt, my worthy Mademoiselle,' he said, 'trusting more to your feelings, to your inner voice, than to what has happened before our eyes, you now wish to test Olivier's guilt or innocence for yourself. If you do not shrink from the gloomy abode of crime, if it is not repugnant to you to see images of every gradation of depravity, the gates of the Conciergerie shall be opened to you in two hours' time. You shall meet this Olivier, whose fate arouses your sympathy.'

In truth, nothing would convince Mlle de Scudéry of the young man's guilt. Everything spoke against him, indeed no judge in the world would have acted otherwise than La Régnie when confronted by such conclusive evidence. Yet the picture of domestic bliss so vividly drawn for her by Madelon outshone all evil suspicion, so that she preferred to assume the presence of an inexplicable mystery rather than believe something against which her whole inner being rebelled.

She intended to get Olivier to go over once more all that had happened in that fateful night and, so far as possible, to unravel a mystery which had perhaps remained impenetrable to the judges because they considered it not worthy of further investigation.

On arrival at the Conciergerie, Mlle de Scudéry was taken into a large, light room. Not long afterwards she heard the clanking of chains. Olivier Brusson was brought in. But the moment he appeared in the doorway, Mlle de Scudéry sank down in a swoon. When she recovered consciousness, Olivier was gone. She vehemently demanded to be taken to her carriage; she wanted to get away, away at once from the haunt of shameless villainy. At the very first glance she had recognized in Olivier Brusson the young man who had thrown a note into her carriage on the Pont-Neuf, who had brought her the casket containing the jewels. Now all doubt was removed, La Régnie's dreadful supposition fully confirmed. Olivier Brusson was a member of the frightful gang of murderers; without a doubt he had also murdered his master! And Madelon? Bitterly deluded by her own emotions as never before in her life, mortally shaken by the power of hell on earth, Mlle de Scudéry despaired of ever knowing the truth. She gave rein to the hideous suspicion that Madelon might be in the plot and share the atrocious blood-guilt. Once a picture has entered it, the human mind diligently seeks and finds colours with which to heighten its tones; thus Mlle de Scudéry, weighing up every circumstance of the crime and the slightest details of Madelon's behaviour, found much to feed her suspicion. A great deal which she had previously regarded as proof of innocence and purity now became a certain sign of villainous malignity, of studied hypocrisy. The heart-rending lamentations, the tears of blood, might just as well have been squeezed from her not by the anguished fear of seeing her sweetheart bleed, but of coming under the executioner's hand herself.

Mlle de Scudéry felt that she must rid herself at once of the serpent she was nourishing in her bosom—with this resolve she dismounted from her carriage. As she entered her room, Madelon threw herself at her feet. Looking up with heavenly eyes, as pure as any angel of God, her hands folded over her heaving bosom, she wailed and loudly implored help and comfort. Mlle de Scudéry, taking a grip on herself and seeking to give her voice as much gravity and calm as she could, said: 'Go—go—rejoice that a just punishment for his shameful deed awaits the murderer. The Holy Virgin grant that no burden of blood-guilt rests upon you yourself.'

'Oh, now all is lost!' With this shrill cry of despair Madelon fell senseless to the ground. Mlle de Scudéry left Martinière to see to the girl and hurried into another room.

Inwardly torn apart and filled with hostility towards everything earthly, Mlle de Scudéry had no wish to go on living in a world pervaded by such demonic deception. She cursed the destiny that had mockingly vouchsafed her so many years in which to strengthen her faith in virtue and honesty, only to destroy in her old age the beautiful picture that had illumined her life.

As Martinière led the girl out, Mlle de Scudéry heard Madelon sigh and softly lament: 'Oh, she too, she too the cruel ones have deceived. Oh, wretched me—oh, poor, unhappy Olivier!'

Madelon's voice cut Mlle de Scudéry to the quick, and once again there stirred in the inmost depths of her soul the presentiment of a mystery, the conviction of Olivier's innocence. Distracted by the most contradictory emotions, Mlle de Scudéry cried out in despair: 'What spirit of hell has entangled me in this hideous affair that will cost me my life?'

At this moment Baptiste entered, pale and terrified, with the news that Desgrais was outside. Since the days of the abominable La Voisin, Desgrais's appearance in a house had been the certain harbinger of some dreadful accusation; hence Baptiste's terror. Mademoiselle therefore asked him with a gentle smile: 'What's the matter with you, Baptiste? I suppose the name Scudéry was on La Voisin's list, eh?'

'Oh, in the name of Christ,' replied Baptiste, trembling from head to foot, 'how can you say such a thing—but Desgrais, the terrible Desgrais, is acting so mysteriously, with such urgency; it seems he simply can't wait to see you!'

'Well then, Baptiste,' said Mlle de Scudéry, 'bring in this man of whom you are so afraid, but who doesn't frighten me in the least.'

'I have been sent to you by President La Régnie, Mademoiselle,' said Desgrais, as soon as he was inside the room, 'with a request which he would not dare hope to see fulfilled, did he not know your virtue and your courage, did not the last means of casting light upon a terrible murder lie in your hands, had you yourself not already taken part in the dreadful trial that now keeps the Chambre Ardente and all of us in suspense. Since seeing you, Olivier Brusson has become half demented. Whereas he seemed previously much disposed to confess, he now once more swears by

Christ and all the saints that he is completely innocent of Cardillac's murder, although he desires to suffer the death he has deserved. Note, Mademoiselle, that this last remark obviously indicates that he is guilty of other crimes. Yet all efforts to drag another word from him have been in vain; even the threat of torture has proved fruitless. He entreats, he conjures us to arrange for him to talk to you; to you, and you alone, he will confess everything. Condescend, Mademoiselle, to hear Brusson's confession.'

'What!' cried Mlle de Scudéry indignantly. 'Am I to serve as an organ of the tribunal, am I to abuse the unhappy man's trust and bring him to the scaffold? No, Desgrais, even if Brusson were a villainous murderer, I could never impose upon him so deceitfully. I wish to know nothing of his secrets, which would remain locked in my breast like a holy confession.'

'Perhaps, Mademoiselle,' retorted Desgrais with a subtle smile, 'you may change your mind when you have heard Brusson. Did you not bid the President himself to be humane? He is doing so, by acceding to Brusson's fantastic request and thus making one last attempt to avoid having to submit Brusson to the torture for which he was long since ripe.'

Mlle de Scudéry involuntarily winced.

'You see, worthy lady,' Desgrais continued, 'no one expects you to return to those gloomy chambers that filled you with horror and repugnance. Under cover of darkness, Olivier Brusson will be brought to you here like a free man. With none to overhear, though there will be guards in the house, he may confess everything of his own free will. That you yourself have nothing to fear from the wretched fellow, I stand surety with my life. He speaks of you with fervent veneration. He swears that only the grim fate which prevented him from seeing you sooner is hurling him to his death. Then it will be in your hands to tell us as much of what Brusson reveals to you as you see fit. Can we compel you to do more?'

Mlle de Scudéry stared in front of her in profound

reflection. She felt as though she must obey the higher power that was demanding of her the solution of some atrocious riddle, as though she could no longer escape the supernatural toils in which she had involuntarily been caught up. Suddenly making up her mind, she said with dignity: 'God will give me composure and fortitude; bring Brusson here, I shall speak to him.'

As when Brusson brought the casket, there was a knock at Mlle de Scudéry's door at midnight. Baptiste, who had been informed of the nocturnal visit, opened it. An icy shudder ran through Mlle de Scudéry as she heard from the soft footsteps and low murmur that the warders who had brought Brusson were taking up positions in the passages of the house.

Finally, the door of her room opened quietly. Desgrais entered, and behind him Olivier Brusson, free from chains and decently dressed. 'Here is Brusson, worthy lady,' said Desgrais, bowing respectfully, and then left the room.

Brusson sank to his knees before Mlle de Scudéry and raised his folded hands imploringly, copious tears streaming from his eyes.

Mlle de Scudéry looked down at him pale-faced and incapable of speaking. Even now, when his features were contorted by grief and anguish, the young man's countenance radiated true goodness. The longer Mlle de Scudéry allowed her eyes to dwell upon Brusson's face, the more vivid was her recollection of some person she had loved, but whom she could not clearly identify. All horror fell from her, she forgot that Cardillac's murderer was kneeling before her. With the pleasant tone of calm benevolence characteristic of her she asked: 'Well, Brusson, what have you to say to me?'

The latter, still kneeling, heaved a sigh of profound, fervent melancholy and then said: 'Oh, noble lady, has all memory of me flown?'

Mlle de Scudéry, looking at him still more closely, replied that she had indeed seen in his features a likeness to someone she had loved, and he must thank this likeness for the fact that she now overcame her deep repugnance to the murderer and listened to him quietly.

Brusson, deeply wounded by these words, quickly rose to his feet and staring gloomily at the floor took a step backwards. Then he asked in a hollow voice: 'Have you entirely forgotten Anne Guiot? It is her son Olivier, whom you often dandled on your knee, who now stands before you.'

'Oh, in the name of all the saints!' cried Mlle de Scudéry, covering her face with her hands and sinking back into the cushions. She had reason enough to feel horrified. Anne Guiot, the daughter of an impoverished burgher, had lived from an early age with Mlle de Scudéry, who brought the dear child up with all a mother's loving care. As she grew up, she was wooed by a handsome, virtuous youth named Claude Brusson. Since he was a highly skilled clockmaker, who earned a good living in Paris, and Anne had fallen wholeheartedly in love with him, Mlle de Scudéry had no hesitation in consenting to her foster-daughter's marriage. The young couple set up house and lived in quiet, happy domesticity, and the bond of love was tied yet tighter by the birth of a beautiful boy, the image of his lovely mother.

Mlle de Scudéry idolized little Olivier, whom she took away from his mother for hours and days at a time, in order to pet and fondle him. As a result, the boy grew attached to her and was as happy to be with her as with his mother. Three years had passed when the professional jealousy of Brusson's fellow craftsmen caused the volume of work that came his way to diminish daily, till in the end he could barely feed himself and his family. To this was added the yearning for his lovely home town, Geneva. So in spite of opposition from Mlle de Scudéry, who promised all manner of support, the little family eventually moved to Geneva. Anne wrote to her foster-mother a few times, then she fell silent, and Mlle de Scudéry could only suppose that her happy life in Brusson's homeland had wiped out the memory of the past.

It was now exactly twenty-three years since Brusson had left Paris for Geneva with his wife and child.

'Oh, horror,' cried Mlle de Scudéry, when she was some-what recovered. 'Are you Olivier? My Anne's son! To find you like this!'

'I do not suppose, worthy lady,' replied Olivier, calm and composed, 'that you ever imagined the boy whom you petted like a fond mother, whom you stuffed with sweets as you dandled him on your knee, to whom you gave the sweetest names, having become a young man, would one day stand before you accused of a hideous murder! I am not blameless, the Chambre Ardente can justly charge me with a crime; but as true as I hope to die blessed, even if it be at the executioner's hand, I am innocent of all blood-guilt; it was not through me, not through my fault that the unhappy Cardillac died!' As he uttered these words, Olivier began to tremble and sway. Mlle de Scudéry silently motioned him to a small armchair standing beside him. He slowly sat down.

'I had plenty of time in which to prepare for my talk with you,' he began, 'which I regard as the last favour of merciful heaven, time in which to gain the calm and com-posure necessary to tell you the story of my atrocious, unheard-of misfortune. Be so merciful as to listen to me calmly, however much the disclosure of a secret of which you certainly have no inkling may astound, indeed horrify you. If only my poor father had never left Paris! My earliest memory of Geneva is of being sprinkled with the tears of my disconsolate parents and brought to tears my-self by their laments, which I did not understand. Later came the clear sense, the full consciousness of the oppres-sive want and profound poverty in which my parents lived. My father found himself disappointed in all his hopes. Crushed by chagrin, he died at the moment when he suc-ceeded in apprenticing me to a goldsmith. My mother spoke a great deal of you, she wanted to acquaint you with her sufferings, but she was overwhelmed by the discourage-ment born of poverty. That, and probably also the false shame which often gnaws at mortally wounded spirits, kept her from carrying out her resolve. A few months after my father's death, my mother followed him into the grave.'

'Poor Anne! Poor Anne!' cried Mlle de Scudéry, overcome by grief.

'Praise be to the eternal power of heaven that she passed over and will not see her beloved son fall under the executioner's hand, branded with shame,' exclaimed Olivier in a loud voice, casting a wild and terrible glance aloft. There was restless movement outside and sound of men walking to and fro. 'Oho,' said Olivier with a bitter smile, 'Desgrais is waking his companions. As though I could flee from here! But to continue: I was harshly treated by my master, although I worked hard and finally far outdid him. One day a foreigner happened to come into our workshop to buy some jewellery. Seeing a fine necklet I had made, he gave me a friendly slap on the back, eyed the ornament, and said: "Well, well, my young friend, that is an excellent piece of work. I really don't know who can surpass you except René Cardillac, who is the finest goldsmith in the world. You should go to him; he will be glad to take you into his workshop, for you are the only person who can be of assistance to him in his magnificent craftsmanship, and he is the only person from whom you can learn." The stranger's words sank deep into my soul. I had no more peace in Geneva, I felt myself drawn away by force. In the end I managed to break free from my master. I came to Paris. René Cardillac received me coldly and gruffly. I refused to be put off, he had to give me work, however paltry it might be. He told me to make a small ring. When I brought him the work he stared at me with his glittering eyes as though trying to see right inside me. Then he said: "You are a first-rate journeyman, you can move in with me and help me in the workshop. I shall pay you well, you will be content with me." Cardillac kept his word. I had been with him for several weeks without seeing Madelon, who, if I am not mistaken, was staying in the country just then with some cousin of Cardillac's. At last she came. Oh, eternal power of heaven, what happened to me when I saw the angelic creature! Has anyone ever loved as I do! And now! Oh, Madelon!'

Olivier's sorrow overcame him and he could say no more. He put both hands over his face and sobbed violently. Finally, mastering his wild anguish with an effort of will, he continued: 'Madelon looked at me with friendly eyes. She came to the workshop more and more frequently. I perceived with delight that she loved me. Strictly as her father kept watch on us, we many times squeezed each other's hands in token of our bond. Cardillac seemed not to notice anything. When once I had gained his favour and could obtain my mastership, I planned to ask him for Madelon's hand. One morning, when I was about to start work, Cardillac came up to me with anger and contempt in his scowling eyes. "I need your labour no longer," he began. "Out of this house within the hour, and let me never set eyes on you again. There is no need for me to tell you why I cannot tolerate your presence here any longer. The sweet fruit after which you aspire hangs too high for you, poor starveling!" I tried to speak, but he seized me with his powerful hand and flung me out of the door, so that I fell and seriously injured my head and arm.

'Blazing with indignation and torn by anguish, I made my way to a kindly acquaintance at the far end of the Faubourg Saint-Martin, who took me into his garret. I had no peace, no rest. At night I prowled round Cardillac's house, fancying that Madelon might hear my sighs, my lamentation, that she might be able to speak to me from the window unobserved. My mind was filled with all sorts of daring plans, which I hoped to persuade her to carry out. Next to Cardillac's house in the Rue Niçaise there is a high wall containing blind niches and old, half-crumbled statues. I was standing one night close beside one of these statues, looking up at the windows of the house, which open on to the courtyard enclosed by this wall. Suddenly I saw a light in Cardillac's workshop. It was midnight. Cardillac was never awake at this hour in the ordinary way, he was in the habit of going to bed on the stroke of nine. My heart pounded with a fearful premonition, I imagined something might happen that would give me entry. But the light immediately disappeared again. I pressed myself against the statue and into the niche, but recoiled in horror when I felt a counter-pressure, as though the statue had come to life. In the grey dusk I then saw the statue slowly rotate and a dark figure slip out and make off down the street with soft footsteps. I sprang to the statue; it was once more standing close against the wall. Involuntarily, as though impelled by an inner force, I crept after the figure. The full light of the bright lamp burning in front of the statue fell upon its face. It was Cardillac! An inexplicable fear, an eerie shudder, came over me. As though under a spell, I had to set out in pursuit of the ghostly somnambulist—for such I took the master to be, although it was not the time of the full moon, which thus bewitches sleepers. Finally, Cardillac vanished into the deep shadows beside him. From the low but familiar sound as he cleared his throat I realized that he had gone into the entrance of a house. "What does this mean, what is he going to do?" I asked myself in amazement, pressing up close to the houses.

'It wasn't long before a man wearing a plumed hat and spurs came out singing and warbling. Like a tiger upon his prey, Cardillac sprang from his place of concealment upon the man, who sank to the ground instantaneously, rattling in his throat. With a cry of horror, I leapt forward; Cardillac was bending over the man as he lay on the ground. "Master Cardillac, what are you doing?" I shouted. "Curses on you!" Cardillac bellowed, ran past me with the speed of lightning and disappeared. Quite beside myself and scarcely capable of moving a step, I approached the fallen man. I knelt down beside him; perhaps he can still be saved, I thought; but there was not a trace of life in him. In my anguish, I barely noticed that I had been surrounded by the Maréchaussée. "Another one laid low by the devils! Hey, young man, what are you doing here? Are you one of the gang? Away with you!"

'Thus they shouted in confusion and seized hold of me.

I was scarcely able to stammer that I could not have committed such a ghastly deed and that they should leave me in peace. Then someone shone a light into my face and cried with a laugh: "That's Olivier Brusson, the journeyman goldsmith, who works with our good, honest Master René Cardillac! He's very likely to murder people in the street—he's just the type! And then you'd expect a murderer to stay lamenting by the corpse and let himself be caught. Come on, lad, tell us what happened."

' "Just in front of me," I told them, "a man fell upon this one here, struck him down, and ran away as fast as lightning when I shouted. I was looking to see whether there was still a chance of saving the victim."

' "No, my son," exclaimed one of those who had lifted up the corpse, "he's dead, stabbed through the heart as usual." "Damnation," said another, "we've come too late again, like the day before yesterday." With this they left, carrying the corpse.

'I simply cannot tell you how I felt; I pinched myself to see whether I was not being deceived by an evil dream; it seemed to me that I should wake up in a moment full of amazement at this crazy figment of my imagination. Cardillac—the father of my Madelon—a villainous murderer! I sank down powerless on the stone steps of a house. Dawn was gradually breaking, a richly plumed officer's hat lay on the pavement in front of me. Cardillac's bloody deed, committed on the spot where I was sitting, suddenly came vividly to me. I rushed away in horror.

'I was sitting in my garret, completely bewildered, almost senseless, when the door opened and René Cardillac came in. "In the name of Christ, what do you want?" I cried to him. Taking no notice of my question, he came towards me, smiling at me with a calm and serenity that only increased my inner repugnance. Since I was unable to rise from my straw pallet, upon which I had thrown myself, he pulled up a rickety old stool and sat down beside me. "Well, Olivier," he began, "how are you, poor lad? I was really terribly over-hasty when I threw you out of the house, I miss you every moment of the day. How would it be if you came and worked with me again? You say nothing? Yes, I know, I have offended you. I didn't want to conceal from you that I was angry about your flirtation with my Madelon. But afterwards I thought things over and came to the conclusion that with your skill, your diligence, and your honesty I couldn't wish a better son-in-law than you. So come with me and see if you can win Madelon for your wife." Cardillac's words pierced my heart, I trembled at his malignity, I couldn't utter a word. "You hesitate," he continued sharply, boring into me with his glittering eyes, "you hesitate? Perhaps you can't come to me today because you have other plans. Perhaps you want to pay a visit to Desgrais or even call upon D'Argenson or La Régnie. Take care, boy, that the claws which you wish to draw out to other people's destruction do not seize and tear you yourself." Then my profound indignation found expression. "Let those who have a hideous crime on their conscience tremble at the names you have just uttered," I cried. "I have no need to—I have nothing to fear from them."

' "As a matter of fact," Cardillac continued, "it would do you honour to work with me. I am the most famous master goldsmith of the day and esteemed everywhere for my honesty and straightforwardness, so that any evil slander would fall back heavily upon the head of the slanderer. As to Madelon, I must confess that it is to her alone that you owe my indulgence. She loves you with a vehemence with which I would not have credited the gentle child. The moment you were gone she threw herself at my feet, embraced my knees, and declared to the accompaniment of a thousand tears that she couldn't live without you. I thought this was simply imagination: all infatuated young things are ready to die on the spot when the first whey-faced youth gives them a friendly look. But my Madelon really did fall ill, and when I tried to talk her out of all this nonsense she cried your name a hundred times. What could I do, if I did not wish her to lapse into despair? Yesterday evening I told her that I consented to everything and would fetch you today. She blossomed out overnight like a rose and is now waiting for you, beside herself with amorous longing."

'May the eternal power of heaven forgive me, I don't know myself how it happened, but suddenly I was standing in Cardillac's house, and Madelon, crying exultantly, "Olivier—my Olivier—my beloved—my husband!" rushed to me, threw her arms round my neck, and pressed herself to my breast, so that in the excess of joy I swore by the Holy Virgin and all the saints that I would never, never leave her.'

Overwhelmed by the recollection of this crucial moment, Olivier fell silent. Mlle de Scudéry, overcome by horror at the crime of a man whom she had regarded as the embodiment of virtue and probity, exclaimed: 'It's terrible! René Cardillac is a member of the gang of murderers that has for so long turned our good city into a den of thieves?'

'Gang, Mademoiselle?' said Olivier. 'There never was any gang. It was Cardillac alone who villainously sought and found his victims throughout the whole city. It was because he was *alone* that he was able to carry out his misdeeds with impunity, that the police could never get on the track of the murderer. But let me continue, the sequel will reveal the secrets of the most villainous and at the same time unhappiest of men. Anyone can imagine the position in which I now found myself with my master. The step had been taken, there was no going back. At times I felt as though I had become Cardillac's accomplice in murder; only in Madelon's love did I forget the inner anguish that tormented me, only in her presence could I shake off all outward sign of the unspeakable affliction under which I laboured. When I worked with the old man in the workshop I could not look him in the face, could scarcely exchange a word with him on account of the horror that set me quivering at the mere presence of this atrocious man, who exhibited all the virtues of the true and tender father, of the good citizen, while the night cast its veil over his crimes. Madelon, the pure, angelic child, idolized him. It cut me to the quick to think that if ever vengeance fell upon the unmasked villain, she, who had been deceived with all the hellish cunning of Satan, would be plunged into the most abysmal despair. This in itself closed my mouth, and I should have kept it closed even if I had had to die a criminal's death. Although I had heard a good deal from the Maréchaussée, Cardillac's crimes, their motive and the manner in which he carried them out, remained a mystery to me; I did not have to wait long for the explanation.

'One day Cardillac, who, to my intense disgust, generally used to be very gay while at work and laugh and joke, was extremely serious and withdrawn. Suddenly he flung aside the piece of jewellery he was working on, scattering gems and pearls in all directions, jumped to his feet, and said: "Olivier, things cannot remain like this between us, the situation is unbearable. What the subtlest cunning of Desgrais and his henchmen failed to discover has been delivered into your hands by chance. You have seen me engaged in the nocturnal labour to which I am driven by my evil star, denial is impossible. But it was your evil star, too, that made you follow me, that wrapped you in a cloak of invisibility and gave such lightness to your footsteps that you walked as soundlessly as the smallest animal; so that I, who can see in the darkest night like the tiger, who can hear the slightest sound, the humming of flies a street away, did not notice you. Your evil star has made you my accomplice. In your present position, betrayal is out of the question. Therefore you shall know all."

' "Never again shall I be your accomplice, hypocritical villain." That was what I wanted to cry out, but the horror that seized me when I heard Cardillac's declaration choked me. Instead of words, I could only utter an unintelligible sound.

'Cardillac sat down on his working-chair again. He wiped the sweat from his brow. He seemed profoundly shaken by his recollection of the past and to have difficulty in gaining control over himself. Finally, he began: "Wise men have a great deal to say about the strange impressions to which pregnant women are susceptible, about the curious in-

fluences which such vivid and involuntary impressions from
outside may exercise upon the child. An extraordinary story
was told me of my mother. During the first month of preg-
nancy she watched, with other women, a magnificent court
festival at Trianon. She caught sight of a cavalier in Spanish
dress with a flashing jewelled necklace, from which she
thereafter could not take her eyes. Her whole being became
a desire for the sparkling gems, which appeared to her of
supernatural worth. Several years earlier, when my mother
was not yet married, the same cavalier had made an attempt upon her virtue, but had been rejected with disgust.
The cavalier observed my mother's yearning, fiery gaze.
He believed that he would be luckier now than he was
before. He managed to approach her and even to lure her
away from her acquaintances to a lonely place. There he
took her passionately in his arms; my mother grabbed at
the beautiful necklace; but the same instant he fell to the
ground, dragging my mother down with him. Either because he had suffered a sudden stroke or for some other
reason, he was dead. My mother sought in vain to extricate
herself from the dead man's rigid arms. With his hollow
eyes, whose light had gone out, directed upon her, the dead
man tossed this way and that with her upon the ground.
Her shrill screams for help finally reached some people
passing in the distance, who hurried to her aid and released
her from the arms of her horrible lover. The shock made
my mother seriously ill. She and I were given up for lost;
but she recovered, and the birth was easier than anyone had
hoped. But the terror of that frightful moment had struck
me. My evil star had risen and shot down sparks that
ignited in me a strange and ruinous passion. Even in my
earliest childhood, I prized sparkling diamonds and the
work of the goldsmith above everything. This was taken for
an ordinary childish liking for pretty things. But it proved
to be something quite different, for as a boy I stole gold and
gems wherever I could lay my hands on them. Like the most
skilled connoisseur, I instinctively distinguished fake jewellery from genuine. Only the genuine article attracted me,

fake gems and rolled gold I ignored. At length my innate urge was forced to yield to my father's savage punishments.

' "But in order to handle gold and precious stones I embraced the goldsmith's profession. I worked with passionate enthusiasm and soon became the leading master in this art. Then there began a period in which my inborn impulse, so long suppressed, forced its way to the surface and grew mightily, eating away everything around it. As soon as I had completed and delivered a piece of jewellery, I lapsed into a state of unrest and despair that robbed me of sleep, health, and the will to live. Like a ghost, the person for whom I had worked stood day and night before my eyes, decked out in my jewellery, and a voice whispered in my ear: 'It's yours—it's yours—take it—what use are diamonds to a dead man?' In the end, I began to steal. I had entry into the houses of the great, I quickly made use of every opportunity, no lock resisted my skill, and soon the jewellery I had made was back in my hands. Then even that did not dispel my restlessness. The eerie voice made itself audible again, mocking me and saying: 'Oho, a dead man is wearing your jewellery!' I myself did not know how it came about, but I began to feel unutterable hatred towards those for whom I had made jewellery. Yes, an impulse to murder them began to stir in the depths of my soul, at which I myself trembled. It was then that I bought this house. I had come to terms with the vendor, we were sitting together in this room, drinking a bottle of wine to celebrate the conclusion of negotiations. Night had fallen, I was about to leave, when the vendor said: 'Listen, Master René, before you go I must acquaint you with a secret of this house.' So saying, he opened a cupboard built into the wall, pushed the back of the cupboard aside, stepped through into a small closet, bent down, and raised a trapdoor. We went down a steep and narrow flight of stairs, came to a narrow gate, which he opened, and emerged into the courtyard. Now the old gentleman walked across to the encircling wall, pushed at a slightly projecting piece of iron, and immediately part of the wall revolved, so that a man could comfortably step through the opening and out into the street. You must see this device some time, Olivier; it was probably made by cunning monks of the monastery that once stood here, so that they could secretly slip in and out. It is a piece of wood, only mortared and whitewashed on the outside, into which a statue, also of wood, has been let; wall and statue together rotate on hidden hinges.

'"Dark thoughts rose in me as I looked at this device, it seemed a preparation for deeds which as yet remained a secret even to myself. I had just delivered to a gentleman of the Court a rich ornament which, as I knew, was intended for a dancer at the opera. I was subjected to terrible torments—the ghost dogged my footsteps—the whispering Satan was ever at my ear! I moved into the house. Bathed in the sweat of terror, I tossed and turned sleepless on my bed. With my mind's eye I could see the man slipping off to the dancer with my jewellery. Full of fury, I jumped up —threw on my coat—went down the secret stairs—and out through the wall into the Rue Niçaise. He came, I fell upon him, he shouted, but I held him fast from behind and plunged my dagger in his heart—the jewellery was mine! This done, I felt such calm, such contentment in my soul as I had never known before. The ghost was gone, the voice of Satan silent. Now I knew what my evil star desired. I had to obey it or perish!

'"Now you understand my actions, Olivier. Do not imagine that because I do what I cannot leave undone I have lost all feeling of pity, of compassion, which is said to be an essential part of man's nature. You know how hard it is for me to deliver a piece of jewellery; how I refuse to work at all for a few people, whose death I do not desire; how sometimes, knowing that tomorrow blood will banish my ghost, I forestall this with a good hard blow with my fist, which stretches the owner of my jewel on the ground and brings it back into my hands."

'Having said all this, Cardillac led me into the secret vault and let me look at his jewel cabinet. The King himself does not own a finer one. Attached to each article was a small label stating exactly for whom it was made and when it was taken by theft, robbery, or violence.

' "On your wedding day, Olivier," said Cardillac in a hollow, solemn voice, "you will swear a sacred oath with your hand on the crucifix that as soon as I am dead you will reduce all these riches to dust by means with which I shall acquaint you. I do not want any human being, and least of all Madelon and you, to come into possession of this hoard bought with blood."

'Caught in this maze of crime, torn by love and repugnance, by bliss and horror, I was like the damned soul whom a lovely angel, gently smiling, beckons up aloft, while Satan holds him fast with red-hot claws, and the holy angel's loving smile, in which all the happiness of high heaven is mirrored, becomes the most agonizing of his torments. I thought of flight, even of suicide—but Madelon! Blame me, worthy lady, blame me for having been too weak to crush by force a passion that bound me to crime; but am I not paying for it with a shameful death?

'One day Cardillac came home unusually gay. He fondled Madelon, gave me a most friendly look, drank a bottle of vintage wine at supper—something which he normally did only on high days and holidays—sang, and exulted. Madelon had left us, I was about to go into the workshop. "Sit where you are, lad," cried Cardillac. "No more work today, let us drink once more to the welfare of the worthiest and most excellent lady in Paris." After I had clinked glasses with him and he had drained his at a gulp, he said: "Tell me, Olivier, how do you like these lines:

> *A lover, afraid of thieves,*
> *Is unworthy of love.*"

'He then told me what had happened in the Marquise de Maintenon's apartment between yourself and the King, adding that he had always revered you above every human being and that you, with your lofty virtue, before which his evil star paled and became powerless, would never arouse any evil spirit, any thoughts of murder, in him, even if you

were to put on the finest jewellery he had ever ma(
"Listen, Olivier," he said, "to what I have decided. A long
time ago I was commissioned to make a necklet and bracelet
for Henrietta of England and to supply the gems myself.
The work surpassed anything I had ever done, and it broke
my heart to think that I must part with these ornaments,
which had become my heart's jewel. You know of the
Princess's unhappy death by assassination. I kept the jewellery and wish now, as a token of my veneration and gratitude, to send it to Mlle de Scudéry in the name of the persecuted band. Besides, if I deliver to Mlle de Scudéry this
token of her triumph, I shall also be pouring upon Desgrais
and his fellows the scorn they merit. You shall take the
jewellery to her."

'As soon as Cardillac spoke your name, Mademoiselle, it
was as though black veils had been torn aside and the beautiful, bright picture of my happy early childhood rose
before me in gay and shining colours. A wonderful feeling
of consolation entered my heart, a ray of hope before which
the gloomy spirits vanished. Cardillac must have perceived
the impression his words made upon me, and he interpreted
it in his own way.

' "You seem to be pleased with my plan," he said. "I may
confess that I was ordered to carry it out by a deep inner
voice, very different from the one that demands blood sacri-
fices from me like a greedy beast of prey. At times a strange
feeling comes over me—I am seized by an inner anxiety,
the fear of something atrocious, the horror of which is
wafted across to the earth from the world beyond. It then
seems to me that what the evil star has committed through
me might be imputed to my immortal soul, which has no
part in it. In such a mood I resolved to make a fine diamond crown for the Holy Virgin in the church of Saint-
Eustache. But every time I tried to start work on it I was
overcome more and more forcibly by this inexplicable
anxiety, till finally I gave up. Now I have the feeling that
I shall be humbly bringing an offering to the embodiment
of virtue and piety, and imploring effective intercession, if

87

I send Mlle de Scudéry the finest jewellery I have ever made."

'Cardillac, who was familiar with every detail of your way of life, Mademoiselle, told me exactly how and when I was to deliver the jewellery, which he enclosed in an elegant casket. I was filled through and through with delight, for heaven itself was showing me, through the monstrous Cardillac, the way to escape from the hell in which I was languishing, an outcast sinner. So I thought. Completely against Cardillac's wishes, I intended to insist upon seeing you personally. As Anne Brusson's son and your foster-child, I meant to throw myself at your feet and tell you everything. Moved by the unspeakable misery that would have descended upon Madelon if it were revealed, you would have kept the secret; but your brilliant mind would have been able to devise some means of controlling his abominable wickedness without revealing it. Do not ask me by what means this could have been done, I do not know; but the conviction that you would save Madelon and me was as deeply implanted in my soul as my faith in the help and comfort of the Holy Virgin.

'You know, Mademoiselle, that my plan miscarried that night. I did not lose hope of being luckier another time. Then suddenly Cardillac lost all his gaiety. He crept gloomily around, staring into space, muttering unintelligibly and striking the air with his hands, as though fighting off some hostile being; his mind seemed to be tormented by evil thoughts. This went on for a whole morning. Finally, he sat down at his work-bench, sprang petulantly to his feet again, looked out of the window, and said in a grave and sombre voice: "I wish Henrietta of England had worn my jewellery."

'These words filled me with horror. Now I knew that his mad brain was once more in the grip of the loathsome murder-spectre, that Satan's voice had once more grown loud in his ears. I saw your life threatened by the murderous fiend. If Cardillac only had his jewellery in his possession again, you would be saved. Then I met you on the Pont-

Neuf, forced my way to your carriage and threw you the note imploring you to bring back to Cardillac at once the jewellery you had received from him. You did not come. My anxiety increased to despair next day, when Cardillac spoke of nothing else than the costly jewellery that had appeared to him during the night. I could only interpret this as referring to your jewellery, and I was certain that he was brooding upon a murderous assault, which he undoubtedly intended to carry out that night. I had to save you, even if it cost Cardillac's life. As soon as Cardillac had shut himself in his room, as usual, after evening prayers, I climbed out of a window into the courtyard, slipped through the opening in the wall, and took up a position close by in deep shadow. It was not long before Cardillac came out and crept quietly away along the street. I followed him. He went towards the Rue Saint-Honoré, my heart trembled. All of a sudden I lost sight of him. I resolved to station myself at your front door. Then, as on the occasion when chance made me the witness of Cardillac's murderous onslaught, an officer passed, singing and warbling, without noticing me. But the same moment a black figure leapt out and fell upon him. It was Cardillac. I wished to prevent this murder; I uttered a loud cry, and in two or three bounds I was on the spot. It was not the officer, but Cardillac, who sank to the ground mortally wounded and with the death rattle in his throat. The officer dropped the dagger, drew his sword from its sheath and, thinking I was the murderer's accomplice, took up a fighting position; but he quickly hurried away when he saw that I paid no attention to him, but merely examined the corpse. Cardillac was still alive. After picking up the dagger which the officer had dropped, I hoisted him on to my shoulders and with an effort carried him home and through the secret passage to the workshop.

'The rest you know. You see, Mademoiselle, that my only crime consists in not having betrayed Madelon's father to the courts, thereby putting an end to his crimes. There is no blood on my hands. No martyrdom will wrest Cardillac's secret from me. I do not wish that now, in despite of the everlasting power of heaven that concealed the father's abominable crimes from the virtuous daughter, the whole misery of the past shall break in upon her with deadly effect, that now the world's vengeance shall grub up the corpse from the soil that covers it, that now the executioner shall put the mark of shame upon the mouldering bones. No, my heart's beloved will weep for me as an innocent victim, time will assuage her grief—but her anguish at the hideous deeds of her dear father would be irreparable!'

Olivier fell silent, but suddenly a river of tears gushed from his eyes, he threw himself at Mlle de Scudéry's feet and entreated: 'You are convinced of my innocence—I am sure you are convinced! Have pity on me, tell me how Madelon is.'

Mlle de Scudéry called Martinière, and a few moments later Madelon flung herself on his breast. 'Everything is all right, now that you are here—I knew the noble-hearted lady would save you!' cried Madelon over and over again, and Olivier forgot the doom that was hanging over him; he felt free and blissfully happy. In the most touching way, they both lamented bitterly what they had suffered on account of one another and then embraced afresh and wept for joy at having found each other again.

If Mlle de Scudéry had not been convinced of Olivier's innocence already, she must certainly have become so now, as she watched the two of them forget the world and their misery and their unspeakable suffering in the bliss of deep and sincere love. 'No,' she cried, 'only a pure heart is capable of such blissful oblivion.'

The bright rays of morning were breaking through the window. Desgrais knocked softly on the door of the room and reminded those within that it was time to take Olivier Brusson away, since this could not be done later without attracting attention. The lovers had to part.

The vague forebodings that had taken possession of Mlle de Scudéry's mind after Brusson's first appearance in her house had now acquired a terrible reality. She saw the son of her beloved Anne innocent, but so entangled by circumstances that there seemed no way of saving him from a shameful death. She honoured the young man's heroism, which made him prefer to die laden with apparent guilt rather than reveal a secret that would cause Madelon's death. She could think of no possible means of snatching the poor fellow from the cruel court. And yet she was determined to shun no sacrifice which might avert the crying injustice that was in the process of being committed. She tormented herself with all kinds of plans, some of them wild and all rejected as soon as conceived. All glimmer of hope grew fainter and fainter, till she was on the verge of despair. But Madelon's unhesitating, childlike trust and the transfiguration that came over her when she spoke of her beloved, whom soon—absolved from all guilt—she would clasp in a wifely embrace, touched Mademoiselle's heart and spurred her to fresh efforts.

In order to do *something*, Mlle de Scudéry wrote a long letter to La Régnie telling him that Olivier Brusson had proved to her complete satisfaction that he had no hand in Cardillac's death, and that only the heroic resolve to take with him to the grave a secret whose revelation would bring ruin upon true innocence and virtue prevented him from making a statement to the court which would free him not merely from the terrible suspicion of having murdered Cardillac but also of having belonged to the band of villainous murderers. Everything burning zeal and brilliant eloquence could produce, Mlle de Scudéry put into her attempt to soften La Régnie's hard heart. A few hours later, La Régnie replied that he was sincerely delighted to hear that Olivier Brusson had convinced his exalted and worthy patroness of his innocence. As to Olivier's heroic resolve to take with him into the grave a secret relating to the murder, he was sorry that the Chambre Ardente could not honour such heroism, but must rather seek to break it by the most forceful means. He hoped within three days to be in possession of the strange secret, which would probably bring miraculous events to light.

Mlle de Scudéry knew only too well what the terrible La Régnie meant by the means that would break Brusson's heroic silence. It was now certain that the luckless young man would be subjected to torture. In her anguish, it finally occurred to Mlle de Scudéry that the advice of a lawyer might be of assistance at least in obtaining a postponement. Pierre Arnauld D'Andilly was at that time the most famous lawyer in Paris. His probity and virtue were equal to his profound knowledge and wide intelligence. Mlle de Scudéry went to him and told him everything, so far as she could without betraying Brusson's secret. She thought that D'Andilly would eagerly assume the innocent man's defence; but her hopes were dashed. D'Andilly listened to everything and then replied, smiling, with Boileau's words: 'Truth may sometimes look improbable.' He pointed out to Mlle de Scudéry that there was the strongest evidence against Brusson, that La Régnie's procedure could in no way be called brutal or hasty, that on the contrary he was entirely within the law, and in fact could not act in any other way without neglecting his duty as a judge. D'Andilly did not believe that he could save Brusson from torture by even the most skilful defence. Only Brusson himself could do that, either by a frank confession or at least by an exact account of the circumstances surrounding Cardillac's murder, which might then bring fresh facts to light.

'Then I shall throw myself at the King's feet and beg for his mercy,' said Mlle de Scudéry, beside herself and in a voice half choked with tears.

'For heaven's sake don't do that, Mademoiselle,' cried D'Andilly. 'Reserve that measure as a last resort; if you try it too soon and without success, it will be lost to you for ever. If the King were to pardon a criminal of that kind at the present juncture he would lay himself open to the bitterest reproaches of the populace, who feel themselves in danger. It is possible that by revealing his secret or by some other means, Brusson will succeed in exculpating himself in the eyes of the people. Then it will be time to implore mercy of the King, who will not ask what has been proved or not proved before the court, but will consult his own inner conviction.'

In view of his wide experience, Mlle de Scudéry had no alternative but to take D'Andilly's advice. She was sitting late that evening in her room, profoundly worried and brooding endlessly on what she could do to save the unfortunate Brusson, when Martinière entered and announced the Comte de Miossens, a colonel in the King's Guard, who urgently wished to speak to Mademoiselle.

'Forgive me, Mademoiselle,' said Miossens, after bowing with soldierly decorum, 'for intruding upon you so late, at such an inconvenient hour. That's how we soldiers do things, and besides a couple of words will gain your pardon. I am here on account of Olivier Brusson.'

Mlle de Scudéry, keenly interested in what she was about to hear, cried out: 'Olivier Brusson? The unhappiest of all men? What have you to do with him?'

'I thought your protégé's name would suffice to win me a sympathetic hearing. The whole world is convinced of Brusson's guilt. I know that you hold another opinion, though, as I have been told, it is supported only by the declarations of the accused. It is different in my case. No one can be more convinced than I am that Brusson had no hand in Cardillac's death.'

'Speak, oh speak,' cried Mlle de Scudéry, her eyes shining with delight.

'It was I,' said Miossens emphatically, 'who struck down the old goldsmith in the Rue Saint-Honoré, not far from your house.'

'By all the saints, you—you!' cried Mlle de Scudéry.

'And I swear to you, Mademoiselle,' Miossens went on, 'that I am proud of my deed. Know that Cardillac was the most abominable and hypocritical villain, that it was he who cunningly murdered and robbed by night and for so long escaped every snare. I do not know myself what aroused my suspicions of the old villain when, in a state of visible unrest, he brought me the jewellery I had ordered,

93

inquired in detail for whom it was intended, and in the craftiest manner questioned my valet as to when I was in the habit of visiting a certain lady. It had long since struck me that the unfortunate victims of this loathsome robber all bore the same fatal wound. I realized that the murderer had practised a particular blow which must kill instantaneously, and that he counted on it. If he missed, it meant a fight. I therefore took a precaution which is so simple I am amazed that others did not think of it before and thereby save their lives from their dastardly attacker. I wore a light breastplate under my waistcoat. Cardillac attacked me from behind. He gripped me with the strength of a giant, but his deadly accurate blow slipped off the iron. The same instant I broke free from his grasp and stabbed him in the chest with the dagger I held ready.'

'And you are silent?' asked Mlle de Scudéry. 'You do not make a statement to the court regarding what happened?'

'Allow me to remark, Mademoiselle,' Miossens continued, 'that such a statement, if it did not ruin me, might at least involve me in the most repugnant trial. Would La Régnie, who scents crime everywhere, immediately believe me if I accused the honest Cardillac, the model of all piety and virtue, of attempted murder? Suppose the sword of justice were pointed at me?'

'That would be impossible,' cried Mlle de Scudéry, 'your birth—your rank . . .'

'Remember the Marshal of Luxembourg,' Miossens broke in, 'who had his horoscope cast by Le Sage and as a result was suspected of poisoning and shut up in the Bastille. No, by St Denis, I shall not sacrifice an hour of my freedom or the lobe of my ear to the raving La Régnie, who would like to set his knife at all our throats.'

'But in this way you will bring the innocent Brusson to the scaffold,' broke in Mlle de Scudéry.

'Innocent?' retorted Miossens, 'You call the villainous Cardillac's accomplice innocent, Mademoiselle? The man who assisted him in his evil deeds, who has deserved death a hundred times over? No, indeed, he will justly bleed; and

94

if I have told you the true facts of the case, Mademoiselle, it was on the understanding that you would know how to use my secret for the benefit of your protégé without delivering me into the hands of the Chambre Ardente.'

Mlle de Scudéry, overjoyed to find her conviction of Brusson's innocence so decisively confirmed, had no hesitation in revealing everything to the Count, since he already knew of Cardillac's crimes. She then asked him to go with her to D'Andilly, who, once he had been told the whole story under the seal of secrecy, would advise them what to do next.

After Mlle de Scudéry had given him as exact an account as she could, D'Andilly inquired again into the smallest details. In particular, he asked Count Miossens if he was quite certain that he had been attacked by Cardillac and whether he would be able to identify Olivier Brusson as the person who carried away the corpse.

'Apart from the fact that I clearly recognized the goldsmith in the moonlit night,' replied Miossens, 'I have also seen in La Régnie's possession the dagger with which Cardillac was stabbed. It is mine, distinguished by the delicate workmanship of the handle. I was standing only a pace from the young man, whose hat had fallen from his head, and could see his every feature; I should have no difficulty in identifying him.'

D'Andilly stared into space for a few moments in silence, then he said: 'There is absolutely no chance of snatching Brusson from the hands of justice by the normal channels. For Madelon's sake he refuses to accuse Cardillac of robbery and murder. There is all the more reason for him to maintain his resolve, because even if he proved this accusation by revealing the secret panel in the wall and the hoard of stolen jewellery, he would still be condemned to death as an accomplice. The same holds good if Miossens were to reveal to the judges what really happened to the goldsmith. Delay is all we can hope to achieve for the present. Let Miossens call at the Conciergerie, have Brusson brought before him, and identify him as the man who carried away

Cardillac's corpse. Let him hasten to La Régnie and say: "I saw a man struck down in the Rue Saint-Honoré; I was standing close to the corpse when another man sprang forward, bent down to the body and, finding that there were still signs of life, hoisted it on to his shoulders and carried it away. I have identified Olivier Brusson as this man." This statement will cause La Régnie to question Brusson afresh in Miossens's presence. Brusson will not be put to the torture, and further investigations will be made. Then it will be time to approach the King himself. It will be left to your ingenuity, Mademoiselle, to do this in the most diplomatic manner possible. In my own view it would be best to tell the King the whole truth. Brusson's confession will be confirmed by Count Miossens's statement, and it may also be confirmed by a secret search of Cardillac's house. The situation cannot be dealt with by a verdict of the court, but only by the King's decision, which, based upon his inner feelings, will pardon where a judge would have to punish.'

Count Miossens carried out D'Andilly's advice to the letter, and everything went as the lawyer had predicted.

The next move was to approach the King, and this was the most difficult step, because he had conceived such an aversion to Brusson, whom alone he considered to be the abominable robber and murderer who for so long had terrorized the whole of Paris, that the slightest reference to the notorious trial put him in a rage. Maintenon, keeping to her principle of never speaking to the King of unpleasant things, refused to act as a go-between; consequently Brusson's fate was left entirely in Mlle de Scudéry's hands. After long thought she reached a decision which she immediately put into execution. She put on a black dress of heavy silk, decked herself out in Cardillac's exquisite jewellery, added a long black veil, and thus attired appeared in Maintenon's apartment at the hour when the King was there. In this solemn garb, the figure of the venerable lady possessed a majesty calculated to arouse deep reverence even among the dissipated individuals accustomed to live out their heedless lives in the antechambers of royalty. Everyone stepped aside for her, and as she entered even the King rose in great surprise and came to meet her.

Then his eye caught the glitter of the exquisite diamonds in her necklace and armlets, and he exclaimed: 'By heaven, that is Cardillac's jewellery!' Turning to Maintenon, he added with a charming smile: 'See, Madame La Marquise, how our lovely bride mourns her bridegroom.'

'Oh, mon Seigneur,' interjected Mlle de Scudéry, as though pursuing the jest, 'how would it befit an anguished bride to adorn herself so magnificently? No, I have completely abandoned the goldsmith and would think no more of him, did not the horrifying picture of his murdered body being carried past just in front of me keep appearing to my eyes.'

'What,' asked the King, 'you saw the poor devil?'

Mlle de Scudéry then told him in a few words how chance (she did not yet mention Brusson's part in the matter) had brought her to Cardillac's house just after the murder was discovered. She described Madelon's frenzied grief, the profound impression the heavenly child had made upon her, and how she had saved the poor girl from Desgrais's clutches to the cheers of the populace. Her tale grew more and more gripping as she described the scenes with La Régnie, Desgrais, and Olivier himself. The King, carried away by the extreme vividness of Mlle de Scudéry's narrative, did not notice that they were talking about the noxious trial of that Brusson who was so repugnant to him; he could not utter a word, and only occasionally gave vent to his emotions in an exclamation. Before he had time to gather his wits, while his mind was still in a turmoil over the fantastic story he had just heard, Mlle de Scudéry lay at his feet imploring mercy for Olivier Brusson.

'What are you doing, Mademoiselle?' burst out the King, taking both her hands and leading her to an armchair. 'You have astounded me. That is a frightful story. Who can vouch for the truth of Brusson's account?'

To this Mlle de Scudéry replied: 'Miossens's statement—the search of Cardillac's house—an inner conviction—

Madelon's virtuous heart that recognized the same virtue in the unhappy Brusson!'

The King, on the point of replying, turned in response to a noise that had broken out by the door. Louvois, who had been working in the next room, entered with a worried mien. The King rose and left the room, followed by Louvois. Both Scudéry and Maintenon considered this interruption dangerous; once having been taken by surprise, the King might fight shy of walking into the trap again. But a few minutes later he returned to the room, walked rapidly up and down a few times, then came and stood in front of Mlle de Scudéry with his hands clasped behind his back and said in a low voice and without looking at her: 'I should like to see your Madelon!'

To this Mlle de Scudéry replied: 'Oh, mon Seigneur, what high, high happiness you are bestowing upon the poor, unhappy child. You have only to give a sign and the little one will be at your feet.' So saying, she tripped as fast as her heavy clothes would let her to the door, called out that the King wished to admit Madelon Cardillac to his presence, and came back weeping and sobbing with delight and gratitude. Mlle de Scudéry had foreseen this favour and had therefore brought Madelon with her, leaving her with the Marquise's chambermaid holding a short petition drawn up by D'Andilly. In a few moments she was lying speechless at the King's feet. Fear, confusion, shy reverence, love, and anguish drove the poor girl's seething blood faster and faster through her veins. Her cheeks were burning red, her eyes glittering with pearly tears that every now and then fell between her silky lashes on to her lovely lily-white bosom.

The King seemed affected by the angelic child's marvellous beauty. He gently raised the girl, then he made as if to kiss the hand he was holding. He lowered it and looked at the sweet child with eyes that were wet with tears, testifying to profound emotion. Maintenon whispered low to Scudéry: 'Isn't the little thing the living image of La Vallière? The King is revelling in sweet memories. Your game is won.'

Quietly as Maintenon had spoken, the King seemed to have heard. He blushed, he cast a glance at Maintenon, read the petition Madelon had handed him, and then said gently and kindly: 'I can well believe, dear child, that you are convinced of your loved one's innocence; but let us hear what the Chambre Ardente has to say about it.' A gentle movement of the hand dismissed the little one, who dissolved into tears.

Mlle de Scudéry observed to her horror that the recollection of La Vallière, helpful though it had seemed at first, had changed the King's mind as soon as Maintenon mentioned the name. Either the King felt that he had been rudely reminded that he was on the point of sacrificing harsh justice to beauty or he had reacted like a sleeper who has been woken by a loud call and whose beautiful dream-figure, which he was about to embrace, vanishes into thin air. Perhaps he no longer saw his La Vallière before him, but thought only of Sœur Louise de la Miséricorde (La Vallière's convent name among the Carmelite nuns), who tormented him with her piety and penitence. There was nothing to do now but quietly await the King's decision.

News of Count Miossens's statement to the Chambre Ardente had meanwhile got about; the populace is easily swayed from one extreme to the other, and the man whom the mob had only a little while earlier cursed as the most villainous of murderers and threatened to tear limb from limb before he ever reached the scaffold, was now lamented as the innocent victim of barbarous justice. Only now did the neighbours recall his virtuous comportment, his great love for Madelon, his loyalty and wholehearted devotion to the old goldsmith. Mass processions appeared before La Régnie's palace, shouting threateningly, 'Set Olivier Brusson free, he is innocent,' and even throwing stones at the windows, so that La Régnie had to seek refuge from the infuriated rabble with the Maréchaussée.

Several days passed without any fresh information whatsoever concerning Olivier Brusson's trial reaching Mlle de Scudéry. Feeling utterly disconsolate, she called to see the

Marquise de Maintenon, who assured her that the King was maintaining complete silence on the matter and that it did not seem advisable to remind him of it. When she then inquired with a strange smile how the little La Vallière was doing, Mlle de Scudéry became convinced that the proud lady was inwardly deeply chagrined by the affair that threatened to lure the over-susceptible King into a region whose magic spell was beyond her control. Hence no help could be expected from the Marquise.

Eventually Mlle de Scudéry, with D'Andilly's assistance, managed to find out that the King had secretly had a long talk with Count Miossens; further, that Bontemps, the King's most trusted valet and *chargé d'affaires*, had been to the Conciergerie and spoken to Brusson; and finally, that the same Bontemps had been to Cardillac's house one night with several men and had spent a long time there. Claude Patru, the occupant of the ground floor, stated that there had been a banging and bumping overhead all night long and that he was sure Olivier Brusson had been present, because he had clearly recognized his voice. It was quite clear, therefore, that the King was trying to ascertain the true facts of the case for himself; but the long delay in coming to a decision remained incomprehensible. La Régnie must be making every possible effort to prevent his victim being snatched from between his jaws. This nipped all hope in the bud.

Almost a month had passed, when the Marquise de Maintenon sent word to Mlle de Scudéry that the King wished to see her that evening in her, Maintenon's, apartment.

Mlle de Scudéry's heart beat wildly, she knew that Brusson's case was about to be decided. She told poor Madelon, who prayed vehemently to the Holy Virgin and all the saints that they might convince the King of Brusson's innocence.

And yet it seemed as though the King had forgotten the whole matter; he passed the time as usual in pleasant conversation with the Marquise de Maintenon and Mlle de

Scudéry, without referring by one syllable to poor Brusson. At length Bontemps appeared, approached the King, and spoke a few words to him in a voice so low that neither of the two ladies caught any of it. Mlle de Scudéry trembled inwardly.

Then the King rose, walked across to Mlle de Scudéry, and said with radiant eyes: 'I congratulate you, Mademoiselle! Your protégé, Olivier Brusson, is free!' Mademoiselle, the tears starting from her eyes, was about to throw herself at the King's feet. He prevented her, saying: 'Come, come, Mademoiselle, you should be an advocate in the Court de Parlement and fight my lawsuits for me, since, by St Denis, no one on earth can resist your eloquence. But,' he added more seriously, 'is not he whom virtue itself defends safe from all evil accusations, from the Chambre Ardente and every court in the world?'

Mlle de Scudéry now recovered her speech and burst out into a flood of gratitude. The King interrupted her, informing her that far more ardent thanks awaited her in her own house than he could claim from her, for the happy Olivier was probably at that very minute embracing his Madelon. 'Bontemps,' concluded the King, 'is to pay over to you a thousand *louis*; give them to the little one as a dowry. Let her marry her Brusson, who does not deserve such happiness, but then let them both leave Paris. That is my will.'

Martinière hurried to meet Mlle de Scudéry, followed by Baptiste, both of them with faces lit by joy and crying exultantly: 'He is here! He is free! Oh, the dear young people!'

The blissful couple flung themselves at Mlle de Scudéry's feet. 'Oh, I knew that you, and you alone, would save my husband,' cried Madelon. 'Oh, faith in you, my mother, was firm in my soul,' cried Olivier. And both kissed the worthy lady's hands and shed a thousand burning tears. Then they embraced one another again and declared that the supernal bliss of this moment outweighed all the unspeakable sufferings of the immediate past and swore never to part even in death.

A few days later they were bound together by the blessing of the priest. Even if it had not been the King's will, Brusson could not have remained in Paris, where everything reminded him of the atrocious period of Cardillac's crimes, where at any moment some chance might reveal the evil secret at present known only to a few, and destroy for ever his peaceful existence. Immediately after the wedding, he moved with his young wife to Geneva, taking with him Mlle de Scudéry's blessings. Splendidly equipped through Madelon's dowry, highly gifted in his trade, and possessed of every civil virtue, he quickly built up a happy, carefree life there. The hopes with which his father had gone down disappointed into his grave were fulfilled in him.

A year had passed since Brusson's departure when a public proclamation appeared, signed by Harloy de Chauvalon, Archbishop of Paris, and the advocate of the Court of Parlement, Pierre Arnauld D'Andilly, to the effect that a repentant sinner had surrendered a hoard of stolen jewellery under the secret of the confessional. Anyone who had been robbed of jewellery, especially by a murderous attack in the open street, was invited to report to D'Andilly, and if his description of the jewellery stolen from him tallied exactly with any item found, and there was no doubt about the justice of his claim, the jewellery would be returned to him.

Many of those who figured in Cardillac's list as not having been murdered, but merely felled with a blow of the fist, gradually called upon the advocate of the Court of Parlement and, to their astonishment, received back the jewellery that had been stolen from them. The rest went to the treasury of the church of Saint-Eustache.

DATURA FASTUOSA

THE GORGEOUS THORN APPLE

Chapter One

Professor Ignatius Helms's glass-house. The young student Eugenius. Gretchen and the Professor's elderly widow. Conflict and decision.

THE young student Eugenius stood in Professor Ignatius Helms's glass-house looking at the beautiful bright-red blossoms which the royal amaryllis (*Amaryllis reginae*) was just unfolding at daybreak.

It was the first mild day of February. The pure azure of the cloudless sky gleamed bright and friendly overhead and the sun shone in through the tall windows. The flowers, still slumbering in their green cradles, shifted as though in a dream disturbed by the presentiment of day, and extended their juicy leaves; but the jasmine, the mignonette, the perpetual rose, the guelder rose, and the violet, awakened to new life, filled the glass-house with the sweetest, loveliest scents, and every now and then little birds that had shyly ventured forth from their warm nests fluttered up and pecked longingly at the panes, as though seeking to lure forth the beautiful, multi-coloured springtime locked up inside the glass-house.

'Poor Helms,' said Eugenius with deep melancholy, 'poor old Helms, never again will you see all this magnificence, all this splendour. Your eyes have closed for ever, you rest in the cold earth! But no, no, I know that you are among all your dear children whom you tended so faithfully; none of those whose early death you lamented is really dead, and only now do you fully understand their life and their love, of which before you had only an inkling.'

At this moment little Gretchen began to clatter and bump

around among the flowers and plants with her watering-can.

'Gretchen, Gretchen!' cried Eugenius. 'What are you doing? I almost believe you are once again watering the plants at quite the wrong time and nullifying all the pains I have taken with them.'

The full watering-can almost fell from poor Gretchen's hands.

'Oh, dear Eugenius,' she exclaimed, as the bright tears came into her eyes, 'don't scold me, don't be angry. You know I'm a silly, simple thing, I always think the poor shrubs and plants, which here no dew and no rain refreshes, look at me as though they were dying of thirst and asking me for food and drink.'

'To give them water now,' Eugenius interrupted her, 'is giving them injurious sweets that will make them sicken and die. I know you mean well by the flowers, but you lack all botanical knowledge, and in spite of my ceaseless instruction you take no trouble over this science, which is most befitting, indeed essential, to any woman; for without it a girl does not even know to which class and order the sweet-scented rose belongs with which she adorns herself, and that is very bad. Just tell me, Gretchen, what are these plants in the pots, which are soon going to blossom?'

'Yes,' cried Gretchen joyfully, 'those are my darling snowdrops!'

'You see,' continued Eugenius, 'you see, Gretchen, you don't even know the proper name of your favourite flowers! You must say *Galanthus nivalis.*'

'*Galanthus nivalis,*' repeated Gretchen in a low voice, as though in awe. 'Oh, dear Eugenius,' she then exclaimed, however, 'that sounds very fine and splendid, but they don't seem to be my darling snowdrops any longer. Do you remember how, when I was still a child . . .'

'Aren't you a child any more?' Eugenius interrupted her.

'Oh, well,' replied Gretchen, blushing to the eyes, 'when you are fourteen you don't think of yourself as a child any longer.'

'And yet,' said Eugenius, smiling, 'it's not so long ago since the big new doll . . .'

Gretchen quickly turned away, jumped to one side, squatted down and busied herself with the flower-pots that were standing on the floor.

'Don't be angry, Gretchen,' Eugenius went on gently. 'Always remain the dear, good, child whom Father Helms took away from her evil kinswoman and, together with his noble wife, brought up as though she were his own daughter. But you were going to tell me something.'

'Oh,' answered Gretchen in a small voice, 'oh, dear Herr Eugenius, it's probably just silly nonsense I've got into my head again, but since you wish me to, I shall tell you frankly what was in my mind. When you called my snow-drops by that splendid name I thought of Fräulein Röschen. As you know, Herr Eugenius, she and I used to be one heart and one soul and—when we were still children—loved to play together. But one day—it must have been about a year ago—Röschen's whole behaviour towards me became ever so strange and serious, and she said I mustn't call her Röschen any more, but Fräulein Rosalinda. I did so, but from that moment on she became more and more of a stranger to me—I had lost my dear Röschen. I think it will be the same with my dear flowers, if I am suddenly to address them by strange, proud names.'

'H'm,' said Eugenius. 'At times there is something very strange in your words, Gretchen. One knows what you mean and yet doesn't really understand what you have said. But that does not affect the magnificent science of botany, and even if your Röschen has now became Fräulein Rosalinda, you can still pay a little attention to the names by which your darlings are called in the learned world. Take advantage of my teaching! For the moment, however, my dear, good child, see to the hyacinths. Push the *Og roi de Buzan* and the *Gloria solis* more into the sunshine. I don't think the *Péruque quarrée* is going to come to very much. The *Emilius Graf Bühren*, which bloomed so proudly in December, has already gone to rest, it won't last much longer; but the *Pastor fido* is making a fine start. You can give plenty of water to the *Hugo Grotius*; that has a lot of growing to do.'

While Gretchen, who had blushed deeply again when Eugenius called her his dear, good child, set joyfully about doing as she was bid, Professor Helms's widow entered the glass-house. Eugenius pointed out to her what a splendid start the springtime flowering had made, bestowing particular praise upon the blossoming *Amaryllis reginae*, which the late Professor had esteemed almost more highly than the *Amaryllis formosissima*, for which reason Eugenius lavished special care upon it, in everlasting memory of his dear teacher and friend.

'You have a good and childlike heart, dear Herr Eugenius,' said the Professor's widow, deeply moved, 'and my dead husband did not feel for any of the other students he took into his house from time to time such esteem, such fatherly love, as he felt for you. But nor did any of the others understand my Helms as you did, none had such an affinity with his inmost being, none entered so profoundly into the true and essential core of his science. "Young Eugenius," he used to say, "is a true, pious youth, that is why the plants and trees love him and flourish merrily under his care. A hostile, peevish, profligate spirit—that is the Satan who sows the weeds that grow in such abundance and whose poisonous breath brings death to the children of God." He used to call his flowers the children of God, you know.'

Tears came into Eugenius's eyes. 'Yes, my dear, esteemed Frau Helms,' he said. 'I shall faithfully maintain this pious love; and this beautiful temple of my teacher, my father, shall thrive in glorious fertility as long as there is breath in my body. If you will permit me, Frau Helms, I shall now move into the little room by the glass-house, which the Herr Professor used to occupy; then I shall be better able to keep an eye on everything.'

'Just now,' replied the Professor's widow, 'my heart grew very heavy at the thought that soon the splendour of all these glorious blossoms must come to an end. It is true that I am quite conversant with the cultivation of plants and flowers and, as you know, not inexperienced in my husband's science. But, heavens above, how can an old woman like myself, however active she be, care for everything like a vigorous young man, even if she is not lacking in love for the work? And since we must now part, my dear Herr Eugenius . . .'

'What!' cried the horrified Eugenius, 'what, you want to cast me out, Frau Helms?'

'Will you please go into the house, dear Gretchen,' said the Professor's widow, 'and fetch me the big shawl, it is very cold out here.'

When Gretchen had gone Frau Helms began very seriously: 'You are perhaps too pure of heart, too inexperienced in the ways of the world, and too noble a youth, dear Herr Eugenius, fully to understand what I am now going to say to you. I shall soon enter upon my sixtieth year, you have barely reached your twenty-fourth, I could easily be your grandmother, and I believe that this difference in age should hallow our life together. But the poisoned arrow of slander does not spare even the matron whose life has been irreproachable, and there will be no lack of malicious persons who, ridiculous as it may sound, will make your presence in my house the subject of evil gossip and sly innuendo. The malice would affect you even more than myself; therefore, dear Herr Eugenius, it is necessary for you to leave my house. I shall, however, aid you in your career as though you were my son, and should have done so even if my Helms had not expressly placed this obligation upon me. You and Gretchen are and will remain my children.'

Eugenius stood mute and dumbfounded. He really couldn't understand what objection could be taken to his continuing to lodge with the Professor's widow, or why this should give rise to malicious gossip. But the lady's clearly expressed desire that he should leave the house that was to him the whole circuit of his life, in which dwelt all his joys, the thought that he was now to part from his darlings, which he had nurtured and tended, seized him with full force and fury.

Eugenius was one of those simple people to whom a small circle, within which they move gaily and freely, is quite enough, who seek and find in the science or art of which their spirit has taken possession the finest and sole aim of their activity and effort; to whom the small domain in which they are at home seems a fertile oasis in the great, barren, joyless desert of the rest of life, which remains unknown to them precisely because they imagine they cannot venture out into it without danger. We know that such people, on account of their mental make-up, remain in a certain sense for ever children, that they appear clumsy and gauche, and even narrow-minded and soulless as a result of a certain petty pedantry which their science imposes on them. They then become the target for a good deal of mockery from uncomprehending scoffers certain of easy victory. But within the innermost heart of such people there often burns the naphtha flame of higher knowledge. Strangers to the hustle and bustle of worldly life, the work to which they have devoted all their love and fidelity is an intermediary between themselves and the everlasting power within all being, and their quiet, inoffensive life is a perpetual service to God in the eternal temple of the world spirit. Such a man was Eugenius.

When Eugenius had recovered from the shock and was able to speak he declared with a vehemence not customary in him that if he had to leave the Frau Helms's house he would consider his earthly career at an end; for once cast out of his home, he would never again achieve peace and contentment. He besought Frau Helms in the most moving terms not to drive the man she had accepted as her son out into the desolate wilderness, for such he must consider any other place, wherever it might be.

The Professor's widow seemed to be striving painfully to reach a decision.

'Eugenius,' she said finally, 'there is one means by which I can keep you in my house under the same conditions as before. Become my husband!'

'It is quite impossible,' she continued, as Eugenius looked

at her in surprise, 'that a mind like yours should harbour the slightest misconception; therefore I do not hesitate for a moment to admit that the proposal I have just made you was by no means a sudden idea, but the outcome of prolonged reflection. You are unfamiliar with the conditions of everyday life and will not quickly, will perhaps never, learn to cope with them. In even the narrowest sphere of life you need someone who will divest you of the burden of dealing with your daily needs, who will care for you down to the smallest detail, so that you may live in complete ease of mind entirely for yourself and science. No one can do this better, however, than a tender, loving mother, and this I wish to be and remain in the strictest sense of the word, even though I appear to the world as your wife. I am sure that no thought of marriage and wedlock has ever entered your head, nor need you reflect upon it any further, for even though the priest has united us with his blessing, it will make not the slightest difference to our relationship, except that this blessing given in a holy place will really consecrate me in all piety your mother, as it will consecrate you my son. I make this proposal, which might appear to many worldlings extremely strange and bizarre, all the more confidently, dear Eugenius, because I am convinced that, if you accept it, nothing will be spoiled thereby. Everything which worldly circumstances demand for a woman's happiness will and must remain alien to you; the compulsion of life, the pressure, the discomfort of so many demands, with which you would be tormented, would quickly destroy your illusions and lay you open to all the grief, all the distress of harsh reality. Hence the *mother* can and must take the place of the *wife*.'

Gretchen came in with the shawl, which she handed to the Professor's widow.

'I do not wish you to reach a quick decision, dear friend,' said the latter. 'Make up your mind when you have thought it all over carefully. Not another word today; it is a good rule that says we should sleep on every problem before coming to a decision about it.'

With this, the Professor's widow left the glass-house, taking Gretchen with her.

Frau Helms was quite right: no thought of marriage and wedlock had ever entered Eugenius's head, and for that very reason her proposal had confounded him, because a completely new picture of life seemed suddenly to appear before his eyes. But when he thought the matter over he could imagine nothing more splendid, more beneficial, than that the Church should give its blessing to an alliance that would afford him a good mother and the sacred rights of a son.

He would have liked to communicate his decision to the old lady at once; but since she had bidden him to say nothing till the following morning, he had to restrain himself, although the expression in his eyes and his whole mien, which was full of quiet, devout joy, might have revealed what was taking place within him.

But when he came to carry out the Professor's widow's advice to sleep on the matter, there appeared to him in the delirium that precedes actual sleep a palely glimmering dream picture made up of figures which under normal circumstances seemed entirely to have vanished from his recollection. At the time when Professor Helms first took him into the house as his amanuensis, a young great-niece— a pretty, pleasant-mannered girl—had been a frequent visitor; but she had made so little impression upon him that when, after having stayed away for a time, she was reported to be returning to the village to marry a young doctor, he couldn't remember her at all. When she did in fact come back to celebrate her wedding to the young doctor, old Helms was ill and unable to leave his room. The devoted child therefore promised to come to the house immediately after the wedding to obtain from the venerable pair the blessing that would bring her and her husband happiness and prosperity.

Now, it so happened that Eugenius came into the room just as the bridal couple were kneeling before the old people. The angelically lovely bride did not seem to him to be the same girl at all; she bore no resemblance to the great-niece he had so often seen in the house, but appeared to be a completely different, loftier being. She was dressed in white satin. The rich garment clung close to her slender body and fell in wide folds. Her dazzling bosom gleamed through costly lace, her daintily braided chestnut hair was charmingly adorned with the symbolic myrtle wreath. A sweet, devout rapture shone upon the beauty's face, all the grace of heaven seemed to have been showered down upon her. Old Helms embraced the bride, then his wife did the same, afterwards leading her to the bridegroom, who pressed the angelic child passionately to his breast with delighted ardour.

Eugenius, whom no one noticed, no one bothered about, didn't know what was happening to him. A wave of icy cold and then of burning heat swept through his limbs, an ineffable pain cut into his chest, and yet it seemed to him that he had never felt such a wonderful sensation. 'Suppose the bride now approached you, suppose you, too, pressed her to your breast?' This thought, which suddenly struck him like an electric shock, appeared to him a monstrous sacrilege; yet the nameless fear that seemed to be crushing him was itself the most fervid longing, the hungriest yearning, for that which would dissolve his whole ego in annihilating pleasure-pain.

Then the Professor noticed him and said: 'Well, Herr Eugenius, here are our happy young bridal pair—you may wish happiness to the blushing bride, that is only fitting.'

Eugenius was incapable of uttering a word, but the lovely bride approached him and with charming friendliness held out her hand, which Eugenius, unaware of what he was doing, pressed to his lips. Then he lost all his senses, he had difficulty in staying on his feet, he didn't hear a word of what the bride was saying to him, and only came to himself when the young couple had long since left the room and Professor Helms was scolding him a little for his incomprehensible shyness, which had rendered him mute and caused him to act like a lifeless being devoid of interest or feeling.

Strangely enough, after Eugenius had gone round for a few days utterly shattered and as though sleepwalking, the whole occurrence faded away within him into a confused dream.

Now it was the figure of the lovely, angelically beautiful bride, as he had seen her that day in Professor Helms's room, that suddenly appeared before his eyes in vigorous, glowing life, and all the nameless anguish of that moment once more constricted his breast. But it seemed to him as though he was himself the bridegroom and the most beautiful one stretched out her arms so that he should embrace her and press her to his bosom. When he sought to rush upon her in an excess of wild delight, however, he felt that he was chained and a voice cried out to him: 'Fool, what are you trying to do? You are no longer your own property, you have sold your youth, no springtime of love and pleasure will blossom for you now, for in the arms of icy winter you have been frozen into an old man.'

With a cry of horror, he woke from his dream, but it was as though he could still see the bride, while behind him stood the Professor's widow striving with ice-cold fingers to press the lids over his eyes, so that he could not see the adorned and lovely young woman. 'Away,' he cried, 'away. My youth is not yet sold, I have not yet been frozen in the arms of icy winter!' Accompanied by an ardent yearning, there flared up in him a profound aversion to the union with the sexagenarian widow.

Eugenius must have looked somewhat out of sorts next morning; the Professor's widow immediately inquired how he was feeling and, since he complained of headache and exhaustion, prepared a cordial with her own hands and tended and pampered him like a spoiled sick child.

'And shall I reward all this motherly love and care with the blackest ingratitude,' said Eugenius to himself, 'shall I wantonly tear myself away from her, from all my joys, from all my life? And that on account of a vision seen in a dream, which can never become real for me, which was perhaps an enticement of Satan, intended to blind me with the base delights of the senses and cast me down into perdition? Is there any further need of thought, of reflection? My decision is firm and unalterable!'

That same evening the Professor's widow, who was almost sixty, became betrothed to young Herr Eugenius, who at the time was still a student.

Chapter Two

The views of worldly-wise youth. The curse of ridicule. Duel for a bride. A serenade that didn't take place and a wedding that did. Mimosa pudica.

EUGENIUS was just pruning some potted plants when Sever, the only friend whom he saw from time to time, came in. The moment Sever saw Eugenius busily working, he stopped in his tracks and burst out laughing.

Anyone else, less susceptible to the bizarre than the jovial, jolly Sever, would probably have done the same.

The Professor's old widow, in all goodness of heart, had presented her bridegroom with her late husband's wardrobe, saying that, even if Eugenius wouldn't go out in the street in these old-fashioned clothes, she would like to see him making use of the fine, comfortable dressing-gowns.

So there stood Eugenius in the Professor's voluminous dressing-gown of Indian fabric dotted with bright-coloured flowers of every kind, and wearing on his head a tall hat on the front of which a glowing *Lilium bulbiferum* (fire lily) was pictured in all its glory; his youthful face amidst this exotic finery gave him the appearance of a bewitched prince.

'God save and preserve us,' cried Sever, when he finally recovered from his laughter, 'I thought you were a ghost. I thought the late Professor had risen from his grave and was moving among his flowers, himself a comely shrub covered with the strangest blossoms! Tell me, Eugenius, where did you get hold of that fancy dress?'

Eugenius answered him that he could see nothing odd in

this garb. The Professor's widow had permitted him to wear her late husband's dressing-gowns, which were comfortable and, moreover, made of such exquisite material as it would now be almost impossible to find anywhere in the world. All the flowers and plants were copied exactly from nature, and among the Professor's things were some rare night-caps that could take the place of a complete *herbarium vivum*. Out of proper respect, however, he intended to wear these only on special feast days. But even the clothes he now had on were of very exceptional interest, because the deceased Professor had written the name of each flower and each plant on the material with his own hand in indelible ink, as Sever could see for himself if he would look more closely at the dressing-gown and the cap; such a dressing-gown served as a wonderful object of study for a young man thirsty for knowledge.

Sever took the night-cap that Eugenius handed to him, and did indeed read a number of names written in a fine, clear hand, for example *Lilium bulbiferum, Pitcairnia angustifolia, Cynoglossum omphaloides, Daphne mezereum, Gloxinia maculata,* and so on. Sever was about to burst out laughing again, but suddenly he became very serious, looked deep into his friend's eyes, and said: 'Eugenius—is it possible —is it true? No, it cannot, it must not be more than a ludicrous, silly rumour put about by evil tongues in mockery of you and Frau Helms! Laugh, Eugenius, laugh uproariously —people say you are going to marry the Professor's widow.'

Eugenius started a little, then he assured his friend with downcast eyes that the rumour was true.

'Then Fate has brought me here in the nick of time,' cried Sever vehemently, 'to pull you back from the ruinous abyss upon whose edge you stand! Tell me, what dreadful madness has come over you, that you should sell yourself in the prime of youth for a mess of pottage?'

As always happened with Sever on such occasions, he worked himself into an ever-increasing state of excitement, and the words came thick and fast, until finally he cursed the Professor's widow and Eugenius himself; he was about

114

to add a few very coarse student's oaths, when Eugenius at last managed to persuade him to be quiet and listen.

Sever's heat had restored all Eugenius's composure. He now explained the situation to Sever, not concealing how the whole plan had originated, and concluded by asking what doubt his friend could have that his union with Frau Helms would bring him unadulterated happiness.

'My poor friend,' said Sever, who had now also grown quite calm, 'my poor friend, in what a close net of mis-understandings you have entangled yourself! But perhaps I may succeed in undoing the tightly tied knot, and once released from these bonds you will feel the value of free-dom!'

'Never,' cried Eugenius. 'My resolve is firm. You are a wretched worldling if you can doubt the gentleness and true mother love with which the worthiest of all women will guide me through life, since I shall always remain a child at heart.'

'Listen,' said Sever. 'You say yourself that you are still a child at heart, Eugenius, and there is some truth in what you say, and because of my greater experience of the world this puts me in a position to give you advice, even though in years I am scarcely older than you. Therefore do not con-sider it presumptuous if I tell you that from where you stand you are quite unable to see the situation clearly. Do not imagine for one moment that I doubt Frau Helms's intentions, that I am not convinced she is only seeking your happiness; but she herself, good Eugenius, is under a gross misapprehension. It is an old and true saying that women can do anything except step outside themselves and enter into the soul of another. What they themselves feel strongly is to them the criterion of all feeling, and their own emo-tions are the model from which they deduce what is locked in the other's breast. From all I know of old Frau Helms I should say that she was never capable of fervid passion, that she has always possessed the phlegmatic constitution which keeps girls and women pretty for a long time— because I must admit that for her years the old woman looks sleek and lively enough. We both know that nobody could have been more phlegmatic than old Helms, and when we also consider that both, in addition to the simple devoutness inspired by traditional morality, were governed by a warm-hearted cheerfulness, it is evident that theirs must have been a truly happy, calm marriage in which the man never criticized the soup and the woman never had the study scrubbed at the wrong time. But the Professor's widow imagines that she can continue undisturbed to play this everlasting *andante* of the marital duet with you, since she credits you with being too phlegmatic ever to want to break out into the world in an *allegro*. So long as everything remains quiet and peaceful within the botanical dressing-gown, it really doesn't matter who is inside, old Professor Helms or the student Eugenius. Oh, no doubt about it, the old lady will look after you, will pamper you; I invite myself here and now to be your guest over the finest Mocha coffee an old woman ever made, and she will be glad to see me smoking with you a pipe of the finest Varinas canaster which she has filled herself, and which I light with a spill that she has cut and folded from notebooks belonging to her late husband that were destined for the flames. But what happens if, in the midst of this calm, which to my mind at least has all the desolation of a barren desert, the storm of life suddenly breaks?'

'You mean,' Eugenius interrupted his friend, 'if mishaps occur—illness . . .'

'I mean,' continued Sever, 'if one day a pair of eyes look in through these panes of glass, a pair of eyes whose fiery rays melt the crust that encloses your heart and the volcano bursts forth in destructive flames. . . .'

'I don't understand you!' cried Eugenius.

'And against such rays,' Sever went on, paying no heed to Eugenius, 'a botanical dressing-gown will afford no protection, it will fall from your body in tatters, even if it be made of asbestos. And, quite apart from disasters of this nature that might befall you, there will be upon you from the outset of this insane union the most deadly of all curses, the curse before which the very smallest blossom of life curls up and dies—the curse of ridicule.'

In his almost childish simplicity of mind, Eugenius really didn't understand what his friend was talking about; he was in the process of learning what he could of the unknown territory Sever was referring to, when the Professor's widow came in.

A thousand ironic little folds twitched across Sever's face and a witticism trembled on his tongue. But when the Professor's widow came towards him with all the cheerful friendliness, all the gracious dignity of a noble matron, when she welcomed him with a few warm words that came straight from the heart as the friend of Eugenius, all irony, all malicious mockery, were wiped out, and it seemed to Sever at that moment as though there were beings and relationships in life of which commonplace worldly understanding had no knowledge, no inkling.

Let us say here that the Professor's widow was bound to make a profoundly appealing impression on anyone whose mind was not closed to the expression of true kindness and honesty, such as speaks to us from Dürer's matrons; for Frau Helms exactly resembled one of these matrons.

So Sever swallowed the witticism that had trembled on his tongue, and the urge to mock did not return even when the Professor's widow actually did invite him, as it was just the right time in the afternoon, to drink coffee and smoke tobacco with Eugenius.

Sever gave thanks to heaven when he was once more outside, for the old lady's hospitality and the noble charm that suffused her whole being had so gripped him that his deepest convictions had been shaken. The fact that, against his will, he had come to believe Eugenius might, after all, be happy in the preposterous union with the old lady struck him as sinister and almost horrifying.

News of Eugenius's strange betrothal had got around, so it was inevitable that next morning, when he entered the only lecture he still attended, everyone looked at him with a smile. More than that, when the lecture was over the students formed double ranks reaching out to the street, and poor Eugenius had to run the gauntlet, while cries rang out from all sides: 'Congratulations, bridegroom,' 'Greet your dear, sweet little bride from us,' 'I suppose the sky seems to him full of violins,' and so on.

The blood rose into Eugenius's head from every vein. Once he was out in the street a coarse fellow in one of the lines called out: 'Greet your bride, the old ——' He uttered a filthy word, but at the same instant all the furies awoke in Eugenius; he smashed his clenched fist into his adversary's face so that he fell over backwards. The student sprang to his feet and raised his thick, knotted stick against Eugenius; several others did the same; but the senior of the students' association jumped between Eugenius and the lad who was cursing him and cried in a loud voice: 'Are you street urchins, to brawl in public like this? What the devil is it to you whether Eugenius is getting married and who to? But Marcell insulted his betrothed in the presence of us all in the open street, and so vulgarly that it was Eugenius's right and duty to return insult for insult on the spot. Marcell knows what he has to do; but if anyone moves a finger now he will have me to deal with.'

The senior took Eugenius's arm and led him home. 'You're a good fellow,' he said to Eugenius, 'you couldn't have acted otherwise. But you live so quietly and so withdrawn that people are inclined to take you for a slyboots. But I'm not going to let you fight; though you're not lacking in courage, you've had no practice, and the bully Marcell is one of our best duellers, he'll have you stretched out at the third thrust. That shall not be; I shall fight in your place, I shall represent your cause; you can rely on that.' The senior then left Eugenius, without waiting for his answer.

'You see?' said Sever. 'You see how my prophecies are already starting to come true?'

'Oh, be silent,' cried Eugenius, 'the blood is still boiling in my veins, I no longer know myself, my whole being is torn in pieces. God above, what evil spirit flared up within me to produce that attack of rage? I tell you, Sever, if I had had a weapon in my hand at that moment I should have struck the unfortunate fellow dead on the spot! But I never imagined that anyone could utter such an insult!'

'Now,' said Sever, 'bitter experience is beginning.'

'Keep your vaunted worldly wisdom to yourself!' exclaimed Eugenius. 'I know that there are hurricanes that suddenly burst upon us and destroy in an instant everything that has been created with care and effort. Oh, I feel as though my finest flowers were lying broken and dead at my feet.'

At this point a student came in Marcell's name to challenge Eugenius to a duel the following morning. Eugenius promised to appear at the agreed time and place.

'You, who have never held a rapier in your hand, mean to fight a duel?' asked Sever in amazement. Eugenius assured him that no power could restrain him from fighting in his own cause, as was only right, and courage and resolution would make up for what he lacked in skill. Sever explained to him that in a duel by thrust and lunge, such as was the custom here, the courageous fighter was bound to be defeated by the skilful one. But Eugenius stuck immovably to his decision, adding that he had perhaps had more practice in fencing than people supposed.

Thereupon Sever embraced him joyfully and cried: 'The senior is right, you are a brave lad through and through, but you shall not go to your death, I am your second, and I shall protect you to the best of my ability.'

Eugenius's face was deathly pale as he came upon the duelling ground, but a sombre fire blazed in his eyes and his whole mien was one of firm courage, the embodiment of calm resolution.

Both Sever and the senior were astonished when Eugenius showed himself a very fair fencer, whose opponent could make no impression upon him at the first exchange. At the second exchange Marcell received an adroit thrust in the chest and fell in a heap.

Eugenius was told to flee, but he refused to move from

the spot whatever danger might threaten him. Marcell, who had been taken for dead, regained his senses and only now, when the surgeon assured him that his opponent would recover, did Eugenius leave the duelling ground and return home with Sever.

'Please,' cried Sever, 'please, friend, help me to wake from my dream, for I am convinced I am dreaming when I look at you. Instead of the peaceful Eugenius, there stands before me a mighty man of valour who fences like the most brilliant senior and possesses the same courage and composure.'

'Oh, Sever,' replied Eugenius, 'would to heaven you were right, if only it were all a bad dream. But no, the whirlpool of life has caught hold of me and who knows upon what rocks the dark power will hurl me, so that I am wounded to death and cannot find my way back into my paradise, which I believed inaccessible to the gloomy, wild spirits.'

'And what are these gloomy, wild spirits that disturb every paradise,' continued Sever, 'but the misconceptions that delude us regarding life that lies serene and clear before us? Eugenius, I conjure you, give up this decision which will ruin you! I spoke of the curse of ridicule; you will feel it more and more. You are brave and resolute, and since it is impossible now to protect your relationship with the old lady from ridicule, it is clear that you will have to fight twenty duels on your bride's account. But the greater the courage and loyalty you show, the more biting will be the acid of derision poured over you and your deeds. All the splendour of your student heroism will pale before the aura of utter Philistinism with which your old bride will surround you.'

Eugenius told Sever to say no more about a matter upon which his mind was firmly made up; he merely assured his friend, in response to his question, that he owed his skill in fencing solely to the late Professor Helms, who as a true student of the old stamp, had attached enormous importance to this art and to everything else appertaining to corporate student life. Almost every day he had spent an hour or so fencing with the old man, largely for the sake of the exercise; as

a result he had acquired considerable skill without ever setting foot in a fencing hall.

Eugenius learnt from Gretchen that the Professor's widow
had gone out and would not be home till the evening, since
she had a lot of shopping to do in town. He was somewhat
surprised to hear this, because it was most unusual for Frau
Helms to leave the house for so long.

Eugenius was sitting in Professor Helms's study, which
had now become his, absorbed in a botanical work that had
just come into his possession; he had almost forgotten the
fateful events of the morning. Dusk had already fallen,
when a carriage drew up outside the house, and soon afterwards Frau Helms entered the room. He was no little
astonished to see her in all the finery she generally wore only
on high festivals. The heavy dress of black bombasine, with
its multiple folds and rich adornment of fine Brabant lace,
the old-fashioned little hood, the costly pearl necklace and
pearl bracelets—the whole turn-out gave the tall, full figure
of the Professor's widow a positively regal and awe-inspiring
appearance.

Eugenius sprang up from his chair, but along with the
unfamiliar apparition all the day's disastrous events some-
how re-emerged from his soul, and from the depths of his
heart he involuntarily cried out: 'Oh, my God!'

'I know,' said the Professor's widow in a tone whose
feigned calm revealed only too clearly the profound per-
turbation of her soul, 'I know all that has happened since
yesterday, dear Eugenius; I cannot, I must not blame you.
My Helms, too, once had to fight a duel on my account
while I was betrothed to him—though I did not hear about
it till we had been married for ten years—and my Helms
was a quiet, God-fearing young man who certainly never
desired anyone's death. That's how things are, though I
have never been able to understand why they should be so.
But women are unable to understand many things that exist
on that dark reverse side of life which, if they wish to be
women and to preserve their womanly honour and dignity,
must always remain remote and obscure to them; with

devout resignation, the woman must believe without question what the man tells her about the dangers of those rocks which he, a bold pilot, has rounded! But what we are dealing with here is something different. Once youth's delight in the senses is past, once the garish pictures of life have paled, are we no longer to understand life at all? Once the spirit is entirely turned towards eternal light, is it not to be able to look upon the pure blue of the heavens without dark clouds and thunderstorms rising from the puddle of earthly life? Oh, when my Helms duelled on my account I was a girl of eighteen in the full bloom of youth, I was called beautiful, people envied him. But you—you duel for a matron, for a relationship which the frivolous world cannot understand, upon which the worthless and ungodly pour scorn. No, that must, that shall not be! I release you from your promise, dear Eugenius! We must part!'

'Never!' cried Eugenius, throwing himself at the Professor's widow's feet and pressing her hands to his lips. 'Shall I not spill my last drop of blood for my mother?'

Shedding hot tears, he besought Frau Helms to keep her word and let the blessing of the Church consecrate him her son.

Then he suddenly cried out: 'Unhappy man that I am, is not everything destroyed, all my hopes, all my joy in life? Marcell may already be dead—at any minute they may drag me off to jail.'

'Rest easy,' said the Professor's widow, while a charming smile spread over her face like the sun breaking through the clouds, 'rest easy, my dear, good son! Marcell is out of all danger; fortunately the thrust struck no vital part. I spent a few hours with the worthy rector of our university. He has discussed the incident with the senior of your students' association, the seconds, and a number of students who saw the whole occurrence. "That was no common brawl," said the noble old man. "Eugenius could not have punished the deep insult in any other way, nor could Marcell have acted otherwise. I have heard nothing, and shall know how to deal with any complaint."'

Eugenius shouted aloud for joy and delight, and carried away by the moment, in which heaven itself seemed to be smiling joyously upon the enthusiastic youth, the Professor's widow yielded to his entreaty that their wedding should be celebrated in a very short time.

Late on the eve of the ceremony, which was to be as quiet as possible, a low murmuring and giggling made itself heard in the street outside the house. It came from a group of students who were gathering there. Bursting into a rage, Eugenius ran to fetch his rapier. But then a rough voice spoke in the street: 'If you wish, I will join you in the pretty little serenade you are about to sing to the bridal pair, but in that case none of you will refuse to partner me in a dance tomorrow, a dance that will last as long as my partner can stay on his feet!'

One after the other, the students slunk silently away. Looking out of the window, Eugenius clearly recognized in the lantern-light Marcell, who stood in the middle of the pavement and did not move from the spot until the last of the assembled students had gone.

'I don't know what is the matter with our Gretchen,' said the Professor's widow, when the few old friends of the late Professor, who had been present at the ceremony, had left. 'She was weeping as though in hopeless grief. No doubt the poor child imagines that we shall pay less attention to her. No—my Gretchen remains my dear, dear little daughter!' So said the Professor's widow and threw her arms round Gretchen, who had just come in.

'Yes,' said Eugenius, 'Gretchen is our dear, good child, and the botany lessons will also go well, I know.' So saying, he too drew her to him and pressed a kiss to her lips, something he would never have done in the ordinary way. But Gretchen collapsed in his arms as though lifeless.

'What is it, Gretchen?' cried Eugenius. 'Are you a little mimosa, to shrink at a touch?'

'The poor child must be ill; the damp, cold air in the church has upset her,' said the Professor's widow, rubbing the child's brow with a stimulant. Gretchen opened her eyes with a deep sigh and said she had suddenly felt as though she were being stabbed in the heart, but it was all over now.

Chapter Three

Quiet family life. Excursion into the world. The Spaniard Fermino Valies. Warnings from an understanding friend.

A T the stroke of five, when the last lovely morning dream of the well-preserved example of some rare plant had fled, Eugenius would leave his bed, put on the Professor's botanical dressing-gown, and study until a small bell rang. This happened on the dot of seven and was a sign that the Professor's widow had got up and dressed, and that coffee was ready in her room. Eugenius would make his way to this room, and after kissing the Professor's widow's hand, precisely as a well-mannered child would wish good morning to his mother, would take the pipe that lay on the table ready filled, and light it from the spill held out to him by Gretchen. An hour would pass in amiable conversation, and at eight o'clock Eugenius would go down into the garden or the hot-house, according to the weather or the season, and occupy himself with botanical work till eleven o'clock. Then he would dress, and on the dot of twelve he would be standing at the laid table on which the soup was steaming. The Professor's widow would be highly delighted if Eugenius then remarked that the fish had just the right degree of spice, that the roast was succulent and flavoursome, and so forth.

'You are just like my Helms,' the Professor's widow would exclaim. 'He always used to praise my cooking, unlike so many husbands, who find the food tastes good everywhere except at home! Yes, dear Eugenius, you have just the same serene and cheerful nature as my late, beloved husband!'

Then there would follow, bit by bit, all sorts of incidents from the simple, quiet life of the dead Professor, which his widow recounted almost garrulously and which still moved

Eugenius deeply, though he knew them all by heart; frequently the little family's simple meal ended with the last drop of wine being drained to the Professor's memory.

The afternoon passed like the morning. Eugenius spent it in study, until the family reassembled at six in the evening. Then Eugenius would devote two hours to instructing Gretchen, in the presence of the Professor's widow, in this, that, or the other science or language. At eight they had supper, at ten they retired to bed. Thus one day was just like another, and only Sunday was different. On Sunday morning Eugenius, splendidly attired in one of the Professor's Sunday coats, many of them strange in colour and even stranger in cut, would go to church with the Professor's widow and Gretchen; in the afternoon, weather permitting, they would go for a walk to a small village not far from the town.

Thus continued the monastically simple life from which Eugenius had no wish to emerge, which seemed to him to encompass all his activity and all his being. But the stuff of wasting disease may be engendered within us when the mind, misconstruing its own organism, opposes itself in unhappy misunderstanding to the essential conditions of life. One could only characterize as disease the hypochondriac self-sufficiency into which all Eugenius's activities became petrified, and which, depriving him more and more of his natural gaiety, made him appear cold, gruff, and shy towards everything that lay outside his own narrow circle. Since he never left the house, except on Sundays in the company of his wife-mother, he lost all contact with his friends; he carefully avoided visits, and even the presence of Sever, his old and faithful friend, caused him such manifest anxiety that even he stayed away.

'Things have come to such a pass with you that you are and must be dead for us. An awakening now would really kill you!'

So said Sever as he left his lost friend for the last time, and it never occurred to Eugenius to wonder what he meant by these words.

The signs of a sickness of the mind soon appeared in Eugenius's deathly pale face. All youthful fire had vanished from his eyes, he spoke the dull language of the self-centred, and seeing him in the garb of the dead Professor, one gained the impression that the old man was trying to drive the young one out of his coat and grow back into it himself. In vain the Professor's widow inquired whether the young man, for whom she trembled, was feeling physically ill and in need of a doctor; he assured her that he had never felt better.

One day Eugenius was sitting in the arbour, when the Professor's widow entered, sat down opposite him, and looked at him in silence. Eugenius, who was absorbed in a book, seemed scarcely to notice her.

'This,' began the Professor's widow at last, 'I did not want, did not foresee, did not for one moment imagine!'

Eugenius, almost startled by the unaccustomed sharp tone in which the Professor's widow uttered these words, jumped from his seat.

'Eugenius,' continued the latter more gently, 'you are completely withdrawing from the world, it is your way of life that is wasting your youth. You think I ought not to reproach you for shutting yourself up in the house in monastic solitude, for living entirely for me and for science; but it isn't right. Far from me be the thought that you should sacrifice the best years of your life to a relationship which you misinterpret when you make this sacrifice for it. No, Eugenius, you must go out into life, which can never be dangerous to your devout nature.'

Eugenius assured her that he felt an inner aversion towards everything that lay outside the narrow circle that was his only home, that he would feel ill at ease among people, and that he really didn't know how to set about emerging from his solitude.

The Professor's widow, regaining her customary amiability, then told him that her late husband, just like himself, had enjoyed a solitary life entirely devoted to study, but notwithstanding this, he had been a frequent, and in his

126

youth almost a daily, visitor to a particular coffee-house frequented especially by scholars, writers, and, above all, foreigners. In this way he had always remained in contact with the world, with life, and very often information he picked up there had proved of great value for his science. Eugenius should do the same.

If his newly wed wife had not insisted, it is unlikely that Eugenius would really have ventured out of his cell.

The coffee-house which she had in mind was indeed a meeting-place of the literary world, and at the same time an establishment much frequented by foreigners, so that during the hours of evening a colourful turmoil swayed this way and that in its rooms.

It is easy to imagine how strange the recluse Eugenius must have felt the first time he found himself in these turbulent surroundings. But he felt his constraint relax when he observed that no one was taking any notice of him. Growing increasingly less tense, he finally took the audacious step of ordering some refreshment from an unoccupied waiter, pushing his way into the smoking room, where he took a seat in a corner and, while listening to the many conversations going on around him, followed his favourite inclination and actually smoked a pipe himself. Only then did he achieve a certain composure as, strangely excited by the gay and noisy activity on all sides, he sat there merrily puffing out the blue clouds.

A man sat down close to him whose appearance and behaviour betrayed the foreigner. He was in the prime of manhood, short rather than tall, but very well built, all his movements were swift and lithe, and his face wore an unusual expression. He was finding it impossible to make himself understood by the waiter he had called over; the more heated and angry he became, the more bizarre grew his stammered German. Finally, he cried in Spanish: 'The man is killing me with his stupidity.' Eugenius understood Spanish very well and did not speak it too badly. Overcoming his diffidence, he went up to the stranger and offered to act as interpreter. The stranger gave him a penetrating look. Then a friendly smile broke over his face and he assured Eugenius that he considered it a piece of great good fortune to have met somebody who spoke his mother tongue, which so few people knew, although it was probably the finest language in existence. He congratulated Eugenius on his pronunciation and concluded by saying that the acquaintance which he owed to fortunate chance must be more firmly cemented, which could be done in no better way than over a glass of the spiritous, fiery wine that grew on the soil of his fatherland.

Eugenius blushed all over his face like a bashful child; but after he had drunk a few glasses of the sherry which the stranger ordered he felt his inner being pervaded by a comforting warmth and began to derive very special enjoyment from his companion's lively conversation.

He should not take it amiss, the stranger finally remarked, after looking at Eugenius for a moment in silence, if he confessed that at first glance he had been somewhat surprised by his appearance. His young face and his whole demeanour were in such singular contrast to his bizarrely old-fashioned clothing that he must have some special motive for appearing thus disguised.

Eugenius blushed afresh, for a fleeting glance at his cinnamon-coloured sleeves with the gold-spun buttons on the cuffs showed him vividly how strange he must look by comparison with everyone else in the room; and especially by comparison with the stranger, who was dressed according to the latest fashion in black and appeared, with his fine, dazzling white linen and the brilliant in his breast-pin, the quintessence of elegance.

Without waiting for Eugenius's answer, the stranger went on, saying that it was quite unlike him to question anyone about the circumstances of his life, but that he felt such a great interest in Eugenius that he could not help confessing to the conviction that he was a young scholar dogged by misfortune and oppressed by poverty. His pale, harassed face bore this out, and the old-fashioned clothes were no doubt a gift from some elderly Maecenas, which he was compelled to wear for lack of any other. He was able and eager to help him, he looked upon him as a compatriot, and on that account he begged him to cast aside all narrow-minded prejudice and to be as frank with him as he would be with the closest and most tried friend.

Eugenius blushed for the third time, but now with bitterness, indeed almost in anger at the misconception which old Helms's unfortunate coat had aroused in the mind not only of the stranger but perhaps of all those present. This very anger, however, loosed his heart and tongue. He disclosed to the stranger all the circumstances of his life, he spoke of the Professor's widow with the enthusiasm which his truly child-like love for the old woman inspired in him, he assured the other that he was the happiest man in the world and that he wished his present situation to last as long as he lived.

The stranger listened to everything very attentively; then he spoke in a meaning, pointed tone: 'I too once lived alone, more alone than you, and believed that in this solitude, which others would have called wretched, destiny had no further call upon me. Then the waves of life billowed high and I was seized by their vortex, which threatened to drag me down into the abyss. But, like a courageous swimmer, I fought my way to the surface and am now sailing gaily and joyfully along on the bright silver flood, no longer fearful of the dread depths concealed beneath the play of the waves. It is only on the heights that people understand life, whose first demand is that we should enjoy and take pleasure in it. Let us empty our glasses to the gay enjoyment of life!'

Eugenius clinked glasses without having entirely understood the stranger. His words, spoken in sonorous Spanish, sounded to him like some strange music that echoed in his inmost being. He felt strangely drawn to the man, he did not know why.

The new friends left the coffee-house arm in arm. At the very moment they parted Sever appeared on the scene and, catching sight of Eugenius, stopped still in amazement.

'Tell me,' said Sever, 'in heaven's name tell me what this means? You in a coffee-house? You on familiar terms with a stranger? And on top of that you look quite excited and heated, as though you had drunk a glass of wine too much!'

Eugenius told his friend all that had happened, how the Professor's widow had insisted on his going to a coffee-house, and how he had then made the acquaintance of the stranger.

'How discerning the old lady is,' cried Sever. 'How well she understands life. She sees that the bird has grown wings, and she lets it try to fly! Oh, what a wise and sagacious woman!'

'Kindly do not speak in that way of my mother,' retorted Eugenius. 'She wants nothing but my happiness, my contentment, and it is to her kindness that I owe my acquaintance with the splendid man from whom I have just parted.'

'The splendid man?' Sever interrupted his friend. 'Well, for my part I wouldn't trust the fellow farther than I could throw him. He is a Spaniard and the secretary of the Spanish Count Angelo Mora, who has recently arrived and moved into the beautiful country house which, as you know, used to belong to the now bankrupt banker Overdeen. But you will have learnt that already from his own lips.'

'Not at all,' replied Eugenius. 'It never occurred to me to ask his name and estate.'

'There we have true cosmopolitanism, gallant Eugen!' cried Sever with a laugh. 'The fellow's name is Fermino Valies and he is undoubtedly a rogue, for every time I see him I am struck by something underhand about him, besides which I have met him in some very odd places. Beware— take care, my pious professor's son!'

'I see,' said Eugenius indignantly, 'that you have been trying to upset and anger me with your unkind criticisms, but you shall not mislead me; the only voice I shall trust and obey is that which speaks within me.'

'May heaven grant,' replied Sever, 'that your inner voice does not prove to be a false oracle!'

Eugenius himself could not understand what had led him to disclose his whole private life to the Spaniard during the first moments of their acquaintance, and if he had attributed to circumstances the strange state of excitement in which he had found himself, he now had to admit—since the image of the stranger remained clear and unfading in his soul— that the mysterious, almost supernatural element in the stranger's personality had worked upon him with truly magic power, and it seemed to him that this element was the cause of the singular distrust which Sever felt towards the Spaniard.

The following day, when Eugenius returned to the coffee-house, the stranger seemed to have been waiting for him impatiently. He told Eugenius that he felt it had been unfair not to have reciprocated his trust the day before, not to have disclosed the conditions of his life to him. His name was Fermino Valies, he was a Spaniard by birth and at present secretary to the Spanish Count Angelo Mora, whom he had met in Augsburg and with whom he had come here.

Eugenius replied that he had learnt all this the previous day from a friend of his called Sever. At this, a hot red suddenly appeared on the Spaniard's cheeks, vanishing again as quickly as it had come. Then he said, with a piercing glance and in an almost bitterly scornful tone: 'I did not imagine that people I had never bothered about would do me the honour of knowing me. But I hardly think your friend will be able to tell you more about me than I myself.'

Fermino Valies now frankly revealed to his new friend that, when little more than a boy, he had been enticed by the malevolent cunning of powerful relations into entering a monastery and taking vows, against which his heart had subsequently revolted. Threatened by the danger of sinking hopelessly into an unending, nameless martyrdom, he had been unable to resist the urge to break free, and when destiny favoured him with an opportunity he had fled from the monastery. Vividly and in the most sombre colours, Fermino then described life in that stringent order whose rules were the product of an inventive but insane fanaticism; all the more flamboyant by contrast appeared the picture which he then drew of his life in the world, which had the colourful richness only to be found in the career of a spirited adventurer.

Eugenius felt as though he were surrounded by magic circles; he imagined that he was seeing in the enchanted mirror of a dream a new world full of glittering figures, and his breast was filled unawares with the yearning to belong to this world himself. He perceived that his wonder at many of the things the Spaniard told him, and in particular the occasional questions he involuntarily interpolated, drew a smile from Fermino Valies, which brought a blush to his own cheeks. He was visited by the humiliating thought that at the age of manhood he was still a child.

Inevitably, the Spaniard daily gained increased dominion over the inexperienced Eugenius. As soon as the accustomed hour struck, he hurried off to the coffee-house and stayed longer and longer, because, even if he did not admit it to himself, he shuddered at the prospect of returning from the gay world to the barren desert of home. Fermino skilfully enlarged the narrow circle in which he had inevitably moved with his new friend. He went with Eugenius to the theatre and to the public promenades, and they generally finished up the evening in some tavern, where fiery beverages intensified Eugenius's mood of excitement to the point of wild exuberance. He came home late at night, threw himself on the bed, not to sleep peacefully as before, but to abandon himself to confused dreams that frequently presented to his eyes scenes which previously would have horrified him. Next morning he felt exhausted and worn out and incapable of scientific work, and not until the hour struck at which he was in the habit of meeting the Spaniard did all the spirits of frenzied life return and drive him forth.

One day around this time, when Eugenius was about to hurry to the coffee-house again, he looked in at the Professor's widow's room, as usual, to take a hasty leave.

'Come in, Eugenius, I want to talk to you!' the Professor's widow called out, and the tone in which she uttered these words was so unusually austere and grave that Eugenius was frozen to the spot in sudden dismay.

He entered the room; he could not bear the old lady's look, in which deep dejection was coupled with crushing dignity.

Speaking calmly and firmly, the Professor's widow now remonstrated with the young man for allowing himself to be enticed into a way of life that scorned all honour, all morality and order and would sooner or later bring about his downfall.

It may well be that the old lady, applying to the life of the young standards belonging to an earlier and more pious era, went too far in her long and at times too vehement homily. Inevitably, therefore, the sense of injustice which first took possession of Eugenius quickly developed into bitter indignation and the growing conviction that he had never yielded to any truly reprehensible impulse. The reproach that does not quite hit the mark always bounces ineffectively off the breast of the guilty party.

When the Professor's widow finally concluded her lecture with a cold, almost contemptuous, 'All right, go and do as you like!' the thought that at the age of manhood he was still a child returned to him with renewed force. 'Miserable schoolboy, will you never escape the rod?' Thus spoke a voice within him! He ran from the spot.

Chapter Four

Count Angelo Mora's garden. Eugenius's delight and Gretchen's grief. The dangerous acquaintance.

A SPIRIT beset by chagrin and torn by contradictory emotions tends to retire into itself; thus Eugenius, when he was already standing outside the coffee-house door, instead of entering hurried away, involuntarily making for the open country.

He came to the wide lattice gate of a garden from which were wafted balmy scents. He looked in and remained rooted to the spot in amazement.

Some powerful spell seemed to have transplanted to this

garden from the remotest and most varied regions the trees and bushes that now flourished luxuriantly in a medley of the strangest colours and shapes, as much at home as though this were their native soil. The broad paths that cut across the magic forest were bordered by exotic plants, shrubs that Eugenius knew only by name and from illustrations, and even flowers which he had cultivated in his own hot-house he here saw growing in a profusion and perfection such as he had never imagined.

Not far from the gate blossomed a *Datura fastuosa* (gorgeous thorn-apple) looking so glorious with its magnificently scented funnel-shaped flowers that Eugenius thought with shame of the wretched specimen of the same plant in his own garden. It was the Professor's widow's favourite flower, and forgetting all his chagrin, Eugenius thought to himself: 'Oh, if only I could get a *Datura* like that into our garden!'

At this moment the sweet notes of an unknown instrument drifted out from among the enchanted bushes, as though carried by the evening breeze, and the glowing and heavenly tones of a woman's voice rose up towards the sky. It was one of those melodies which only the amorous passion of the South can conjure up from the depths of the heart: the hidden woman was singing a Spanish *romanza*.

The young man was seized by all the sweet, nameless pain of ardent melancholy, all the glow of passionate yearning; he was overcome by an intoxication of the senses that called up before his eyes a far-away enchanted dreamland filled with vague but lovely shapes. He fell to his knees and pressed his head against the lattice.

The sound of steps approaching the gate startled him to his feet, and he walked quickly away, not wishing to be surprised by strangers in his agitated state.

In spite of the fact that dusk had already fallen, Eugenius found Gretchen still in the garden busy with the flowers.

Without looking up, she said in a low, shy voice: 'Good evening, Herr Eugenius!'

'What is the matter with you?' cried Eugenius, struck by

the girl's strange constraint. 'What is the matter, Gretchen? Look at me!'

Gretchen looked up at him, but the same instant bright tears welled up in her eyes.

'What is the matter, dear Gretchen?' repeated Eugenius, taking the girl's hand. But at this a sudden pain seemed to run through her. All her limbs trembled, her bosom rose and fell, her weeping turned into violent sobbing.

A singular emotion, something more than pity, pervaded the young man.

'For heaven's sake,' said Eugenius with the most anguished sympathy, 'for heaven's sake, what is the matter with you, what has happened, my dear Gretchen? You're ill, very ill! Come, sit down, tell me everything!'

With this Eugenius led the girl to a garden bench, sat down beside her, and, squeezing her hand, repeated: 'Tell me everything, my dear Gretchen!'

'I suppose I'm a silly, simple thing,' she murmured in a low voice and with downcast lids, 'and it's all imagination, nothing but imagination! And yet,' she then cried in a louder voice, the tears welling up in her eyes again, 'and yet it's true—it's true!'

'Compose yourself,' said Eugenius, quite bewildered, 'compose yourself, dear Gretchen, and trust in me, tell me what evil has befallen you, what has so disturbed you.'

At last Gretchen began to speak. She told Eugenius that while he was away an unknown man had come into the garden through the gate, which she had forgotten to bolt, and had inquired after him very insistently. There was something unusual about the man's whole person; he had looked at her with such strange, fiery eyes that an icy shiver had run through all her limbs and she could scarcely stir for fear and trembling. Then the man had asked various questions in very odd words which she barely understood, since he didn't speak proper German at all, and finally he had asked—here Gretchen suddenly stopped and her cheeks looked like fire lilies. But when Eugenius pressed her to tell him everything, everything, she went on to say that the stranger had asked her whether she wasn't fond of Herr Eugenius. Straight from the heart she had replied: 'Oh, yes, terribly fond of him!'

Thereupon the stranger had come up close to her and gazed at her once more with his repulsive, piercing eyes, so that she had to look down at the ground. More than that! The stranger had tapped her impudently and shamelessly on her cheeks, which were burning with fear and trepidation, and said: 'You pretty little thing, go on being fond of him!' Then he laughed so maliciously that her heart trembled in her body. At this moment the Professor's widow had come to the window and the stranger had asked her whether that was Herr Eugenius's lady wife, and when she replied, 'Yes, that is our mother,' he had exclaimed derisively: 'Ay, what a beautiful lady! I suppose you're jealous, little one?' After this he uttered a sly and malevolent laugh such as she had never heard from anyone before; then, after staring once more straight into the Professor's widow's eyes, he had quickly left the garden.

'But, dear Gretchen,' said Eugenius when she had finished, 'I can see nothing in all this to have so profoundly, so painfully upset you.'

'O Lord above,' burst out Gretchen, 'O Lord above, how often has our mother told me that devils in human form walk the earth sowing weeds among the wheat and setting all sorts of dangerous snares for good people! O merciful God, the stranger was the devil who . . .'

Gretchen stopped. Eugenius had realized at once that the stranger who had surprised Gretchen in the garden could be none other than the Spaniard Fermino Valies, and he knew very well what Gretchen meant.

No little perplexed by Valies's visit, he now asked Gretchen whether there had really been such a great change in his own behaviour recently.

Thereupon everything Gretchen had kept locked up in her bosom came pouring out. She complained to the young man that while he was at home he was always gloomy, taciturn, indeed at times so grave and sombre that she didn't even dare to speak to him. That he never now honoured her with an evening's teaching, which she had so much enjoyed, which in fact had been the best thing in the world to her. That he took no more joy in the beautiful plants and flowers—that yesterday he hadn't spared so much as a glance for the balsam trees which were now flowering so magnificently and which she had so carefully tended all on her own, that he no longer gave any thought whatever to the dear, good . . .

A flood of tears choked Gretchen's words.

'Calm yourself, don't let wild fancies take possession of you, my good child !'

As Eugenius uttered these words his eyes fell upon Gretchen, who had risen from the bench on which they had been sitting; and as though a magic mist that had been obscuring his vision had suddenly been dissipated, he now became aware that it was not a child, but a sixteen-year-old maiden with all the charm of fully developed youth who was standing before him. A strange surprise overwhelmed him, so that he could not go on. Finally gaining control of himself, he said in a low voice, 'Calm yourself, my good Gretchen, everything will be different,' and slipped out of the garden, into the house, and up the stairs.

If Gretchen's grief and her aversion to the unknown visitor had strangely stirred the young man's heart, his rancour towards the Professor's widow, to whom in his befuddled state he attributed all Gretchen's suffering and distress, was for that very reason intensified.

When he now entered the old lady's room and the latter began to address him he interrupted her with the vehement reproach that she had stuffed the young girl's head with all kinds of nonsense and passed judgement on his friend, the Spaniard Fermino Valies, whom she did not know and never would know, since the yardstick of an old Professor's widow was too small to measure figures that were truly life-size.

'So it has come to that !' cried the old lady in the most

anguished tone and raising her eyes and folded hands to heaven.

'I don't know what you mean by that,' said Eugenius morosely, 'but at least I haven't come to keeping company with the devil!'

'Oh, yes,' cried the Professor's widow, raising her voice, 'oh, yes, you are in the devil's snare, Eugenius; the Evil One already has you in his power, he is already stretching out his claws to drag you down into everlasting perdition! Eugenius, turn from the devil and his works, it is your mother who is entreating you, conjuring you. . . .'

'Am I to be buried between these bleak walls?' Eugenius interrupted the Professor's widow bitterly. 'Am I to sacrifice the vigorous life of a young man in joyless drudgery? Are the harmless enjoyments offered by the world works of the devil?'

'No,' cried the Professor's widow, sinking back exhausted in her chair, 'no, but . . .'

At this moment Gretchen entered and asked whether they would not come to supper, since everything was ready.

The three of them sat down at table mute and gloomy, prevented from speaking by the hostile thoughts that filled their hearts.

Early next morning Eugenius received the following note from Fermino Valies:

'You were at our garden gate yesterday. Why did you not come in? We spotted you too late to invite you. You saw our little botanists' Eden, didn't you? This evening you will be awaited at the same garden gate by

'Your fervent friend,

'Fermino Valies.'

According to the cook, the note had been brought by a terrifying man who was all black—probably a Moorish servant of the Count.

Eugenius felt his whole heart swell at the thought that he was now to enter this paradise full of glorious enchantments. He heard the heavenly notes that had risen from among the bushes and his breast quivered with passion and longing. All his ill-humour had vanished, to be replaced by joyful anticipation.

At table he told them where he had been and how complete had been the change in the banker Overdeen's garden outside the gates, which now belonged to Count Angelo, and that it was now a garden of enchantment for a botanist. His friend Fermino Valies had kindly offered to take him into it this evening, and he would see with his own eyes in nature all the things he at present knew only from descriptions and pictures. He spoke at length about all the wonderful trees and bushes from distant regions, named them, and expressed his profound astonishment at the way they flourished here in a climate so different from that of their native lands. Then he went on to talk about the shrubs and plants, assuring his listeners that everything in this garden was completely strange and out of the ordinary, that, for example, he had never in his life seen such a *Datura fastuosa* as the one blooming in this garden. The Count must possess mysterious magic powers, for without such powers no one could have conjured all this into being during the short time the Count had been living there. Then he spoke of the heavenly notes of the female voice that had risen from the bushes, and described in great detail the bliss he had felt while listening to it.

In his joyful enthusiasm, Eugenius did not notice that he was the only one speaking and that the Professor's widow and Gretchen were sitting mute.

When the meal was over the old lady, rising from her seat, said very seriously and calmly: 'You are in a dangerously over-excited state, my son. The garden you have described so enthusiastically, and whose wonders you ascribe to the foreign Count's evil magic powers, has been exactly the same for many, many years and its strange, indeed apparently miraculous, appearance is the work of a skilled foreign gardener who was employed by Overdeen. I have been there a few times with my husband, who, however, found it all too artificial and used to say that the violence done by man to nature in so startlingly mingling alien and incompatible plants weighed heavily on his heart.'

Eugenius counted the minutes; at last the sun went down and he was able to set out.

'The gate of perdition is open and the servant stands ready to receive the victim!' cried the Professor's widow in grief and anger; Eugenius, however, assured her that he hoped to return unscathed from the place of perdition.

The man who brought the stranger's note was all black and utterly repulsive, Gretchen told him.

'Well, then,' said Eugenius with a smile, 'it must have been Lucifer himself, or at least one of his head chamberlains, eh? Gretchen, Gretchen, are you still afraid of the chimney sweep?'

Gretchen blushed and lowered her eyes; Eugenius hurried off.

Eugenius was beside himself with amazement at the botanical splendour and magnificence that met him in Count Angelo Mora's garden.

'There are treasures of which you knew nothing, are there not, Eugenius?' said Fermino Valies at length. 'Things look different here from the way they look in your Professor's garden.'

Note that by now the two were on such friendly terms that they invariably addressed one another by their first names.

'Oh, do not speak of the wretched, barren spot in which I have languished like a sick, etiolated plant and lived a life utterly devoid of joy,' replied Eugenius. 'Oh, what splendour, what trees, what flowers, oh, to stay here, to live here!'

Fermino remarked that if Eugenius would approach Count Angelo Mora, which he, Fermino, would willingly arrange, his wish could easily be granted, provided it was possible for him to part from his wife, at least for so long as the Count remained here.

'But I don't suppose that's possible,' Fermino continued mockingly. 'How could a young husband like yourself fail to be still in the seventh heaven of love and unwilling to be deprived of his bliss for a moment? I saw your wife yesterday. She is indeed a bright and lively little woman for her advanced age. It is astonishing how long Cupid's torch burns in some women's hearts. Tell me, how do you feel when you embrace your Sarah, your Ninon? We Spaniards have a fervid imagination, you know, and hence I cannot think of your marital joys without bursting into flames! You aren't jealous, are you?'

The sharp and deadly dart of ridicule struck the young man's breast. He thought of Sever's warnings, he felt that if he responded to the Spaniard's prompting by revealing his true relationship with the Professor's widow he would stimulate the latter's mockery even further. But once again it was clearly revealed to his soul that a false mirage had cheated him, an inexperienced youth, of his life. He remained silent, but the burning red that mantled his cheeks must have betrayed to the Spaniard the effect of his words.

'It is beautiful here,' Fermino continued, without waiting for his friend's reply, 'beautiful and splendid, but do not therefore call your garden barren and joyless. In your garden yesterday I found something that far, far surpasses all the shrubs, plants, and flowers in the world. You know that I cannot have anything else in mind than the angelic girl who lives in your house. How old is the little one?'

'Sixteen, I believe,' stammered Eugenius.

'Sixteen!' repeated Fermino. 'Sixteen! The loveliest age in this country. As a matter of fact, the moment I saw the girl a great deal became clear to me, my dear Eugenius! Your little household must be quite idyllic, everything peaceful and friendly, the good old woman is content, so long as her little husband keeps cheerful—sixteen! Do you think the girl may still be innocent?'

All Eugenius's blood boiled at the Spaniard's impudent question.

'Your question is wanton profanity,' he blazed at him, 'filth that cannot fleck the heavenly clear mirror of the girl's pure mind.'

'Come, come,' said Fermino, casting a malicious glance at the young man, 'come, come, do not work yourself into a passion, my young friend! The purest, clearest mirror reflects life's images most vividly, and these images—but I see that you do not like to hear the girl discussed, so I shall say no more.'

The fierce indignation that shook him was indeed written on his face. Fermino really did appear to him sinister, and in the depths of his heart the thought germinated that Gretchen, with a child's intuition, might have been right when she took the Spaniard for a Satanic being.

At this moment a few chords rang out from among the bushes like billowing waves and that voice rose up which yesterday had inspired in the young man's breast all the delights of sweet melancholy.

'Oh God above!' cried the young man, standing transfixed.

'What is it?' asked Fermino; Eugenius made no reply, but listened to the song, completely lost in bliss and pleasure.

Fermino looked at him with eyes that seemed to be trying to penetrate his soul.

When the song ended at last Eugenius sighed deeply, and as though all the sweet melancholy could only now rise from his constricted breast, bright tears welled up in his eyes.

'The song seems to have moved you deeply,' said Fermino with a smile.

'Whence do they come,' cried Eugenius rapturously, 'whence do they come, those heavenly notes? They cannot dwell in any human breast.'

'Oh, yes, they can,' replied Fermino. 'It is the Countess Gabriela, my master's daughter, who, as is the custom in our country, is strolling through the garden singing *romanzas* and accompanying herself on the guitar.'

All of a sudden the Countess Gabriela, the guitar under her arm, stepped out from among the dark bushes and stood before Eugenius.

It must be said that the Countess Gabriela was beautiful

in every respect. The exuberance of her figure, the fiery glance in her big black eyes, the great charm of her demeanour, the full, sonorous, silvery tone of her deep voice —all this revealed that she had been born under sunny southern skies.

Such charms may be dangerous, but even more dangerous to the young man with no experience of life is that indescribable expression in the face, in the whole being, which indicates that the fires of love have already been awakened and are blazing fiercely within. To this expression is then added the mysterious art that enables a woman afire with love so to choose and arrange her clothes and her jewellery that a harmonious whole causes the charm of each individual part to shine forth with an even more dazzling brilliance.

Since the Countess Gabriela was in this respect the very goddess of love, it was inevitable that her appearance should strike Eugenius, already excited by her singing, like a flash of lightning that set him ablaze.

Fermino introduced the young man to the Countess as a new friend who understood and spoke Spanish perfectly and was also a brilliant botanist, for which reason this garden gave him exceptional pleasure.

Eugenius gabbled a few unintelligible words, while the Countess and Fermino exchanged meaning glances. Gabriela looked hard into the young man's eyes, so that he felt he would sink into the ground.

Then the Countess gave her guitar to Fermino and took Eugenius's arm, declaring in her most charming manner that she too knew a little about botany, but would like to learn more about many singular shrubs, and therefore must insist upon Eugenius taking another stroll through the garden.

Trembling with sweet fear, the young man wandered away with the Countess, but his breast became freer when the Countess inquired about this, that, or the other strange plant, and he was able to release his emotions in a flood of scientific explanations. He felt the Countess's sweet breath on his cheek; the electric warmth that permeated him filled him with a nameless pleasure; he no longer recognized himself in the rapture that seemed suddenly to have made him a totally different being.

Ever denser, ever darker grew the veils in which evening wrapped wood and field. Fermino remembered that it was time to go and visit the Count in his room. Eugenius, completely beside himself, pressed the Countess's hand fervently to his lips and then strode away as though carried by the air and filled with a bliss his heart had never known before.

Chapter Five

The dream figure. Fermino's fateful gift. Consolation and hope.

As might have been expected, the turmoil in Eugenius's heart kept all sleep at bay. When, after day had already begun to dawn, he finally fell into the slumber that is more a condition of stupefaction between waking and sleeping than true sleep, there appeared to him in all the dazzling brilliance of her charm and beauty and dressed as on her wedding day, the figure of that bride whom once already he had seen in a dream; and the terrible battle in his heart that he had fought before was renewed with redoubled violence.

'Why do you stay far from me?' said the figure in a sweet voice. 'Do you doubt that I am yours? Do you believe that the happiness of your love is lost? Just look up! The bridal chamber is adorned with sweet-scented roses, with blossoming myrtles! Come, my beloved, my sweet bridegroom! Come to my breast!'

As fleeting as a breath, Gretchen's features glided over the dream figure, but as it drew closer, stretching out both its arms to embrace the young man, it was the Countess Gabriela.

In a frenzy of passion, Eugenius tried to throw his arms

around the heavenly figure; but an icy paralysis held him fast, so that he remained motionless as the dream figure grew paler and paler, uttering frightened, dying sighs.

A strangled cry of horror was torn from the young man's breast.

'Herr Eugenius, Herr Eugenius! Wake up, you seem to be having a nightmare!'

Thus cried a loud voice. Eugenius started up out of his somnolent state, the bright sun shone into his face. It was the housemaid who had called him and now told him the foreign gentleman had already been there and had spoken to the Professor's widow, who was down in the garden and very worried about Herr Eugenius sleeping so late, fearing he might be indisposed. Coffee was ready in the garden.

Eugenius was no little astonished to find the Professor's widow standing in the garden in front of a magnificent *Datura fastuosa* and bending down over the great funnel-shaped flowers to inhale their sweet scent.

'Hey,' she cried to Eugenius, 'hey, you lie-a-bed! Do you know that your foreign friend has already been here asking to speak to you? Well, it looks as though I was unfair to the gentleman and paid too much heed to my evil forebodings! Just think, dear Eugenius, he had this wonderful *Datura fastuosa* brought here from the Count's garden, because he heard from you that I was particularly fond of this flower. So in your paradise you thought of your mother, dear Eugenius. The beautiful *Datura* shall be carefully tended.'

Eugenius didn't know what to make of Fermino's action. He felt almost inclined to believe that by this attention Fermino wished to make amends for having derided a relationship he knew nothing about.

The Professor's widow now told him that the stranger had invited him to the garden again that evening. The great good humour expressed today in the good lady's whole demeanour acted like balm upon the young man's sore and battered spirits. It was as though his feeling for the Countess was of such a lofty nature that it could have nothing in common with the ordinary circumstances of life. Love, which relates to earthly pleasure, therefore seemed to him the wrong name for this emotion; in fact, he felt that it would be profaned by the slightest thought of sensual enjoyment, although the fateful dream should have taught him otherwise. As a result of all this, however, he was merry and gay as he had not been for a long time, and the old lady was far too light-hearted herself at this moment to notice the strange tension that showed through his gaiety.

Only Gretchen, with her child's intuition, clung to the conviction that Herr Eugenius had become an entirely different man, when the Professor's widow commented that he was now his old self again.

'No,' said the little one, 'he is no longer as fond of us as he used to be; he only pretends to be so friendly so that we should not ask about things he wants to keep to himself.'

Eugenius found his friend in a room of the big greenhouse busy filtering various liquids, which he then poured into phials.

'I am working in your field,' he cried to the young man, 'though probably in a different fashion from anything you have ever done.'

He then explained that he possessed the secret of certain preparations that increased the growth, and in particular the beauty, of plants, shrubs, creepers, and so on, which was the reason why everything in the garden grew and flowered with such splendour. Thereupon, Fermino opened a small cupboard in which Eugenius saw a multitude of phials and little boxes.

'Here,' said Fermino, 'you see a whole collection of the rarest and most secret preparations, the effects of which are quite miraculous.'

Now it was a juice, now a powder, which, when mingled with the soil or water, served to make the colour and scent of this or that flower more beautiful and splendid, to give an added lustre to the leaves of this or that creeper.

'If, for example,' continued Fermino, 'you put a few drops of this juice in the water which you pour over *Rosa centifolia* from a watering-can like gentle rain, you will be astonished by the splendour revealed by the opening buds. But the effect of this dust-like powder is even more marvellous. When strewn in the calyx of a flower it mingles with the pollen and enhances the scent, without changing its nature. This powder may be employed with excellent results in many flowers, but especially in *Datura fastuosa*; only great caution must be exercised in using it. Half the quantity that will go on the tip of a knife is enough; the whole contents of the phial, or even half that quantity, would kill the strongest man instantaneously, leaving all the signs of death from shock, so that no one would suspect poison. Take it, Eugenius, I make you a present of this mysterious powder. The experiments you make with it will not fail, but be careful, and remember what I have told you about the deadly power of this insignificant-looking, colourless, and odourless powder.

So saying, Fermino handed Eugenius a small sealed blue phial, which the latter, catching sight of the Countess Gabriela in the garden, put into his pocket without further thought.

Suffice it to say that the Countess—the embodiment of love and pleasure, a woman who carried in the core of her being the art of that higher coquetry which consists in affording only a foretaste of enjoyment and so arousing and maintaining the insatiable thirst of passionate longing—systematically reduced the young man to a state of ever more vehement, ever more consuming desire. Only the hours, the moments, when he saw Gabriela counted in his life; his house seemed to him a dark and bleak prison, the Professor's widow the evil spirit born of childish delusion that kept him there under a spell. He did not notice the deep, silent grief that was gnawing at his wife's heart, nor the tears shed by Gretchen because he hardly spared her a glance and did not answer when she passed a friendly remark.

Several weeks had gone by like this when Fermino called to see Eugenius one morning. There was a tension in his whole demeanour that seemed to point to some unusual happening.

After a few casual words, he looked the young man hard in the eyes and said in a strange incisive tone: 'Eugenius—you love the Countess, and to possess her is all you long and strive for.'

'Unhappy man!' cried Eugenius, quite beside himself. 'Unhappy man! You plunge your murderous hand into my breast and destroy my paradise! No, what am I saying, you shake the madman out of his infatuated dream! I love Gabriela—I love her as probably no one on earth has ever been loved before, but this love is leading me to hopeless perdition!'

'I don't agree with you,' said Fermino coldly.

'To possess her,' went on Eugenius, 'to possess her! Ha, is the poor beggar to strive after the finest gem of rich Peru? A wretched man lost in the paltry misery of a misunderstood life, who has nothing to offer but the frank admission of a passionate and hopeless longing, and she—she—Gabriela!'

'I don't know whether it is simply the admittedly wretched circumstances of your life that make you such a coward, Eugenius,' said Fermino. 'A loving heart may proudly and audaciously strive for the highest.'

'Do not arouse illusory hopes that can only increase my misery,' Eugenius said to his friend.

'H'm,' replied Fermino. 'I don't know whether illusory hope and hopeless misery are the right expressions, when a man's love is returned with the highest passion that can burn in a woman's breast.'

Eugenius was about to fly into a frenzy. 'Quiet!' cried Fermino. 'Relieve your feelings in shouts and exclamations when I have said all I have to say and left, but now listen to me calmly.

'It is only too certain,' Fermino continued, 'that the Countess loves you and loves you with all the devastating fire that flames in the hearts of Spanish women. She lives only for you, her whole being belongs to you. So you are no wretched beggar, you are not lost in the paltry misery of a misunderstood life; no, in Gabriela's life you are infinitely rich, you stand at the golden gates of a gorgeous Eden that is open to you. Do not imagine that your social position will be an obstacle to your union with the Countess. There are certain circumstances that will make the proud Spaniard forget his exalted rank and give him cause ardently to wish you his son-in-law. I am the one who should tell you what these circumstances are, my dear Eugenius, and if I told you now I should avoid the suspicion of unfriendly secrecy, but it will be better if I say nothing for the present—all the more so, since a gloomy black cloud has just drifted into the sky of your love. You can imagine that I have told the Countess nothing about your circumstances; hence I have no idea how the Countess can have learnt that you are married and to a woman over sixty. She poured out her heart to me, she is completely dissolved in grief and despair. At one minute she curses the moment she met you, curses you yourself; the next she is once more speaking of you by the tenderest names and accusing herself, accusing the madness of her love. She never wants to see you again, that was what she . . .'

'Merciful heaven,' shrieked Eugenius, 'can there be for me any more terrible death?'

'That was what she resolved in the frenzy of disappointed love,' Fermino continued, smiling roguishly. 'But, so I hope, you shall see Countess Gabriela tonight at midnight. This is the moment when the flowers of the *Cereus grandiflorus*, the great-flowered torch-thistle, open in our greenhouse—flowers which, as you know, begin to wither again as soon as the sun rises. As little as the Count can stand the spicy, penetrating scent of these flowers, so greatly does Gabriela love them. Or rather, Gabriela's sentimental mind sees in the miracle of this cactus the very mystery of love and death, which is celebrated in this nocturnal blossoming through a rapid unfolding to the acme of bliss followed by an equally rapid withering. In spite of her grief and despair, therefore, the Countess is bound to come into the greenhouse, where I shall conceal you. Think of some way of breaking free from your bonds, flee your prison cell! But I shall leave everything to love and your lucky star! I pity you more than the Countess, and therefore I shall bend all my energies to the task of bringing you to happiness.'

Fermino had scarcely left the young man, when the Professor's widow came to him.

'Eugenius,' she said with the deep, despondent gravity of the venerable matron, 'Eugenius, things cannot remain like this between us any longer.'

At this, the thought shot through the young man like a sudden flash of lightning that his union was not indissoluble, that the difference in their ages was in itself a ground for judicial separation.

'Yes,' he cried in triumphant scorn, 'yes, Madam, you are quite right, things cannot remain like this between us any longer! Let us put an end to a relationship that was born of madness and is dragging me to perdition. Separation—divorce—I agree wholeheartedly.'

The Professor's widow turned deadly pale and her eyes filled with tears.

'What,' she said in a trembling voice, 'will you deliver me up to the scorn and derision of evil people, me who warned you when you preferred tranquillity, the inner peace of the soul, to the mad bustle of the world, me, your mother? No, Eugenius, you will not, you cannot, do that! Satan has blinded you! Look within yourself! Have things come to such a pass that you despise and wish to leave your mother who nurtured and cared for you, who wanted nothing but your temporal and your eternal welfare? Oh, Eugenius, no earthly judge will be required to divorce us. Soon the Father of Light will call me from this world of grief and lamentation! When I am lying in my grave, long since forgotten by my son, then enjoy your freedom—all the happiness which the illusions of earthly existence may afford you.'

A flood of tears choked the old lady's voice; holding her handkerchief to her eyes, she slowly walked away.

The young man's heart was not so hardened that the

good lady's mortal anguish did not cut him to the quick. He realized that every step he might take towards a separation would inflict a feeling of humiliation upon her and inevitably hasten her death, and he knew that this was not the way in which to gain his freedom. He wanted to be patient —to sacrifice himself; but a cry of 'Gabriela!' rang out in his heart, and the deepest and most malevolent rancour towards the old lady once more found room in his soul.

Last Chapter

IT was a dark, sultry night. The breath of nature rustled audibly through the black bushes and flashes of lightning writhed like fiery serpents on the far horizon. The whole area around the Count's garden was filled by the wonderful scent of the blossoming torch-thistle. Drunk with love and passionate desire, Eugenius stood before the lattice gate; at last Fermino appeared, opened the gate, and led him into the dimly lit greenhouse, where he hid him in a dark corner.

It was not long before the Countess Gabriela appeared, accompanied by Fermino and the gardener. They took up a position in front of the blossoming *Cereus grandiflorus* and the gardener seemed to be expatiating at great length on this wonderful cactus and the care and skill with which he had tended it. At last Fermino led the gardener away.

Gabriela stood as though immersed in a sweet dream, she sighed deeply, then she said in a low voice: 'If only I could live and die like this blossom! Oh, Eugenio!'

At this, the young man rushed out of his hiding-place and threw himself at the Countess's feet.

She uttered a cry of terror and tried to flee. But with the desperation of amorous frenzy the young man clasped her in his arms, and she too clasped him in her lily-white arms—not a word—not a sound—only burning kisses!

Footsteps approached; the Countess pressed the young man once more to her bosom. 'Be free—be mine—you or death!' she murmured, then gently thrust him from her and fled quickly into the garden.

Fermino found his friend stupefied and dazed with delight.

'Did I exaggerate?' said Fermino at last, when Eugenius seemed to have awakened. 'Could anyone be more fervently, more passionately loved than you are? But after this rapturous moment of amorous bliss I, your friend, must cater for your earthly needs. Although lovers do not usually attach much importance to other bodily enjoyments, nevertheless do me the favour of taking some refreshment before you leave here with the break of day.'

Mechanically, as though in a dream, Eugenius followed his friend, who led him into the small room where he had previously found him engaged in chemical operations.

He enjoyed some of the highly spiced foods which he found set out, and the fiery wine which Fermino pressed upon him appealed to him even more.

As may be imagined, Gabriela, and Gabriela alone, was the subject of the conversation that Fermino and Eugenius engaged upon, and every hope of the sweetest amorous bliss glowed in the young man's breast.

Dawn had broken, Eugenius wished to leave. Fermino conducted him to the lattice gate. As they parted, Fermino said: 'My friend, remember Gabriela's words, "Be free, be mine!" and come to a decision that will bring you quickly and certainly to the goal. Quickly, I say; for at dawn the day after tomorrow we are leaving here.'

With this, Fermino slammed the lattice gate and made off down a side alley.

Half swooning, Eugenius could not move from the spot. She was going and he could not follow? All his hope was destroyed by this sudden blow. At length he ran from the place with death in his heart. The blood in his veins seethed more and more fiercely once he was back in his house; the walls seemed to be crashing down upon him, he ran out into the garden. He caught sight of the lovely *Datura fastuosa* in full blossom; the Professor's widow was in the habit of bending down over the flowers and inhaling

152

their balmy and delicious perfume. Then the thoughts of hell rose within him, Satan took possession of him, he drew out the little phial which Fermino Valies had given him and which he was still carrying on his person, opened it, and with averted face shook the powder into the calyx of the *Datura fastuosa.*

It seemed to him now as though everything around him was enveloped in a fiercely blazing fire; he flung the phial far away from him and ran on and on, until he sank to the ground exhausted in the neighbouring forest. His mind was as confused as if he were dreaming. Then the voice of the Evil One spoke within him: 'What are you waiting for? Why do you hesitate? The deed has been done and yours is the triumph! You are free! Go to her—go to her whom you have won at the price of your salvation; all the most intense pleasure, all the nameless delights of life are yours!'

'I am free, she is mine!' cried Eugenius loudly, rising to his feet and running swiftly to Count Angelo Mora's garden.

It was high noon by now; he found the lattice door firmly shut, and no one came in answer to his knocking.

He had to see her, to take her in his arms, to enjoy all the abundance of happiness he had won in the first flush of his dearly bought liberty. The urgency of the moment gave him unwonted agility; he scaled the high wall. Deathly stillness reigned throughout the garden, the alleys were deserted. Finally, Eugenius thought he could hear low whispering in the summer-house he was approaching.

'If it were she!' The thought throbbed within him with all the sweet trepidation of ardent desire. He crept closer and closer—looked through the glass door—and saw Gabriela wantonly sinning in Fermino's arms!

With a roar like a mortally wounded beast, he flung himself against the door and smashed it in pieces; but at the same instant an icy shudder ran through him and he fell senseless on the stone threshold of the summer-house.

'Take the madman away!' These words rang in his ears; he felt himself lifted up with a giant's strength and hurled out of the gate, which shut behind him with a clinking sound.

He clung convulsively to the lattice, uttering terrible curses and imprecations against Fermino, against Gabriela! Then a malicious laugh rang out in the distance and he seemed to hear a voice crying *'Datura fastuosa!'* Grinding his teeth, Eugenius repeated *'Datura fastuosa'*; but suddenly a ray of hope penetrated his soul. He rose to his feet and ran as fast as he could to the town and into his house. On the stairs he was met by Gretchen, who was profoundly shocked by his appearance. The breaking glass had cut his head all over and the blood was flowing down over his face; to this was added the distracted look in his eyes, the expression of the terrible turmoil in his heart, to which his whole demeanour bore witness. The dear child was unable to utter a word when Eugenius, grasping her hand, asked in a wild voice: 'Has Mother been in the garden?' Then he cried in mortal fear: 'Gretchen, be merciful, speak, tell me—has Mother been in the garden?'

'Oh,' replied Gretchen at last, 'oh, dear Eugenius, Mother—no, she hasn't been in the garden. Just now, when she was on the point of going out, such fear came over her. She felt ill, stayed upstairs, and went to bed.'

'Just God!' cried Eugenius, falling on his knees and raising his hands to heaven, 'just God, you have been merciful to the vile sinner!'

'But, dear Herr Eugenius,' said Gretchen, 'what terrible thing has happened?'

Without answering, Eugenius raced down into the garden, tore the deadly plant furiously out of the soil, and trampled its blossoms in the dust.

He found the Professor's widow in a gentle slumber. 'No,' he said to himself, 'no, the power of hell is broken, Satan's arts cannot touch this saint!' Then he went up to his room; utter exhaustion brought him rest.

But soon he saw in his mind's eye the horrible picture of the hellish deception that had brought him inescapable ruin. He believed that he could atone for his crime in no other way than by a voluntary death. But vengeance, terrible vengeance must precede this death.

With the gloomy, baleful quiet which follows the most furious storms and in which the most fearful decisions mature, he bought a good double-barrelled pistol, powder, and lead, loaded the weapon, slipped it in his pocket, and set out for Count Angelo Mora's garden.

The lattice gate was open, Eugenius did not notice that it was occupied by armed police; he was about to enter, when someone caught hold of him from behind.

'Where are you going? What are you going to do?' It was Sever who had gripped him and now spoke.

'Do I bear the mark of Cain upon my brow?' asked Eugenius in the sombre voice of one who has abandoned all hope. 'Do you realize that I am on my way to commit murder?'

Sever took his friend by the arm and drew him gently away, saying: 'Do not ask me, dearest Eugenius, how I know everything, but I do know that you have been enticed by the arts of hell into the most dangerous of snares, that a Satanic deception turned your head, that you wish to avenge yourself upon the shameful scoundrel. But your vengeance comes too late. Both of them, the so-called Count Angelo Mora and his fine accomplice, the renegade Spanish monk Fermino Valies, have been arrested on orders from the Government and are on their way to the Residence. The Count's supposed daughter has been recognized as an Italian dancer who performed at the Teatro San Benedetto in Venice last carnival season.'

Sever gave his friend a few moments' peace in which to compose himself, then he exercised upon him the power possessed by every firm and lucid mind.

As Sever gently explained to him that it was man's earthly heritage often to be unable to withstand evil temptation, but that heaven frequently saved him in a miraculous fashion, and that there was atonement and consolation to be found in this salvation, the young man's heart, which had been turned to stone by despair, softened. A flood of tears poured from his eyes and he allowed Sever to take the pistol from his pocket and discharge it in the air.

Eugenius himself did not know how he suddenly came to find himself standing with Sever outside the Professor's widow's door, trembling from head to foot with a criminal's guilty fear.

The old lady lay sick in bed. But she smiled indulgently at the two friends and then said to Eugenius: 'My evil foreboding did not deceive me. The Lord of Light has saved you from hell. I forgive you everything, dear Eugenius— but, O heavenly Father, can I speak of forgiveness, when I must accuse myself? Only now, in old age, do I have to admit that earthly man is bound to the earthly by bonds from which he may not release himself, since the will of the everlasting power itself has knotted them. Yes, Eugenius, it is an insane sacrilege to attempt to deny the just demands of life that spring from the very nature of our existence on earth; it is arrogant presumption to believe we have risen above them! It was not you, but I alone who was at fault, and I wish to atone and bear the mockery of evil people with patience. Be free, Eugenius!'

At this, the young man, utterly crushed by the bitterest remorse, knelt before the old lady's bed and, taking her hand and covering it with kisses and tears, swore that he would never leave his mother and that he only hoped, by living in the peaceful aura of her piety and saintliness, to win forgiveness of his sins.

'You are my good son,' said the Professor's widow, her face suffused by the gentle smile of heavenly transfiguration. 'Soon, I feel it, soon heaven will reward you!'

Curiously enough, the Spanish monk had also set the same snare for Sever as for the inoffensive Eugenius, who had allowed himself to be caught, whereas the worldly wise Sever had easily escaped. It was, of course, happy coincidence that Sever had received information about the dubious relations between the so-called Count Angelo Mora and his retinue.

Both the Count and Fermino were, in fact, nothing else than emissaries of the order of the Jesuits, and it is a well-known principle of this order to seek adherents and reliable agents everywhere. Eugenius had doubtless first caught the monk's attention through his knowledge of Spanish. Once the monk discovered, on closer acquaintance, that he was dealing with an utterly inexperienced and innocent youth who, moreover, was living in thoroughly frustrating and life-denying circumstances, he inevitably concluded that it would be easy to train this youth to serve the aims of the order. It is equally well known that the order employs the strangest hocus-pocus to gain adherents; but nothing binds people more firmly than crime, and hence Fermino rightly believed that there was no better way of making certain of the young man than by arousing the slumbering passion of love with the maximum intensity, so that it should lead him to commit the abominable deed.

Soon after all this had happened, the Professor's widow's health rapidly declined. Like the Professor himself, she passed away peacefully in the arms of Gretchen and Eugenius when all the trees and bushes had lost their leaves.

But when she had been carried to the grave, the thought of his hideous, execrable crime returned to Eugenius. Even though this crime had remained without practical consequences, Eugenius nevertheless accused himself of being his mother's murderer, and his heart was rent by the furies of hell.

Even his faithful friend Sever was unable to bring the despairing Eugenius back to his senses. He sank into a state of silent, brooding grief, never left his room, saw no one and ate just enough to keep body and soul together.

A few weeks had passed like this, when one day Gretchen came to him in travelling clothes and said in a trembling voice: 'I have come to say goodbye to you, dear Herr Eugenius! My kinswoman in the little town three miles from here wants to have me back. Goodbye. . . .'

She could go no farther.

At this, a terrible anguish invaded the young man's breast, and through this anguish there suddenly shone the naphtha flame of the purest love.

'Gretchen!' he cried. 'Gretchen, if you leave me I shall

die the agonizing death of the despairing sinner! Gretchen —be mine!'

Oh, with what a true heart had Gretchen, without knowing it herself, long loved him. Half swooning with sweet trepidation, with heavenly bliss, the maiden sank upon the young man's breast.

Sever entered and, seeing the happy lovers, said gravely and solemnly: 'Eugenius, you have found the angel of light who will restore peace to your soul, and you will be blessed here on earth and in heaven above.'

THE KING'S BRIDE

A FAIRY TALE AFTER NATURE

Chapter One

in which information is given regarding various persons and their relationships, and the way is prepared in pleasant fashion for all the astonishing and most marvellous things contained in subsequent chapters.

IT was a bountiful year. In the fields wheat and barley, oats and rye sprouted and blossomed magnificently, the country lads went among the peas and the cattle among the clover; the trees were so weighted down with cherries that the whole host of sparrows, despite their ardent wish to gobble up everything, had to leave half the fruit untouched to provide food for others. All things ate their fill day after day at Nature's hospitable table. More than all else, however, the vegetables in Herr Dapsul von Zabelthau's kitchen garden did so surpassingly well that it was no wonder Fräulein Ännchen was quite beside herself with joy.

Some explanation must at once be given concerning the identity of this Herr Dapsul von Zabelthau and Fräulein Ännchen.

It is possible that at some time in your travels, dear reader, you have entered the lovely region through which flows the friendly Main. Balmy morning winds were breathing their scented breath over the meadow shimmering in the golden glitter of the risen sun. You could not bear to remain in the confinement of your carriage, you alighted and wandered through the little wood beyond which, once you began to descend into the valley, you discerned a small village. Suddenly you saw approaching you through this wood a tall, gaunt man whose strange attire riveted your gaze. He was wearing a little grey felt cap perched on a jet-black wig, clothes that were all of grey: coat, waistcoat and trousers, grey stockings and shoes, indeed even his very long stick was painted grey. The man came towards you with long strides, staring at you with big, deep-set eyes and yet seeming not to notice you at all. 'Good morning, good sir,' you cried out to him as he almost ran into you. Then he started, as though woken abruptly from a deep dream, raised his cap, and spoke in a hollow, tearful voice. 'Good morning? O good sir, how glad we can be that we have a good morning—we poor inhabitants of Santa Cruz—two earthquakes have only just taken place and now the rain is pouring down in torrents!' You were at a loss, dear reader, as to what to answer this strange man, but while you were still thinking it over he had already gently touched your brow and gazed into the palm of your hand with a 'By your leave, good sir!' In a voice as hollow and tearful as before, he then said, 'Heaven bless you, good sir, your stars are auspicious,' and strode on.

This singular man was none other than that Herr Dapsul von Zabelthau, whose one and only meagre inheritance was the little village of Dapsulheim, which lay before you in the most charming and smiling landscape, and which you were about to enter. You wanted breakfast, but things looked dismal in the inn. All its provisions had been consumed during the *kermis*, and since you were not prepared to content yourself with nothing but milk, you were directed to the manor house, where the gracious Fräulein Anna would kindly regale you with whatever she had to offer. You lost no time in making your way thither.

There is really no more to be said about this manor house than that it had windows and doors like those of the former castle of Baron von Tondertonktonk in Westphalia. Over the front door hung the arms of the Zabelthau family carved in wood in the New Zealand style. The house had an odd look, however, through the fact that the north side came into direct contact with the encircling wall of an ancient ruined castle, in such a way that the back door was the old castle gate and opened straight into the castle fore-court, in the centre of which the tall, circular watch-tower stood completely intact. From out of the front door sur-mounted by the armorial bearings there stepped a red-cheeked young girl, who could be considered quite pretty with her clear blue eyes and fair hair and a figure that was perhaps just a trifle too buxom and robust. Friendliness itself, she pressed you to come into the house and, as soon as she realized your need, plied you with the most excellent milk, a substantial slice of bread and butter, ham that appeared to you to have been cured in Bayonne, and a small glass of beetroot brandy. As she did so, the girl, who was none other than Fräulein Anna von Zabelthau, spoke gaily and freely of everything appertaining to agriculture, of which she exhibited no small knowledge.

But suddenly there rang out, as though from the air, a loud and terrible voice: 'Anna—Anna! Anna!' You started with fright, but Fräulein Anna remarked quite amiably: 'Papa has come back from his walk and is calling for break-fast from his study.' 'Calling—from his study?' you asked in amazement. 'Yes,' replied Fräulein Anna, or Fräulein Änn-chen as people called her, 'yes, Papa's study is up there in the tower and he is calling through the tube.' And then, beloved reader, you saw Ännchen open the narrow door of the tower and run up the stairs with the same early lunch you yourself had just enjoyed, that is to say a good solid helping of ham and bread accompanied by beetroot brandy.

She was with you again in a twinkling, however, and took you round the splendid kitchen garden, talking so much about curly kale, rampion, English turnips, little green-head, montrue, great mogul, yellow prince's head, and so forth that you must have been quite staggered, especially if you did not know that all these grand names referred to nothing more than various species of cabbage and other vegetables.

I imagine that the brief visit which you, dear reader, paid to Dapsulheim will have given you an idea of what life was like in the house of which I am about to relate all sorts of strange and wellnigh unbelievable things. During his youth Herr Dapsul von Zabelthau rarely left the castle of his parents, who owned considerable property. His tutor, after instructing him in foreign, and especially Oriental, languages, encouraged his interest in mysticism, or rather hocuspocus. The tutor died and left young Dapsul a whole library of books on the occult sciences, in which he became absorbed. His parents also died, and now young Dapsul set off on journeys to distant places; impelled by the desires implanted in him by his tutor, he made his way to Egypt and India. When he returned, after many years, he found that the cousin to whom he had entrusted his fortune had administered it with such zeal that there was nothing left of it but the little village of Dapsulheim. Herr Dapsul von Zabelthau was too intent upon the sun-born gold of a loftier world to have much use for earthly wealth; hence he was profoundly grateful to his cousin for having preserved for him the cheerful village of Dapsulheim with the beautiful high watch-tower, which seemed built for astrological operations and at the very top of which Herr Dapsul von Zabelthau immediately installed his study.

The prudent cousin then persuaded Herr Dapsul von Zabelthau that he ought to marry. Dapsul saw the necessity and at once married the young lady his cousin chose for him. The lady left the house as quickly as she had entered it. She died, after bearing him a daughter. The cousin saw to wedding, baptism, and funeral, so that Dapsul, in his tower, noticed very little of it all, especially since just at this time a very remarkable comet appeared in the sky, with whose conjunctions the melancholy Dapsul, always forecasting disaster, believed his destiny to be entwined. To the great joy of the old great-aunt responsible for her upbringing, his little daughter developed a liking for agriculture. Fräulein Ännchen had to rise from the ranks, as the saying goes. She worked her way up from goose girl, through maid, upper maid, and housekeeper, to lady of the house, so that theory was clarified and consolidated by beneficial practice.

She was quite unusually fond of geese and ducks, chickens and pigeons, cattle and sheep; even the rearing of well-shaped little piglets by no means left her indifferent, although she did not deck out a little white piglet with a ribbon and bell and make a lap animal of it, as one young lady is said to have done somewhere. Above all, and far above fruit-growing, however, she liked the vegetable garden. Benefiting from her great-aunt's agricultural erudition, Fräulein Ännchen, as the gentle reader will have observed, had in fact acquired a pretty good theoretical knowledge of vegetable growing; while the soil was being dug over, the seed scattered, and plants set, Fräulein Ännchen did not merely stand and watch, but took an active part. Fräulein Ännchen was handy with a spade, there was no denying that. Thus, while Herr Dapsul von Zabelthau was absorbed in his astrological observations and other mystic matters, Fräulein Ännchen, once her aged great-aunt was dead, ran the estate; while Dapsul was studying heavenly affairs, Ännchen saw with industry and skill to those of the earth.

As we have said, it was no wonder Ännchen was almost beside herself with joy at the magnificent burgeoning of the kitchen garden that year. One bed of carrots, however, surpassed everything else in luxuriant growth and promised a quite exceptional crop.

'Oh, my lovely, dear carrots!' cried Fräulein Ännchen time and again, clapping her hands, jumping up and down, dancing around and generally behaving like a child who has received a generous profusion of Christmas presents. And it really seemed as though the carrot children in the earth rejoiced over Ännchen's joy, for the thin laughter that rang out clearly rose from the soil. Ännchen paid no particular attention to it, but ran to meet the farmhand, who, holding up a letter, cried out: 'For you, Fräulein Ännchen, Gottlieb brought it with him from the town.' Ännchen immediately recognized from the address that the letter was from none other than young Herr Amandus von Nebelstern, the only son of a neighbouring landowner, who was at the university. While still living in his father's village,

Amandus had paid daily visits to Dapsulheim and had become convinced that never in his whole life could he love anyone but Fräulein Ännchen. Equally, Fräulein Ännchen knew for sure that she could never feel the slightest affection for anyone but Amandus with the curly brown hair. Hence both of them, Ännchen and Amandus, had agreed that they would marry, and the sooner the better, and that they would be the happiest married couple in the whole wide world.

Amandus, in the normal way, was a gay and carefree youth, but at the university he fell into the hands of some person unknown who not only persuaded him that he was a world-shaking poetic genius but also led him to wallow in sentimentality. He did this so successfully that in a short time he had hoisted himself up above everything which the drearily prosaic call sense and reason and which they erroneously assert can perfectly well exist side by side with the most active imagination. As we have said, the letter which Fräulein Ännchen now received was from young Herr Amandus von Nebelstern. Opening it joyfully, she read:

'Heavenly maid,

'Can you see, can you feel, can you picture your Amandus, himself a flower, enveloped by the orange-blossom breath of the scented evening, lying on his back in the grass and gazing aloft with eyes full of pious love and reverent yearning! Thyme and lavender, roses and carnations, as well as yellow-eyed narcissi and modest violets, he weaves into a garland. And the flowers are thoughts of love, thoughts of you, O Anna! But is sober prose a fitting language for the lips of passion? Hear, oh hear, how I can love and speak of my love only in the form of a sonnet.

'Upon a myriad thirsty suns love flares,
Seeking its joy within another's heart;
Down from the dark sky stars do dart
And mirrored are in springs of loving tears.

'*Tremendous rapture thrills and tears*
  The sweet fruit born of bitter seed apart,
  And longing calls its distant counterpart;
  My being melts away in lover's cares.

'*In waves of fire the storm-tossed waters roar;*
  The fearless swimmer girds his loins and leaps
  Into the turmoil of the surf below.

'*A hyacinth blooms upon the other shore;*
  The true heart opens like a bud, out seeps
  Warm blood, in which the roots of love best grow.

'O Anna, when you read this sonnet of sonnets, may you be pervaded by all the heavenly delight in which my whole being dissolved as I wrote it and afterwards read it aloud with divine enthusiasm to like-minded friends, people with a feeling for the highest things in life. Think, oh, think, sweet maid, of your faithful, enraptured Amandus von Nebelstern.

'P.S. When you reply, O lofty virgin, do not forget to send me a pound of the Virginian tobacco you grow yourself. It burns well and tastes better than the Porto Rico the lads smoke here when they go visiting taverns.'

Fräulein Ännchen pressed the letter to her lips and then said: 'Oh, how sweet, how beautiful! And the lovely verses that rhyme so prettily! Oh, if only I were clever enough to understand it all, but I suppose only a student can do that. I wonder what he means about the roots of love. Oh, I'm sure he must be referring to the long red English carrots or even the rampion, the dear fellow!

That very day Fräulein Ännchen made it her business to pack up the tobacco and hand over twelve of the finest goose quills to the schoolmaster, so that he could cut them carefully. Fräulein Ännchen resolved to sit down the same day and begin her answer to the exquisite letter. Once again a very audible laugh followed her as she ran from the kitchen garden, and if Ännchen had paid only the slightest attention

165

she could not have failed to hear the thin voice that called:
'Pull me out, pull me out—I am ripe—ripe—ripe!' But as
we have said, she paid no attention to it.

Chapter Two

*which contains an account of the first miraculous
happening and other things worth reading about,
without which the promised fairy tale could not
develop.*

HERR DAPSUL VON ZABELTHAU generally descended from
his astronomic tower at midday to share with his
daughter a frugal meal that lasted a very short time and
passed almost in silence, since Dapsul was not fond of conversation. Ännchen did not bother him by talking herself,
all the less because she knew that if her Papa were to start
speaking at all he would come out with a farrago of queer,
incomprehensible stuff that would make her head spin. Today, however, her mind was in such a turmoil over the
blossoming of the kitchen garden and the letter from her
beloved Amandus that she talked incessantly of both
jumbled together. In the end Herr Dapsul von Zabelthau
dropped his knife and fork, covered both ears with his
hands, and cried: 'Oh, what vapid, drab and muddled
babble!' But when Fräulein Ännchen lapsed into a dis-
mayed silence he said in his characteristic drawling, tearful
tone: 'As regards the vegetables, my dear daughter, I have
long known that the conjunction of the stars this year is
particularly propitious to such fruits, and earthly man will
doubtless enjoy cabbages and radishes and lettuces so that
his terrestrial substance may multiply and withstand the fire
of the World Spirit like a well-kneaded pot. The gnomic
principle will resist the assaults of the salamander, and I
look forward to eating parsnips, which you cook so excel-
lently. As to young Herr Amandus von Nebelstern, I have
not the slightest objection to your marrying him as soon as
he returns from the university. Just send word to me

166

through Gottlieb when you are going to your wedding with your bridegroom, so that I may escort you to the church.'

Herr Dapsul remained silent for a few moments and then, without looking at Ännchen, whose face was glowing all over with joy, he continued, smiling and tapping his glass with his fork (two actions which he always liked to combine, though he rarely had an opportunity): 'Your Amandus is someone who should and must be, I mean a gerund, and I will admit, my dear Ännchen, that I long ago worked out this gerund's horoscope. The conjunctions of the planets are all quite auspicious. He has Jupiter in the ascending node, which Venus looks upon in the sextile aspect. Only the orbit of Sirius intersects it, and precisely at the point of intersection there stands a great danger, from which he will save his bride. The danger itself is inexplicable, since there enters the picture a strange being that seems to baffle all astrological science. It is, however, apparent that Amandus will save you with that singular state of mind which men call madness or lunacy. O my daughter'—here Herr Dapsul relapsed into his usual tearful tone—'O my daughter, let no sinister power cunningly concealed from my clairvoyant eyes step suddenly into your path, let not young Herr Amandus von Nebelstern have need to save you from any other danger than that of becoming an old maid!' Herr Dapsul heaved a series of deep sighs, then he went on: 'But once this danger has passed, the orbit of Sirius is suddenly interrupted, and Venus and Jupiter, previously far apart, are reunited and reconciled.'

It was years since Herr Dapsul von Zabelthau had spoken so much as he had that day. Quite exhausted, he rose and climbed his tower again.

Early the following day Ännchen was ready with her answer to Herr Amandus von Nebelstern. It read:

'My dearly beloved Amandus,

'You have no idea what joy your letter gave me. I told Papa about it and he promised to escort us to the church for the wedding. Do hurry and come back from the university. Oh, if only I could quite understand your dearest verses which rhyme so prettily! When I read them aloud to myself it all sounds so wonderful and I imagine I understand every word, then it all slips away and I feel as though I had simply been reading disconnected words. The schoolmaster says it's supposed to be that way, that is the new refined speech, but I—oh!—I'm a silly, simple thing! Write and tell me if I can't perhaps become a student for a time, without neglecting my domestic duties? No, that's impossible? Then I shall have to wait till we are man and wife, then perhaps I shall pick up some of your learning and the new refined speech. I'm sending you the Virginian tobacco, my darling Amandchen. I have stuffed my hatbox absolutely full—so much wanted to go in—and placed my straw hat for the time being on Charlemagne, who stands in our guest room, though without legs because he is, as you know, only a bust. Don't laugh at me, Amandchen, I have also written a few lines of verse and they rhyme quite well. Do write and tell me how it is that one knows so well what rhymes without being taught. Now listen:

> *'I love you though you now be far away*
> *And long with all my heart your wife to be.*
> *The sky above my head, blue like the sea,*
> *At night is bright with golden stars that play.*
> *Love me always, dear, and never leave me,*
> *O sweetheart promise you will ne'er deceive me.*
> *Virginian tobacco I send you now in haste*
> *And wish you much enjoyment from its taste!*

'Take the will for the deed; when I understand refined speech I shall do better. The yellow stone-head has done splendidly this year, and the broad beans have made a fine start, but my dachshund, little Feldmann, gave the big gander a terrible bite in the leg yesterday. Well, we can't have everything perfect in this world. A hundred kisses in thought, my dearest Amandus, your faithful bride, Anna von Zabelthau.

'P.S. I have written in a great hurry, that's why the letters are a bit crooked in places.

'P.S. You mustn't hold that against me, even if I write a bit crooked my heart is straight and I am always your faithful Anna.

'P.S. Good gracious, I nearly forgot, scatterbrain that I am. Papa sends his best wishes and told me to tell you that you are one who should and must be and will one day save me from a great danger. I am very pleased about this and am once more your ever-loving, ever-faithful Anna von Zabelthau.'

Fräulein Ännchen felt much relieved when she had finished this letter, which had been a great effort to write. She became completely light-hearted and gay when she had also prepared the envelope, sealed it without burning either the paper or her fingers, and given the letter and the tobacco box, on which she had painted distinctly with a brush the letters A. v. N., to Gottlieb, who was to take them both to the town by the mail coach.

After seeing to the poultry in the yard, Fräulein Anna ran quickly to her favourite spot, the kitchen garden. When she came to the carrot bed she thought to herself that it was now obviously time to provide for the gourmets in town and pull up the first carrots. The maid was called to help her with the work. Fräulein Anna stepped carefully into the middle of the bed and seized hold of a magnificent tuft of carrot leaves. But the moment she pulled a strange sound made itself heard. The reader must not think of the mandrake root and the horrible whimpering and whining that rends the human heart as it is pulled out of the earth. No, the sound that seemed to come from the earth resembled a thin, joyful laugh. Nevertheless, Fräulein Ännchen let go of the tuft of leaves and exclaimed in some dismay: 'Why, who is that laughing at me?' But since there was no further sound, she took a fresh grip on the tuft of leaves, which seemed taller and more luxuriant than any of the others, gave it a hearty tug, disregarding the laughter that rang out again, and pulled out of the soil the finest and tenderest of carrots. But the moment Fräulein Ännchen looked at the carrot she uttered a shout of mingled joy and terror, so that the maid rushed over to her and, like Fräulein Anna, cried out aloud at the pretty wonder she perceived. Firmly encircling the carrot there was a magnificent gold ring with a fierily sparkling topaz. 'Ah,' cried the maid, 'that is meant for you. Fräulein Ännchen, that is your wedding ring, you must put it on immediately.' 'What nonsense you are talking,' replied Fräulein Ännchen, 'I must receive my wedding ring from Herr Amandus von Nebelstern, not from a carrot!'

The longer Fräulein Ännchen looked at the ring, the better she liked it. The workmanship was so fine and delicate that it seemed to surpass anything ever produced by human art. The band was formed of hundreds and hundreds of tiny little figures, entwined in the most diverse groups, which it was impossible to distinguish at the first glance with the naked eye, but which, on looking at the ring longer and more intently, seemed to grow in size, to come to life and to dance in graceful rows. And then the gem had such a special fire that it would have been difficult to match it even among the topazes in the Green Vault of the Royal Palace at Dresden.

'Who knows,' said the maid, 'how long the beautiful ring may have been lying deep in the earth, and then it was raised by the spade and the carrot grew through it.'

Fräulein Ännchen now pulled the ring off the carrot, and strangely enough the latter slipped through her fingers and vanished into the soil. Neither the maid nor Fräulein Ännchen paid much heed to this, however; they were too profoundly absorbed in contemplation of the magnificent ring, which Fräulein Ännchen, without more ado, now placed on the little finger of her right hand. As she did so, a stabbing pain ran from the root of her finger to the tip, but ceased as quickly as it began.

At midday, of course, she gave Herr Dapsul von Zabelthau an account of the strange thing that had happened to her in the carrot bed, and showed him the beautiful ring the carrot had been wearing. She tried to pull the ring off her finger so that her Papa could examine it more closely. But she felt the same stabbing pain she had felt when she put the ring on, and this pain continued as long as she tugged at the ring, till finally it became so unbearable that she had to let go. Herr Dapsul scrutinized the ring on her finger with close attention, made Anna describe a variety of circles with outstretched finger towards all the points of the compass, sank into profound meditation, and then climbed the tower without uttering another word. Fräulein Anna heard her Papa sighing and groaning loudly as he mounted the stairs.

The following morning, while Fräulein Ännchen was out in the yard chasing the big cock which got up to all sorts of mischief and in particular quarrelled with the pigeons, Herr Dapsul von Zabelthau wailed so terrifyingly down the speaking-tube that Ännchen was quite shaken and shouted up through her cupped hand: 'Why do you howl so mercilessly, dearest Papa, it's driving the fowls crazy!' Thereupon Herr Dapsul yelled down the speaking-tube: 'Anna, my daughter Anna, come up to me at once.'

Fräulein Ännchen was greatly surprised by this command, for her Papa had never before ordered her to come into the tower; on the contrary, he had kept the gate carefully locked. She was seized with a certain trepidation as she mounted the narrow spiral stairs and opened the heavy door that led into the tower's one and only room. Herr Dapsul von Zabelthau was sitting in a large armchair of peculiar shape, surrounded by all kinds of strange instruments and dusty books. In front of him was a stand bearing a sheet of paper stretched in a frame with various lines drawn on it. He was wearing a tall, pointed, grey cap on his head and a wide cloak of grey callimanco and had a long white beard on his chin. Because of the false beard, Fräulein Ännchen did not at first recognize her Papa and looked anxiously around to see if he wasn't in one of the corners of the room; when she realized that the man with the beard was really

Papa she laughed heartily and asked whether it was already Christmas and Papa was dressed up as Father Christmas.

Paying no heed to Ännchen's talk, Herr Dapsul von Zabelthau picked up a small piece of iron, touched Ännchen's forehead with it, and then stroked her right arm several times from the shoulder down to the tip of the little ring finger. After this she had to sit in the armchair, which Herr Dapsul had vacated, and place her little beringed finger against the paper in the frame in such a way that the topaz come in contact with the focal point upon which all the lines converged. Immediately yellow rays spurted from the gem in all directions, until the whole sheet of paper had turned dark yellow. Then the lines jiggled up and down and it was as if the little men on the band of the ring were hopping merrily all over the sheet. Herr Dapsul, keeping his eyes glued to the paper, had meanwhile picked up a thin metal plate; he held it high in the air with both hands and was about to press it down on the paper, when he slipped on the smooth stone floor and fell very un-gently on his hindquarters, while the metal plate, which he had instinctively dropped in an attempt to break his fall and preserve his coccyx, fell to the floor with a clinking noise. Fräulein Ännchen awoke with a soft 'Oh!' from the strange, dreamy state into which she had sunk. Herr Dapsul rose to his feet with an effort, put back the grey sugar-loaf hat that had fallen from his head, and sat down facing Fräulein Ännchen on a pile of folio-volumes.

'My daughter,' he said then, 'my daughter Anna, what was your state of mind just now? What did you think, what did you feel? What shapes did you see with the eye of the spirit within you?'

'Oh,' replied Fräulein Ännchen, 'I felt wonderful, more wonderful than I have ever felt before. Then I thought of Herr Amandus von Nebelstern. I saw him clearly before my eyes, but he was even handsomer than usual, and he was smoking a pipe of the Virginian leaves I sent him, which suited him extremely well. Then I suddenly had a tremendous appetite for young carrots and little sausages and was

172

quite delighted when the dish stood in front of me. I was about to set to, when I awoke from the dream with a sudden painful jerk.'

'—Amandus von Nebelstern—Virginian canaster—carrots—sausages!' Thus spoke Herr Dapsul von Zabelthau very thoughtfully and signed to his daughter, who was about to leave, that she should stay.

'Happy, ingenuous child,' he began in a tone that was far more tearful than ever before, 'happy not to have been initiated into the deep mysteries of the universe, not to know the dangers that threaten you from all sides. You know nothing of the supernatural science of the sacred Cabbala. It is true that on that account you will never share in the heavenly pleasure of the wise, who, once they have reached the highest stage, need neither eat nor drink except for pleasure, and remain unaffected by all human considerations; but in compensation you are not subject to the fear that comes on the way up to this stage, like your unhappy father, who is seized by far too much human vertigo and in whom what he laboriously discovers by research arouses only horror and dismay, and who is still compelled to eat and drink and—everything else—from pure earthly necessity. Know, my lovely and happily ignorant child, that the deep earth, the air, water, and fire are full of spiritual beings of a higher yet more limited nature than man. It seems unnecessary to explain to you, my little stupid one, the peculiar nature of the gnomes, salamanders, sylphs, and undines, you would not be able to grasp it. To indicate the danger in which you may possibly be, it will be sufficient to tell you that these beings strive for union with mortals, and since they know that mortals normally fight shy of such a union, the aforesaid spirits employ all sorts of cunning devices to entice the human beings upon whom they have bestowed their favour. They may use a twig, a flower, a glass of water, a flash of fire, or any other apparently insignificant thing as a means of attaining their aim. It is correct to say that such a union often turns out very advantageous, as was the case with two priests, of whom the

Prince of Mirandola relates that they lived for forty years in happy wedlock with one such spirit. It is also correct that the greatest sages sprang from unions between a human being and a spirit of the elements. Thus the great Zoroaster was the son of the salamander Oromasis, thus great Apollonius, wise Merlin, the brave Count of Cleve, and the great Cabbalist Ben Sira, were the offspring of such unions, while according to the statement of Paracelsus the beautiful Melusine was nothing else than a sylph. But in spite of these possible advantages, the danger of such a union is too great, for apart from the fact that the elemental spirits demand that the brightest light of the profoundest wisdom shall blaze forth upon those on whom they bestow their favour, they are also extremely sensitive and wreak terrible vengeance for any slight. Thus it once came about that when a sylph who was united with a philosopher heard him speak with his friends a trifle too enthusiastically of a beautiful woman she immediately displayed her snow-white and beautifully shaped leg in the air, as though to convince his friends of her beauty, and then killed the poor philosopher on the spot. But why should I speak of others? Why do I not speak of myself? I know that for twelve years a sylph has loved me, but she is shy and bashful, and I am tormented by thoughts of the danger of trying to enslave her by Cabbalistic means, because I am still far too dependent upon earthly needs, and hence lack the necessary wisdom. Every morning I resolve to fast and happily allow breakfast to pass, but when midday comes—O Anna, my daughter Anna—you know well—I guzzle terribly!'

Herr Dapsul von Zabelthau uttered these words almost in a howl, while the bitterest tears ran down over his emaciated, hollow cheeks; then he continued more calmly: 'But I take care to behave with the greatest refinement, the most exquisite gallantry towards the elemental spirit that bears me affection. I never venture to smoke a pipe of tobacco without observing the appropriate Cabbalistic precautions, since I do not know whether my gentle spirit of the air likes the brand and might not be sensitive to the pollution of her element, for which reason those who smoke hunter's canaster or shag can never grow wise and enjoy the love of a sylph. I take the same precautions every time I cut a hazel wand, pick a flower, eat fruit, or strike fire, for I make every possible effort to avoid coming into conflict with any spirit of the elements. And yet—you see that nutshell on which I slipped and, falling over backwards, spoiled the whole experiment that would have revealed to me the secret of the ring in its entirety? I do not remember ever having eaten nuts in this room that is dedicated exclusively to the pursuit of knowledge (you know now why I always lunch on the stairs), and it is therefore all the clearer that there was a little gnome hidden in this shell, perhaps for the purpose of lodging with me and listening in to my experiments. For the spirits of the elements love human sciences, especially such as uninitiated people, if they do not call them foolish and insane, at least consider beyond the power of the human mind and therefore dangerous. Hence they often slip in to observe divine magnetic operations. In particular, the gnomes, who are incorrigible jokers, make a practice of finding some magnetizer who has not yet attained the stage of wisdom which I described to you just now and is still too dependent upon earthly needs, and substituting an infatuated child of the earth at the moment when he believes that he is embracing a sylph in totally pure and clarified air.

'When I trod on the little student's head he grew angry and threw me down. But the gnome doubtless had a deeper reason for preventing me from uncovering the mystery of the ring. Anna!—my daughter Anna!—hear me—I should have disclosed that a gnome had bestowed his favour upon you, one who, to judge by the construction of the ring, must be a wealthy, distinguished, and at the same time extremely refined man. But, my precious Anna, my dearly beloved little stupid, how can you enter into a union with one of these elemental spirits without running the most terrible risk? If you had read Cassiodorus Remus you could retort that according to his true account the famous Magdalena de la Cruz, abbess of a convent at Gordova in Spain, lived in agreeable matrimony with a little gnome for thirty years, that the same thing happened with a male sylph and young Gertrude, who was a nun in the convent of Nazareth at Cologne; but think of the learned preoccupations of those spiritual ladies and of your own. What a difference! Instead of reading in wise books, you very often feed chickens, geese, ducks, and other creatures that are a source of irritation to every Cabbalist; instead of observing the sky, the course of the stars, you dig the earth; instead of following the track of the future in artistic horoscopical diagrams, you churn milk into butter and pickle *sauerkraut* to meet the base needs of winter, though I myself should not like to go without this dish. Tell me, can all that continue for long to please a sensitive philosophical spirit of the elements? For, O Anna, through you Dapsulheim flourishes and your spirit never may and never can escape from this earthly vocation. And yet you felt concerning the ring, even though it caused you sudden violent pain, an unrestrained and thoughtless joy! For your salvation I wished by this operation to break the power of the ring, to free you utterly from the gnome who is pursuing you. The ritual failed through the cunning of the little student in the nutshell. And yet I feel a courageous readiness to combat the elemental spirit such as I have never before experienced! You are my child —whom I did not beget with a sylph, a female salamander, or any other elemental spirit, but with that poor country maid from the best family, whom wicked neighbours mockingly referred to as the Lady of the Goats, on account of her idyllic nature, which induced her to pasture a small flock of pretty white goats on the green hills every day all by herself, while I, at that time an infatuated fool, blew the shawm on my tower. You are and remain my child, my blood! I shall save you; this mystic file here shall free you from the baneful ring!'

So saying, Herr Dapsul von Zabelthau picked up a small file and began to file the ring. But no sooner had he scraped the file this way and that a few times than Fräulein Ännchen cried out in pain: 'Papa—Papa, you're filing my finger off!' And as she cried, thick, dark blood did indeed well up from under the ring. Thereupon, Herr Dapsul von Zabelthau dropped the file, sank half-fainting into the armchair, and cried out: 'Oh!—oh!—oh!—I'm done for! Perhaps this very hour the gnome will come and bite through my throat, if the sylph does not save me!—O Anna—Anna—go—flee!'

Fräulein Ännchen, who had wished herself miles away as soon as her Papa began his strange outburst, raced downstairs with the speed of the wind.

Chapter Three

in which an account is given of the arrival of a remarkable man in Dapsulheim and further events are described.

HERR DAPSUL VON ZABELTHAU had just embraced his daughter with many tears and was about to ascend the tower, where he dreaded to be visited at any moment by the irate gnome, when the clear and merry notes of a horn were heard and a little rider of rather curious and droll appearance galloped into the courtyard. The yellow horse was not at all large, consequently the little man, in spite of his big, shapeless head, did not look so very dwarf-like, but towered above the horse's head. This was solely due to the length of his body, however, for the legs and feet dangling from the saddle were so small as to be scarcely worth taking into account. For the rest, the little man wore a very pleasant riding habit of golden-yellow satin, a tall hat of the same material with a splendid bunch of grass-green feathers and riding boots of highly polished mahogany wood. With a penetrating 'Whoa!' the rider pulled up his mount directly in front of Herr Dapsul von Zabelthau. He seemed about to dismount, then slid down with the speed of lightning under the belly of his horse, flung himself up on the other side two, three times in succession twelve ells high in the air, in such a way that at each ell he turned six somersaults, and ended by standing on his head on the pommel of his saddle. In this position he galloped forwards, backwards, sideways in all sorts of astonishing twists and turns, while his little feet beat trochees, Pyrrhics, dactyls, and so on in the air. When the elegant gymnast and equestrian finally stood still and uttered a polite greeting there could be seen on the soil of the courtyard the words: 'Cordial greetings to you and your lady daughter, honoured Herr Dapsul von Zabelthau!' He had ridden these words into the earthly element in beautiful roman uncial letters. After this, the little man jumped off his horse, turned three cartwheels, and then said that he had been instructed to present to Herr Dapsul von Zabelthau the compliments of his gracious master, Baron Porphyrio von Ockerodastes, called Corduanspitz, and if Herr Dapsul von Zabelthau had no objection, the Baron would like to pay him a friendly visit for a few days, since he hoped in the future to become his closest neighbour.

Herr Dapsul von Zabelthau looked more like a dead man than a living one, so pale and rigid was he as he stood there leaning on his daughter. Scarcely had the words 'It—will—be—a—great—pleasure' with difficulty passed his lips, than the little rider made off at lightning speed, after the same ceremonial he had performed on arrival.

'Oh, my daughter,' now cried Herr Dapsul von Zabelthau, wailing and sobbing, 'oh, my daughter, my poor unhappy daughter, it is only too evident that it is the gnome who is coming to abduct you and wring my neck! But we will summon the last ounce of courage that remains to us! Perhaps it will be possible to placate the enraged elemental spirit, we must behave towards him with all the propriety we can muster. I shall immediately read to you, my precious child, a few chapters from Lactantius or Thomas Aquinas on how to deal with elemental spirits, so that you shall not commit any terrible *faux pas*. . . .'

But before Herr Dapsul von Zabelthau had time to fetch Lactantius, Thomas Aquinas, or any other authority on elemental spirits, there rang out from quite close by the sort of music that is performed by musical children at Christmas. Then a fine long column wound its way up the road. In the front came some sixty or seventy little riders on small yellow horses, all dressed like the emissary in yellow riding habits, pointed caps, and boots of polished mahogany. They were followed by a coach of purest crystal drawn by eight yellow horses, which again was followed by about forty other, less sumptuous, coaches, some drawn by six and some by four horses. Alongside the column swarmed a multitude of pages, runners, and other servants decked out in glittering clothes, so that the whole *cortège* presented a picture as gay as it was singular. Fräulein Ännchen, who had never before guessed that there could be such pretty little things in the whole world as these tiny horses and people, was beside herself and forgot everything, even to shut her mouth, which she had opened wide in joyful exclamation.

The coach drawn by eight horses stopped just in front of Herr Dapsul von Zabelthau. Riders jumped down from their horses, pages and servants hurried forward, the coach-door was opened, and he who now gracefully descended from the coach and out of the arms of his servants was none other than Baron Porphyrio von Ockerodastes, called Corduanspitz. In stature, the Baron was far from being an Apollo of the Belvedere, in fact he wasn't even to be compared with the dying warrior. For apart from the fact that he was less than three feet tall, a third part of this small body consisted of the obviously too large, fat head, which, moreover, was embellished by a big, long, hooked nose and a pair of large, round, bulging eyes. Since the body was also somewhat long, only some four inches were left for the legs. This small space was well utilized, however, for in themselves the baronial legs were the daintiest one could possibly see. Of course, they appeared too weak to bear the dignified head; the Baron had a tottering walk and frequently tripped and fell; but he was on his feet again in a trice, like a cork-tumbler, so that his falls looked more like the attractive capers of a dance. The Baron wore a close-fitting habit of gleaming gold material and a little cap almost like a crown, topped by an enormous bush of many plant-green feathers.

As soon as the Baron was standing on the ground, he rushed up to Herr Dapsul von Zabelthau, grasped him with both hands, bounded up to his neck, which he clasped, and cried in a voice that boomed far more loudly than one would have expected from his small stature: 'O my Dapsul von Zabelthau—my dearly beloved Father!'

Having said this, the Baron swung himself down from Herr Dapsul's neck as agilely and adroitly as he had gone up, jumped or rather hurled himself at Fräulein Ännchen, seized the hand of the beringed finger, smothered it with noisy, smacking kisses, and boomed as loudly as before: 'O my most beautiful Fräulein Anna von Zabelthau, my best beloved bride!'

Thereupon the Baron clapped his hands, and immediately the shrill children's music struck up again and more than a hundred tiny gentlemen sprang out of the coaches and down from the horses, and danced as the courier had done—now on their heads, now on their feet—the most elegant trochees, spondees, iambics, Pyrrhics, anapests, tribrachs, bachs, antibachs, choriambics, and dactyls, so that it was a joy to behold. While this rejoicing was going on, however, Fräulein Ännchen recovered from the great shock caused by the terms in which the little Baron had addressed her and became preoccupied by all sorts of well-founded domestic qualms. 'How,' she thought, 'can our small house lodge all these little people? Should I be forgiven if, out of necessity, I bedded at least the servants in the big barn, and would there be room for them even there? And what shall I do with the nobles, who have come in coaches and are undoubtedly used to sleeping in soft beds in fine rooms? Must the two plough-horses also be turned out of their stable, and even if I were so unmerciful as to drive lame old Fox out to grass, would there be enough room then for all these little beasts of horses the ugly Baron has brought with him? And it's the same with the hundred coaches! But then comes the worst thing of all—will our whole year's stock of provisions be sufficient to satisfy all these little creatures for as long as two days?'

This last worry was the worst of all. Fräulein Ännchen could see everything being gobbled up, all the new vegetables, the flock of sheep, the poultry, the salt meat, even the beetroot brandy, and this brought the sparkling tears to her eyes. It seemed to her as though just at this moment Baron Corduanspitz made a thoroughly impudent and malicious face; this gave her the courage, while his retinue was still dancing with all their might, to tell him in plain words that, much as her father esteemed his visit, a stay at Dapsulheim of more than two hours was out of the question; since space and everything else necessary to the proper reception and appropriate entertainment of such a fine and wealthy gentleman with his numerous attendants was totally lacking. At this, little Corduanspitz suddenly looked as sweet and tender as a marzipan loaf and, pressing Fräulein Ännchen's rather rough and none too white hand to his lips with closed eyes, assured her that nothing could be farther from his wishes than to cause the dear Papa and the loveliest daughter even the very slightest inconvenience. Everything demanded by kitchen and cellar he had brought with him, but as regards a lodging he asked no more than a patch of ground and the open sky above, so that his people could erect the usual travelling palace, in which he and his whole retinue and all their animals would lodge.

Fräulein Ännchen was so delighted by Baron Porphyrio von Ockerodastes's words that, to show she did not in the least mind parting with her titbits, she was on the point of offering the little man doughnuts she had saved from the last *kermis* and a glass of beetroot brandy—unless he preferred double-bitter, which the upper maid had brought from the town and recommended as beneficial to the stomach. But at this moment Corduanspitz added that he had chosen the vegetable garden for the erection of his palace, and Ännchen's joy was at an end!

While the retinue, to celebrate their master's arrival in Dapsulheim, continued their Olympic Games, butting one another in their pointed stomachs with their fat heads and turning back-somersaults, flinging themselves up into the air, playing games of skittles in which they themselves took the part of skittles, ball, and skittlers, and the like, little Baron Porphyrio von Ockerodastes plunged into a conversation with Herr Dapsul von Zabelthau that seemed to grow more and more weighty, till the two of them went off hand in hand and mounted the astronomic tower.

Terrified at the thought of what she might find, Fräulein Ännchen now ran as fast as she could to the vegetable garden, to save what could still be saved. The upper maid was already standing in the field staring open-mouthed in front of her, motionless, as though she had been changed into a pillar of salt like Lot's wife. Fräulein Ännchen went equally rigid beside her. Finally, both of them yelled so that their words echoed far and wide: 'Merciful heavens, what a disaster!'

They found the whole beautiful vegetable garden transformed into a desert. There was not a green plant, not a shrub, nothing but a barren, desolate field. 'No,' cried the enraged maid, 'there is no other possibility, that must have been done by the accursed little creatures who have just arrived. They came in coaches? They want to pass themselves off as people of breeding? Ha, ha! They are goblins, believe me, Fräulein Ännchen, nothing but an unChristian witches' brood, and if only I had a piece of crosswort with me you would see a miracle. But just let them come, the little beasts, I'll strike them dead with this spade!' So saying, the upper maid swung her fearsome weapon aloft, while Fräulein Ännchen wept loudly.

In the meantime four gentlemen from Herr Corduanspitz's retinue approached with such pleasant, elegant mien and courtly bows, and looking at the same time so extremely strange, that the upper maid, instead of striking out as she had intended, let the spade slowly sink, and Fräulein Ännchen ceased her weeping.

The gentlemen announced themselves as the closest friends of Baron Porphyrio von Ockerodastes, called

Corduanspitz; they belonged, as their clothes symbolically indicated, to four different nations, and gave their names as Pan Kapustowicz from Poland, Herr von Schwarzrettig from Pomerania, Signor di Broccoli from Italy, and Monsieur de Roccambolle from France. They assured Ännchen in mellifluous tones that in no time at all the builders would come and give the beautiful young lady the great pleasure of watching a lovely palace of pure silk go up in the twinkling of an eye.

'What good is a silken palace to me?' cried Fräulein Ännchen, weeping loudly in profound grief. 'What is your Baron Corduanspitz to me anyway, since you wicked people have destroyed all my lovely vegetables and all my joy is gone?' But the courteous gentlemen consoled Ännchen, assuring her that they were not responsible for the devastation of her vegetable garden, that, on the contrary, it would soon be a picture of luxuriant growth such as Fräulein Ännchen had never seen here or in any other vegetable garden in the world.

The little builders came indeed, and such a wild and confused turmoil broke out in the field that both Fräulein Ännchen and the upper maid ran away in terror to the shelter of a bush, from where they watched to see what would happen.

Although they could not understand how such a thing could take place by natural means, in a few minutes a sumptuous and lofty tent of golden-yellow material, decorated with multi-coloured garlands and feathers, went up before their eyes; it occupied the whole of the big vegetable garden, and its guy-ropes passed right over the village to the nearby forest, where they were attached to large trees.

No sooner was the tent ready than Baron von Ockerodastes came down with Herr Dapsul von Zabelthau from the astronomic tower, and after repeated embraces climbed into his coach and drove with all his followers, in the same order in which they had come to Dapsulheim, into the silken palace, which closed behind the last man.

Fräulein Ännchen had never seen her Papa as he was

now. All trace of the grief that normally plagued him had vanished from his face, he seemed almost to be smiling, and at the same time there was a transfigured look in his eyes that seemed to indicate some great and unexpected stroke of luck. Without a word, Herr Dapsul von Zabelthau took his daughter's hand, led her into the house, embraced her three times in succession, and at last burst out: 'Happy Anna—immensely happy child!—happy father! O daughter, all worry, all distress, all grief of the heart is now past! You have been vouchsafed a destiny that rarely comes to mortals! Know that this Baron Porphyrio von Ockerodastes is no malignant gnome, although he is descended from one of these spirits of the elements, but one who succeeded in purifying himself and developing his higher nature through the instruction of the salamander Oromasis. From this purifying fire there sprang love for a mortal woman, with whom he was united, becoming the ancestor of the most illustrious family whose name ever embellished parchment. I believe that I have already told you, beloved daughter Anna, that the pupil of the great salamander Oromasis, the noble gnome Tsilmenech—a Chaldean name meaning Dunderhead—fell in love with Magdalena de la Cruz, abbess of a convent at Cordova in Spain, and lived with her for thirty years in happy and agreeable wedlock. Now, the dear Baron Porphyrio von Ockerodastes—who has assumed the surname Corduanspitz, from Cordovan or Spanish leather, to indicate his origin in Cordova and also to distinguish himself from a prouder, but fundamentally less worthy collateral line that bears the surname Saffian, from Saffian or Moroccan leather—is a scion of the sublime family of supernatural beings that developed from this union. The fact that Spitz, meaning lace, was added to the Corduan must have some elemental, astrological explanation; I have not yet reflected upon this point. Following the example of his great forefather, the gnome Tsilmenech, who loved Magdalena de la Cruz ever since her twelfth year, the excellent Ockerodastes bestowed his love upon you when you were only twelve. He was happy to receive a little gold ring from you, and now you have also put on his ring, so that you have irrevocably become his betrothed!'

'What,' cried Fräulein Ännchen, full of terror and dismay, 'what?—his bride? I'm to marry that repulsive little goblin? Have I not long been the betrothed of Herr Amandus von Nebelstern? No—I shall never take the ugly sorcerer for a husband, even if he is made a thousand times of cordovan or saffian!'

'There!' replied Herr Dapsul von Zabelthau, growing more serious, 'I see to my regret how little heavenly wisdom is able to penetrate your stubborn earthly mind! You call the noble, elemental Porphyrio von Ockerodastes ugly and repulsive, perhaps because he is only three feet tall and apart from his head carries little that is impressive in the way of torso, arms and legs, and other irrelevant features, while the legs of the sort of earthly dandy you have in mind cannot be long enough, because of his coat tails. O my daughter, into what a heinous error you have fallen! All beauty lies in wisdom, all wisdom in thought, and the physical symbol of thought is the head! The more head, the more beauty and wisdom, and if man could cast off all his other limbs as noxious luxuries and sources of evil he would have attained the loftiest ideal form! Whence come all diseases, all affliction, all discord, all dispute, in short all the corruption of the earthly realm, but from the damned luxuriance of the limbs? Oh, what peace, what tranquillity, what bliss on earth, if mankind existed without belly, rump, arms, or legs, if it consisted solely of the bust! Happy, therefore, is the artists' idea of portraying great statesmen or great scholars as busts, in order to indicate symbolically the higher nature that must dwell in them by virtue of their responsibilities or their books! Well, then, my daughter Anna, no more talk of ugliness, repulsiveness, or other denigratory comments upon the noblest of the spirits, the magnificent Porphyrio von Ockerodastes, whose betrothed you are and will remain. Know that through him your father will shortly attain to the highest degree of happiness, after which he has so long striven in vain. Porphyrio von Ockerodastes is informed that the sylph Nehahilah (Syrian, meaning Pointed Nose) loves me and he will aid me with all his powers to become worthy of union with this being of a higher spiritual nature. I am sure you will be pleased with your future step-mother. May kind fate so dispose that our two weddings may be celebrated at the same happy hour!' With this, Herr Dapsul von Zabelthau dramatically left the room, casting his daughter one more meaning glance.

Fräulein Ännchen's heart was heavy as she recalled that long ago, when she was still a child, a small gold ring had inexplicably slipped from her finger. Now she was sure that the repulsive little sorcerer had lured her into his snare, leaving her small chance of escape. The thought plunged her into the deepest grief. She had to unburden her oppressed heart, and this she did with the aid of a goose quill, with which she swiftly wrote as follows to Herr Amandus von Nebelstern.

'My best beloved Amandus,

'Everything is finished, I am the unhappiest person in the whole world and sob and weep so bitterly for sorrow that even the domestic animals have pity and compassion on me, and how much more deeply will you be moved. As a matter of fact, the disaster affects you as much as it does me, and you will be equally filled with grief. You know that we love one another as warmly as any couple can love and that I am your betrothed and that Papa was going to escort us to church? Well, a horrid little yellow man has suddenly come along in a coach and eight and claims that I have exchanged rings with him and that we are bride and bridegroom! And just think how terrible it is! Papa also says I must marry the little monster, because he comes of a very distinguished family. That may be, to judge by the retinue and the gorgeous clothes they wear, but the man has such a ghastly name that for this reason alone I never want to be his wife. At the same time, he is also called Corduanspitz, and that is his family name. Write and tell me whether the Corduanspitzes are really so noble and distinguished; they will know that in the town. I can't understand what has come over Papa in his old age, he wants to marry as well, and the horrible Corduanspitz is to couple him off with a woman who floats in the air. God protect us! The upper maid shrugs her shoulders and says she doesn't think much of mistresses that fly in the air and float on water and that she would give notice at once and that she hopes for my sake that my step-mama will break her neck at the next witches' ride on Walpurgis Night. These are nice goings on, I can tell you. But you are my one and only hope. I know that you are the one who should and must, and will save me from great danger. The danger is here, come quick and save

'Your mortally afflicted, but
ever faithful betrothed,
Anna von Zabelthau.

'P.S. Couldn't you challenge the little yellow Corduan-spitz to a duel? You would be bound to win, because he is rather weak in the legs.

'P.S. I beg you once more, put on your clothes at once and hurry to your unhappy, but, as I said above, ever faithful betrothed, Anna von Zabelthau.'

Chapter Four

which describes the court of a powerful king, but first reports a bloody duel and other strange happenings.

FRÄULEIN ÄNNCHEN felt as if paralysed in every limb by dejection. She sat at the window with arms folded and stared out, paying no heed to the clucking, crowing, quacking, and squawking of the poultry, which, as dusk was falling, wanted to be put to rest by her. Indeed, with the greatest indifference she allowed this task to be carried out by the maid and did not even protest when the latter struck the rooster—who resented this change in routine and rose in revolt against the substitute—a violent blow with the whip. The love pains that rent her own breast robbed her of all feeling for the suffering of the favourite pupil of her sweetest hours, which she devoted to his education.

Corduanspitz had not put in an appearance the whole day, but had remained with Herr Dapsul von Zabelthau in the tower, where important operations were no doubt being performed. Now, however, Fräulein Ännchen observed the little man tottering across the courtyard in the glow of the setting sun. In his bright yellow habit he looked to her more repulsive than ever, and the droll way in which he hopped this way and that, seeming at every instant to trip and fall and bounce up again—at which anyone else would have laughed himself sick—only caused her more chagrin. Finally, indeed, she put both hands over her face to shut out the sight of the loathsome buffoon. Then suddenly she felt a tug at her apron. 'Down, Feldmann,' she cried, thinking it was the dog tugging at her. But it was not the dog; when Fräulein Ännchen took her hands from her face she saw Baron Porphyrio von Ockerodastes, who bounded with unparalleled nimbleness on to her lap and threw both arms around her neck. Fräulein Ännchen screamed loudly with terror and disgust and jumped up from her chair. But Corduanspitz hung on to her neck and seemed all of a sudden to weigh at least twenty hundredweight, so that he pulled poor Ännchen down with the speed of an arrow into the chair in which she had been sitting. Now, however, Corduanspitz slipped down off Ännchen's lap, dropped as elegantly and politely as his lack of balance would allow on to his little right knee, and said in a clear, rather curious, but not unpleasant voice: 'Adored Fräulein Anna von Zabelthau, most excellent lady, chosen bride, do not be angry, I beg, I beseech you! Do not be angry, do not be angry! I know you think my people have laid waste your beautiful vegetable garden in order to build my palace. O powers of the universe! If only you could look into my small body and see my heart that is jumping with love and generous impulses! If you could discover all the cardinal virtues gathered in my breast beneath this yellow satin!

Oh, how far removed I am from that deed of horrid violence which you ascribe to me! How could a gentle prince
possibly harm his own sub . . . but no, stop, what are words,
what are speeches?! You must see for yourself, my betrothed, all the splendours that await you! You must come
with me to my palace, where a joyful people await the
adored mistress of their lord!'

It is easy to imagine how horrified Fräulein Ännchen was
by Corduanspitz's demand, how she struggled against moving one step to follow the terrifying buffoon. But Corduanspitz continued to describe in such emphatic terms the
extraordinary beauty, the boundless wealth of the vegetable
garden that was really his palace that she finally decided
at least to peep into the tent, which could do her no harm
at all. The little man turned at least a dozen cartwheels in
succession for joy and delight, then took Fräulein Ännchen
very tenderly by the hand and led her through the garden
to his silken palace.

Fräulein Ännchen stopped dead as though rooted in the
soil, with a loud 'Oh!', as the entrance curtains were drawn
aside to reveal the prospect of an endless kitchen garden
more splendid than she had ever seen in her loveliest dreams
of vegetable luxuriance. Every kind of green and root vegetable, of salad, pea and bean, flourished there in a radiant
splendour beyond the power of words to describe. The
music of pipes and drums and cymbals rang out with
redoubled vigour, and the four courtly gentlemen whom
Fräulein Ännchen had already met, to wit Herr von
Schwarzrettig, Monsieur de Roccambolle, Signor di Broccoli, and Pan Kapustowicz, approached with many ceremonious bows.

'My chamberlains,' said Porphyrio von Ockerodastes with
a smile as, preceded by these gentlemen, he led Fräulein
Ännchen through the double rank formed by the guard of
English red carrots to the centre of the field, where stood
a sumptuous high throne. Round this throne the great ones
of the kingdom were gathered, the lettuce princes with the
bean princesses, the cucumber counts with the melon dukes

at their head, the cabbage ministers, the onion and beetroot generals, the kale ladies, and so on, all in the most magnificent attire appropriate to their rank and estate. And among them a hundred or so of the dearest lavender and fennel pages ran about spreading sweet odours. As Ockerodastes mounted the throne with Fräulein Ännchen, the Lord High Chamberlain Turnip waved his long staff, and immediately the music ceased and everyone listened in silent reverence. Then Ockerodastes raised his voice and, speaking very solemnly, said: 'My faithful and beloved subjects, behold here at my side the noble Fräulein Anna von Zabelthau, whom I have chosen as my consort. Richly endowed as she is with beauty and virtue, she has long looked upon you with the eyes of mother-love and has provided and tended a soft and fertile bed for you. She will always be and remain a true and worthy mother of our country. Now show your dutiful approval and orderly jubilation at the act of benevolence which I am about to perform towards you!'

At a second sign from the Lord High Chamberlain Turnip a thousand-voiced roar of jubilation went up, the bulb artillery fired their salvo, and the band of the Carrot Guards struck up the well-known anthem 'Lettuce, lettuce and green parsley'.

It was a sublime moment that drew tears of rapture from the great ones of the kingdom, and especially the kale ladies. Fräulein Ännchen was thoroughly bemused, when suddenly she noticed that the little man beside her had a crown sparkling with diamonds on his head and a golden sceptre in his hand. 'Oh, oh!' she cried, clapping her hands together in astonishment. 'Heaven preserve us! You are much more than you seem, are you not, my dear Herr von Corduanspitz?'

'Adored Anna,' replied Ockerodastes very gently, 'the stars compelled me to appear to your respected father under a borrowed name. Know, my dearest child, that I am one of the mightiest kings and rule an empire whose frontiers cannot be traced, because cartographers have forgotten to mark them on their maps. It is the King of the Vegetables, Daucus Carota I, who is offering you, O sweetest Anna, his hand and his throne. All the vegetable princes are my vassals, and only on one day a year, in accordance with ancient tradition, does the Bean King reign.'

'Then I am to be a queen and possess this splendid and magnificent vegetable garden?' cried Fräulein Ännchen joyfully.

King Daucus Carota assured her once again that such was the case, and added that all vegetables which sprouted from the soil would be subject to his and to her dominion. Fräulein Ännchen had not expected anything like this, and she considered that from the moment little Corduanspitz had turned into King Daucus Carota I he had become far less ugly than before and that the crown and sceptre and the royal cloak suited him exceedingly well. When Fräulein Ännchen also took account of his pleasant manner and the riches that would come to her through union with him, she could not escape the conviction that no young country maid could hope to make a better match than she, who in the twinkling of an eye had become a king's bride. Fräulein Ännchen was therefore delighted beyond measure and asked her royal bridegroom whether she could not remain in the beautiful palace there and then, and whether the wedding could not be celebrated the following day. King Daucus replied that, charmed as he was by the ardour of his adored bride, he must postpone his happiness on account of certain conjunctions of the planets. For one thing, it was imperative that Herr Dapsul von Zabelthau should not learn of his son-in-law's royal estate, because otherwise the operations destined to effect the desired union with the sylph Nehahilah might be disturbed. For another, he had promised Herr Dapsul von Zabelthau that both weddings should be celebrated on the same day. Fräulein Ännchen had to promise solemnly that she would not let slip a syllable to Herr Dapsul von Zabelthau concerning what had happened to her; she then left the silken palace to the accompaniment of loud and clamorous jubilation from the populace, who were completely enraptured by her beauty and her courteous and affable behaviour.

In her dreams she saw the kingdom of the entrancing King Daucus Carota again and dissolved in bliss.

The letter she had sent to Herr Amandus von Nebelstern had affected the poor lad most terribly. It was not long before Fräulein Ännchen received the following reply:

'Idol of my heart, celestial Anna,

'The words of your letter were daggers, sharp-pointed, red-hot, poisoned, murderous daggers that transpierced my breast. O Anna! Are you to be torn from me? What a thought! I can't understand why I didn't go mad on the spot and kick up some frightful, savage rumpus! But, outraged by my dreadful destiny, I fled from men, and immediately after supper, instead of playing billiards as usual, I rushed out into the forest, where I wrung my hands and cried out your name a thousand times! It began to rain terribly hard and I happened to be wearing a brand new cap of red velvet with a gorgeous golden tassel on top. People say no cap has ever suited me so well as this one. The rain was liable to ruin this superbly tasteful article of dress, but what does amorous despair care for caps, for velvet and gold! I wandered around until I was soaked through, frozen stiff, and assailed by a terrible belly-ache. This drove me to the nearby tavern, where I had some excellent mulled wine prepared and smoked a pipe of your heavenly Virginia with it. I soon felt myself possessed by divine inspiration, I whipped out my notebook and hastily scribbled down a dozen splendid poems, and—such is the wondrous power of poesy!—both amorous despair and belly-ache were gone. I shall communicate to you only the last of these poems and you, O ornament of virgins, will be filled, like me, with joyful hope!

> *Shroud me in my grief,*
> *Candles of love are out*
> *Within my empty heart*
> *Raided by a thief.*

192

Yet the spirit lives,
Word and rhyme it gives.
When the poem's down,
My face has lost its frown.
Once more within my heart
Love's candles brightly burn,
Gone is all my grief,
Forgotten is the thief.

'Yes, my sweet Anna, I shall soon hasten to your aid, a guardian knight, and wrest you from the scoundrel who seeks to rob me of you! So that in the meantime you shall not despair, I am writing you a few divine, consoling aphorisms from my Treasury of Masterpieces, from which you may draw comfort.

'The breast expands, the spirit takes on wings?
Be gay like Owlglass, heart, who always jests and sings!

'Love may feel for love a bitter hate,
And time itself may sometimes be too late.

'Love is the scent of flowers, existence without let.
O youth, wash thou the fur, but do not get it wet!

'Say you in winter that a cold wind blows?
Fur coats are warm, friend, as every man knows!

'What divine, sublime, pregnant maxims! And how simply, how unassumingly, how concisely expressed! Once more, then, my sweetest maid! Be consoled, carry me in your heart as always. I shall come, I shall save you, I shall press you to my breast shaken by passion's storm,

'Your ever true
Amandus von Nebelstern.

'P.S. Whatever happens I cannot challenge Herr von Corduanspitz to a duel. For, O Anna, every drop of blood that might flow from your Amandus at the hostile onslaught of a foolhardy adversary is glorious poet's blood, the ichor of the gods, which may not be spilt. The world is justly entitled to claim that a spirit such as mine shall be preserved by every possible means. The poet's weapon is the word, the song. I shall have at my rival with Tyrtaeic battle songs, strike him down with pointed epigrams, beat him to the ground with dithyrambs full of amorous frenzy—these are the weapons of the true poet which, ever victorious, secure him against any attack, and thus armed and accoutred, I shall appear and win your hand in battle, O Anna!

'Farewell, once more I press thee to my breast! You may hope everything from my love and especially from my heroic courage, which will shrink from no peril to set you free from the shameful net into which, by all appearances, a demonic monster has lured you!'

Fräulein Ännchen received this letter just as she was playing tig with her future bridegroom, King Daucus Carota I, in the meadow beyond the garden, deriving great amusement from ducking quickly down while running at full speed, so that the little king shot straight over her head. Contrary to her usual practice, she slipped her beloved's letter into her pocket without reading it, and we shall see in a minute that it had come too late.

Herr Dapsul von Zabelthau was completely at a loss to understand why Fräulein Ännchen had suddenly changed her mind and fallen in love with Herr Porphyrio von Ockerodastes, whom she had previously found so repulsive. He sought an explanation from the stars, but when the latter gave him no satisfactory answer he was forced to conclude that the human mind was more impenetrable than all the mysteries of the cosmos and not to be understood by any conjunction of the planets. He could not suppose that the bridegroom's higher nature had swayed Ännchen's affections in spite of his obvious lack of all physical beauty. Although, as the gentle reader has already heard, Herr Dapsul von Zabelthau's conception of beauty was infinitely far removed from that held by young ladies, he had at least sufficient worldly experience to know that the said young ladies regard understanding, wit, intelligence, and feeling as desirable tenants only when they occupy a fine house, and that man upon whom a fashionable frock coat does not sit well—even if he be in other respects a Shakespeare, a Goethe, a Tieck, or a Friedrich Richter—runs the risk of being driven from the field by any tolerably well-built hussar in the state uniform the moment he takes it into his head to march against a young girl. Things had turned out differently with Fräulein Ännchen; it was not a question either of beauty or understanding, however, but simply that a poor country maid does not often have a chance of becoming a queen. Herr Dapsul von Zabelthau was unaware of this, however; especially since on this point, too, the stars had let him down.

As may well be imagined, these three people—Herr Porphyrio von Ockerodastes, Herr Dapsul von Zabelthau, and Fräulein Ännchen—were one heart and one soul. Things went so far that Herr Dapsul von Zabelthau left his tower more often than ever before in order to chat with his esteemed son-in-law about all sorts of entertaining subjects; in particular, he now regularly took his lunch down in the house. At this time of day Herr Porphyrio von Ockerodastes also emerged from his silken palace and allowed himself to be fed by Fräulein Ännchen with bread and butter.

'Oh, oh,' Fräulein Ännchen frequently giggled into his ear, 'oh, oh, if Pape knew that you are really a king, best Corduanspitz.'

'Contain yourself, dear heart,' replied Daucus Carota I, 'contain yourself, dear heart, do not dissolve in rapture. Near, near is your day of joy!'

It happened that the schoolmaster presented Fräulein Ännchen with a bunch of the most magnificent radishes from his garden. Fräulein Ännchen was delighted, because Herr Dapsul von Zabelthau was very fond of radishes, but Ännchen could not take anything from the vegetable garden over which the palace had been built. Moreover, it now occurred to her that among the various leaf and root plants in the palace she had seen everything except radishes.

Fräulein Ännchen quickly cleaned the gift radishes and took them to her father for breakfast. Herr Dapsul von Zabelthau had already mercilessly cut off the crown of leaves from several of them, dipped them in the salt-cellar, and eaten them with relish, when Corduanspitz entered. 'O Ockerodastes, my friend, have some radishes,' Herr Dapsul von Zabelthau cried out to him. There was still one large, exceptionally fine radish on the plate. Corduanspitz had no sooner caught sight of it than his eyes began to blaze and he shouted in a terrifyingly booming voice: 'What, unworthy duke, you still dare to appear before my eyes and even to force your way with atrocious impertinence into a house that is protected by my power? Did I not banish you for ever, you who sought to contest my lawful throne? Away with you, traitorous vassal!'

Two little legs suddenly grew under the fat head of the radish, and with them he quickly jumped off the plate. He then took up a position close in front of Corduanspitz and spoke as follows: 'Cruel Daucus Carota I who sought in vain to destroy my clan! Did ever one of your race have such a big head as I and my relatives? Understanding, wisdom, sagacity, we are gifted with all that, and while you frequent kitchens and stables and are of some value only at the height of your youth, so that it is the *diable de la jeunesse* alone that affords your brief, ephemeral joy, we enjoy social intercourse with persons of rank and eminence and are greeted with jubilation the moment we raise our green heads! But I challenge you, O Daucus Carota, even if you are a clumsy great oaf like all your kind! Let us see which of us is the stronger!'

So saying, the Radish Duke brandished a long whip and without more ado set upon King Daucus Carota I. But the latter swiftly drew his little dagger and defended himself bravely. The two little men chased one another about the room in a series of the most astonishing and fantastic leaps, until Daucus Carota had the Radish Duke in such straits that he was forced to make a bold leap out of the open window and take to his heels. Daucus Carota, with whose exceptional agility the gentle reader is already familiar, bounded after him and pursued the Radish Duke across the field.

Herr Dapsul von Zabelthau had watched the frightful hand-to-hand combat in mute, dumbfounded dismay. Now he burst out weeping and wailing: 'O daughter Anna! O my poor, unhappy daughter Anna! We are lost—you—I— we are both lost!' And with these words he ran out of the room and climbed as quickly as he could up into his astronomic tower.

Fräulein Ännchen had no idea what on earth had cast her father into a state of such boundless distress all at once. The whole incident had given her exceptional pleasure, and she was joyful at heart to have observed that her bridegroom possessed not only rank and wealth but also courage, for there is probably no girl in the world who can love a coward. Now that she had been convinced of King Daucus Carota's courage she felt very resentful of Herr Amandus von Nebelstern's unwillingness to fight him.

Had she still been in doubt whether to sacrifice Herr Amandus to King Daucus Carota I, she would now have made up her mind to do so, since all her bridegroom's magnificence had been revealed to her. She instantly sat down and wrote the following letter:

'My dear Amandus,
' "Everything in the world may change, everything passes," says the schoolmaster, and he is quite right. You too, my dear Amandus, are far too wise and learned a student not to agree with the schoolmaster or to be in the least surprised when I tell you that there has also been a slight change in my mind and heart. You can believe me when I say that I am still very fond of you and can well imagine how fine you must look in the red velvet cap with the gold tassel, but as to marriage—you know, dear

Amandus, clever as you are and pretty as are the little verses you write, you will never, never become a king, and—do not jump out of your skin, dearest—little Herr von Corduanspitz is not Herr von Corduanspitz, but a mighty king named Daucus Carota I who rules the whole great realm of vegetables and has chosen me for his queen! Since the day my dear little king cast off his incognito he has also grown much better looking, and I can now see how right Papa was when he asserted that the head is a man's crowning glory and hence cannot be too big. At the same time Daucus Carota I—you see how well I can remember and write his beautiful name, now that it seems quite familiar to me—I was going to say, at the same time my little royal bridegroom behaves in such a pleasant and endearing manner that it is quite indescribable. And what courage, what audacity the man has! Before my eyes he put to flight the Radish Duke, who seems to be an ill-mannered, refractory fellow, and you should have seen how Daucus jumped out of the window after him! Nor do I think my Daucus Carota would bother much about your verses; he seems to be a man of fortitude upon whom verses, be they ever so fine and pointed, would have little effect. Well, dear Amandus, accept your destiny like a pious man and do not take it amiss that I am going to become a queen, instead of your wife. But be consoled, I shall always remain your affectionate friend, and if in the future you wish to be appointed to the Carrot Guard or, since you prefer knowledge to weapons, to the Parsnip Academy or the Ministry of Pumpkins, you have only to say the word and your fortune will be made.

'Farewell and do not be angry with your
        former betrothed but now
            affectionate friend and future queen,
                            Anna von Zabelthau
(soon to be no longer von Zabelthau, but simply Anna).
'P.S. You shall also be kept regularly supplied with the finest Virginian leaves, you can firmly rely on that. Although I am inclined to think that there will be no smoking at my court, a few beds not far from the throne shall immediately

be planted out with Virginian tobacco under my special supervision. This will promote culture and morality, and my little Daucus shall have a special law written on the matter.'

Chapter Five

in which news is given of a frightful disaster and the further course of events is reported.

FRÄULEIN ÄNNCHEN had just sent off her letter to Herr Amandus von Nebelstern, when Herr Dapsul von Zabelthau came into the room and said in the tearful tone of utter despondency: 'O my daughter Anna, how shamefully we have both been betrayed! That infamous scoundrel who lured you into his snare, who made me believe he was Baron Porphyrio von Ockerodastes, called Corduanspitz, a scion of the illustrious family founded by the gnome Tsilmenech in alliance with the noble Cordovan abbess, this infamous scoundrel—learn, and fall in a swoon!—is himself a gnome, but of the lowest order, that which tends vegetables! The gnome Tsilmenech belonged to the noblest order, that entrusted with the care of diamonds. Then comes the order of those who prepare metals in the realm of the Metal King. Then follow the flower gnomes, who are not so high in rank because they are dependent upon the sylphs. The basest and least noble, however, are the vegetable gnomes, and not merely is the deceitful Corduanspitz such a gnome—no, he is actually the king of this race and is called Daucus Carota!'

Instead of swooning, or showing the slightest sign of dismay, Fräulein Ännchen gave her lamenting Papa a friendly smile; the gentle reader already knows why! But when Herr Dapsul von Zabelthau showed great amazement at this and insisted upon trying to bring home to Fräulein Ännchen the enormity of her fate and making her grieve over it, Fräulein Ännchen felt that she could no longer keep the secret entrusted to her. She told Herr Dapsul von Zabelthau that the so-called Baron von Corduanspitz had long since disclosed his true rank to her himself and had thereafter appeared to her so lovable that she desired no other husband. She then went on to describe all the wondrous beauties of the vegetable kingdom into which King Daucus Carota I had introduced her, not forgetting to pay fitting tribute to the strange charm of all the manifold inhabitants of this great realm.

Herr Dapsul von Zabelthau struck his hands together time after time and wept bitterly at the sly malice of the gnome king, who had employed the most ingenious means, which were also the most dangerous to himself, in order to drag the unhappy Anna down into his gloomy demoniac empire.

Splendid and beneficial as the union of any ordinary elemental spirit with a human principle might be, Herr Dapsul von Zabelthau now explained to his attentive daughter—citing as an example the marriage between the gnome Tsilmenech and Magdalena de la Cruz, the success of which was the reason why the treacherous Daucus Carota claimed to be a scion of this family—the position was quite different in the case of the kings and princes of these races of spirits. Whereas the salamander kings were merely irascible, the sylph kings merely haughty, the undine queens merely very infatuated and jealous, the gnome kings, on the contrary, were sly, malicious, and cruel; for no other reason than to avenge themselves upon the children of the earth, who abducted their vassals, they would seek to entice one of them; the victim was then entirely divested of his or her human form—becoming just as misshapen as the gnomes themselves—and forced to descend into the earth, never to reappear.

Fräulein Ännchen seemed unwilling to believe all the evil which Herr Dapsul von Zabelthau imputed to her beloved Daucus; on the contrary, she began once more to enumerate all the wonders of the vegetable kingdom over which she would soon be ruling.

'Blind and foolish child!' cried the enraged Herr Dapsul von Zabelthau. 'Do you not credit your father with suffi-

cient Cabbalistic wisdom to know that everything the infamous Daucus Carota has shown you is nothing but a snare
and a delusion? No, you do not believe me; to save you I
must convince you, and to do this I must employ the most
desperate means. Come with me!'

For the second time, Fräulein Ännchen had now to
ascend with her father into the astronomic tower. From a
large box Herr Dapsul von Zabelthau took out a quantity of
yellow, red, white, and green ribbons and, to the accompaniment of a curious ceremonial, wrapped Fräulein Ännchen
in them from head to toe. He did the same with himself and
then the two of them, Fräulein Ännchen and Herr Dapsul
von Zabelthau, cautiously approached the silken palace of
King Daucus Carota I. On her father's orders, Fräulein
Ännchen slit open a seam with a pair of scissors she had
brought with her and looked inside.

Heaven preserve us, what did she see instead of the beautiful vegetable garden, instead of the Carrot Guard, the
kale ladies, the lavender pages, the lettuce princes, and
everything that had seemed to her so magnificent? She
looked down into a deep puddle that appeared to be filled
with colourless, nauseating mud. And in this mud there
wriggled and squiggled all kinds of horrible creatures from
the womb of the earth. Fat-rain worms writhed slowly in
tangled masses, while beetle-like creatures stretched out
their short legs and crawled laboriously away. On their
backs they carried large onions that had ugly human faces
and grinned and squinted at one another with murky yellow eyes and tried to grasp each other's long, crooked noses
with the little claws that grew just under their ears, and
drag one another down into the slime, while long, naked
slugs slowly weltered in a seething mass and stretched up
their long horns out of the depths. Fräulein Ännchen
almost swooned with horror at this loathsome sight. She put
both hands over her face and ran away as fast as her legs
would carry her.

'Now do you see,' Herr Dapsul von Zabelthau said to her,
'how shamefully the detestable Daucus Carota deceived

you, by showing you a magnificence that lasts only for a brief moment? He had his vassals don gala dress and his guards the uniform of the state in order to entice you with their dazzling splendour! But now you have seen the kingdom over which you would rule in its négligé, and once you were the horrible Daucus Carota's wife you would be forced to remain in the subterranean realm and never emerge again upon the surface of the earth! And if . . . oh . . . oh . . . what do I see, unhappiest of fathers!'

Herr Dapsul von Zabelthau now lapsed into such a state of frantic distress that Fräulein Ännchen was left in no doubt that some fresh disaster must have descended upon them. Fearfully, she asked the cause of her Papa's heart-rending laments; but he was sobbing so bitterly he could only stammer: 'O—daugh-ter—just—look—at—yourself!' Fräulein Ännchen ran into the house, looked at herself in the mirror, and started back in mortal terror.

She had good cause to be terrified. The situation was this: just as Herr Dapsul von Zabelthau was trying to open the eyes of King Daucus Carota's bride to the risk she was running of gradually losing her appearance and shape and changing bit by bit into the true image of a gnome queen, he perceived something terrible already taking place. Fräulein Ännchen's head had grown much fatter and her skin had turned saffron-yellow, making her look quite horrible. Although Fräulein Ännchen was not particularly vain, she was nevertheless girl enough to realize that to become ugly was the most terrible misfortune that could befall one here on earth. How often had she pictured the glorious joy she would feel, when, as a queen, she drove to church beside her royal husband in the coach and eight with a crown on her head, dressed in satin and decked out with diamond and gold necklaces and rings, amazing all the women, not excluding the schoolmaster's wife, and imposing respect even upon the proud gentry of the village to whose diocese Dapsulheim belonged; yes—how often had she indulged in these and other bizarre dreams! Fräulein Ännchen burst into tears!

'Anna—my daughter Anna, come up to me at once!'
Thus Herr Dapsul von Zabelthau called down through the
speaking-tube.

Fräulein Ännchen found her Papa dressed in a kind of
miner's outfit. Speaking with composure, he said: 'When
need is greatest, help is often nearest at hand. I have just
ascertained that Daucus Carota will not leave his palace
today or, indeed, until tomorrow noon. He has assembled
the princes of the house, the ministers, and the other great
ones of the land in order to confer on the subject of the
future crop of winter cabbage. The meeting is an important
one and may last so long that we get no winter cabbage at
all this year. I intend to employ this time, when Daucus
Carota is so absorbed by matters of state that he does not
notice me and my activities, to devise a weapon by means
of which I can perhaps combat and defeat the base gnome,
so that he is compelled to flee and leave you your freedom.
While I am at work, gaze fixedly through this tube at the
tent and tell me at once if you see anyone looking out or
actually emerging from it.'

Fräulein Ännchen did as she was bid, but the tent remained closed. In spite of the fact that Herr Dapsul von
Zabelthau was hammering away hard at metal plates a few
paces behind her, however, she frequently heard wild shouting that seemed to come from the tent and then loud slap-
ping sounds, as though someone's ears were being boxed.
She reported this to Herr Dapsul von Zabelthau, who was
delighted and said that the more violently they quarrelled
inside, the less likely they were to notice what was being
forged to their ruin outside.

Fräulein Ännchen was no little surprised when she saw
that Herr Dapsul von Zabelthau had hammered out of
copper a few absolutely charming saucepans and equally
delightful frying-pans. Looking at them with an expert eye,
she could see that the tinning was exceptionally well done
and that her Papa had fully conformed with all the laws
governing the work of coppersmiths; she asked whether she
might not take the fine utensils and use them in the kitchen.

At this, Herr Dapsul von Zabelthau smiled mysteriously and merely replied: 'All in good time, my daughter Anna, all in good time, now go downstairs and wait and see what happens in our house tomorrow.'

Herr Dapsul von Zabelthau had smiled, and it was this which gave the unhappy Änchenn hope and confidence.

The following day, as noon approached, Herr Dapsul von Zabelthau came down with his saucepans and frying-pans, went into the kitchen, and requested Fräulein Ännchen and the maid to leave, as he wished to prepare the midday meal on his own today. He particularly exhorted Fräulein Ännchen to be as amiable and affectionate as possible towards Corduanspitz, who would no doubt shortly make his appearance.

Corduanspitz, or rather King Daucus Carota I, did indeed soon appear, and if he had previously acted as though deeply in love, today he was the very embodiment of delight and rapture. To her horror, Fräulein Ännchen noticed that she had already grown so small that Daucus had no difficulty in jumping up on to her lap and hugging and kissing her, which the unhappy girl had to endure in spite of her profound aversion to the horrid little monster.

At last Herr Dapsul von Zabelthau entered and said: 'O excellent Porphyrio von Ockerodastes, will you not accompany my daughter and myself into the kitchen and see how neatly and hospitably your future wife has arranged everything there?'

Fräulein Ännchen had never before seen in her father's face the sly, malicious expression it wore as he took little Daucus by the arm and dragged him almost forcibly out of the room into the kitchen. At a sign from her father, Fräulein Ännchen followed them.

Fräulein Ännchen's heart leapt when she saw the splendidly crackling fire, the glowing coals, and the pretty copper saucepans and frying-pans on the stove. As Herr Dapsul von Zabelthau led Corduanspitz close to the stove, the hissing and bubbling in the saucepans and frying-pans grew louder and louder. Then the hissing and bubbling turned into frightened whimpering and groaning, and from one of the saucepans a voice wailed: 'O Daucus Carota, O my king, save thy faithful vassals, save us poor carrots! Cut in pieces, flung into injurious water, painfully stuffed with butter and salt, we languish in unspeakable suffering which noble parsley youths share with us!' And from a frying-pan came the lament: 'O Daucus Carota, O my king, save thy faithful vassals, save us poor carrots! We are frying in hell and we have been given so little water that terrible thirst compels us to drink our own heart's blood.' And from another saucepan a voice whimpered: 'O Daucus Carota, O my king, save they vassals, save us poor carrots! A brutal cook has hollowed us out, chopped up our inside and stuffed it back in again mixed with all sorts of foreign matter, with eggs, cream, and butter, so that all our senses and powers of understanding are in confusion and we ourselves no longer know what we are thinking!' Then a babble of voices screamed and cried from all the saucepans and frying-pans: 'O Daucus Carota, mighty king, save, oh save thy faithful vassals, save us poor carrots!'

Thereupon Corduanspitz screeched loudly, 'Damned, idiotic foolishness!', bounded with his usual agility up on to the stove, looked into one of the saucepans, lost his balance, and fell in. Herr Dapsul von Zabelthau quickly sprang towards him and tried to close the lid of the saucepan, exclaiming jubilantly: 'Caught!' But Corduanspitz sprang out of the saucepan with the force of a spring and struck Herr Dapsul von Zabelthau several cracking blows across the mouth, crying: 'Impertinent simpleton of a Cabbalist, you shall pay for that! Out, boys, all together, out!'

At this, a sound came from all the pots and pans like the onrush of Wotan's Host, and hundreds and hundreds of horrible little fellows the length of a finger hooked themselves firmly all over Herr Dapsul von Zabelthau's body and hurled him backwards into a large basin and prepared him for cooking by pouring over him the scalding contents of all the vessels and sprinkling him with chopped eggs, mace, and grated wheaten rolls. Then Daucus Carota bounded out of the window and his subjects did likewise.

Fräulein Ännchen sank down in horror before the basin in which her poor father lay ready to be cooked; she took him to be dead, since he did not give the slightest sign of life. She began to lament: 'Oh, my poor Papa—oh, now you are dead and nothing can save me from the fiendish Daucus!' At this, however, Herr Dapsul von Zabelthau opened his eyes, leapt with renewed energy out of the basin, and yelled in a terrifying voice Fräulein Ännchen had never heard him use before: 'Ha, despicable Daucus Carota, my powers are not yet exhausted! You will soon see what the impertinent simpleton of a Cabbalist can do!'

Fräulein Ännchen quickly brushed off the chopped eggs, mace, and grated wheaten rolls with the kitchen broom. Then Herr Dapsul seized a copper saucepan, set it on his head like a helmet, took a frying-pan in his left hand and a big iron ladle in his right, and, thus armed and accoutred, rushed out of the house. Fräulein Ännchen saw Herr Dapsul von Zabelthau running at full speed towards Corduanspitz's tent and yet not moving from the spot. She fell senseless at the sight.

When she came to, Herr Dapsul von Zabelthau had vanished, and she fell into a state of terrible anxiety when he did not return in the evening, during the night, or even the following morning. She could not help surmising that some fresh enterprise had come to a still more disastrous end.

Chapter Six

which is the last and at the same time the most edifying of all.

FRÄULEIN ÄNNCHEN was sitting alone in her room, plunged in profound grief, when the door opened and who should come in but Herr Amandus von Nebelstern? Overcome with shame and regret, Fräulein Ännchen let loose a flood of tears and begged in the most doleful tones: 'O my best beloved Amandus, forgive what I wrote you in my blindness! But I was bewitched and probably still am. Save me, save me, my Amandus! I look yellow and repulsive, woe is me, but I have kept my faithful heart and do not want to be a queen!'

'I don't know what you are complaining about, my dear young lady,' replied Amandus von Nebelstern, 'since the finest, most splendid lot has fallen to you.'

'Oh, do not mock me,' cried Fräulein Ännchen. 'I have been punished severely enough for my stupid pride in wanting to become a queen!'

'I really don't understand you, my dear young lady,' continued Herr Amandus von Nebelstern. 'If I am to be honest, I must admit that your last letter put me in a state of rage and despair. I beat the serving lad, then the poodle, smashed a few glasses—and, you know, there's no joking with a student who is breathing vengeance! But once I had worked off my rage, I decided to hurry here and see with my own eyes why and to whom I had lost my beloved bride. Love knows neither rank nor estate, I wanted to question King Daucus Carota himself and ask him whether he really was going to marry my betrothed or not. But everything worked out differently when I got here. As I was passing the fine tent that has been set up outside, King Daucus Carota stepped out and I soon perceived that I had before me the most amiable of all possible princes, although I have never seen one before; just imagine, my dear young lady, he immediately sensed in me the sublime poet, lauded to the skies my verses which he has not yet read, and offered me the post of court poet in his service. Such a position has long been the splendid goal of my most ardent desires, and I therefore accepted his offer with delight. O my dear young lady, with what inspiration I shall sing your praises! A poet can be in love with queens and princesses, or rather it is part of his duties to choose such an exalted personage as the lady of his heart, and if this renders him slightly mad it produces the divine delirium without which there can be no poetry, and nobody should be surprised at the poet's rather strange behaviour; they should think of the great Tasso, who also suffered a certain clouding of his common sense as a result of falling in love with the Princess Leonora d'Este. Yes, my dear young lady, though you will soon be a queen, you shall yet remain the lady of my heart, whom I shall raise to the lofty stars in the most sublime and godly verses!'

'What, you have seen the knavish goblin and he . . .' Fräulein Ännchen burst out in amazement; but at this moment the object of her wrath, the little gnomic king, entered in person and said in tender tones: 'O my dear, sweet bride, idol of my heart, have no fear that I am angry on account of Herr Dapsul von Zabelthau's little slip. No— and all the less because it actually furthered my happiness and as a result of it my solemn wedding to you, my most lovely one, can already be celebrated tomorrow, something I had not previously been able to hope for. You will be glad to know that I have chosen Herr Amandus von Nebelstern to be our court poet, and I should like him at once to afford us a specimen of his talent and sing us something now. But let us go to the arbour, for I love the open air; I shall sit on your lap and you, dearest bride, can scratch my head a little during the song, which is something I enjoy on such occasions!'

Petrified with fear and horror, Fräulein Ännchen meekly obeyed. Daucus Carota sat on her lap in the arbour, she scratched his head, and Herr Amandus von Nebelstern, accompanying himself on the guitar, began the first of the twelve dozen songs which he had himself written and set to music and bound together in a thick tome.

It is a pity that these songs are not written down in the Chronicle of Dapsulheim, from which the whole of this story is taken; there is merely a remark to the effect that passing peasants stopped and inquired curiously who was suffering such agonies in Herr Dapsul von Zabelthau's arbour that he had to give vent to these fearful cries of pain.

Daucus Carota twisted and turned on Fräulein Ännchen's

lap and groaned and whimpered more and more bitterly, as though he were suffering from a terrible colic. Fräulein Ännchen observed to her astonishment that while Amandus was singing Corduanspitz was growing smaller and smaller. Finally, Herr Amandus von Nebelstern sang the following sublime lines (the only song that is actually recorded in the Chronicle):

'List how the singer sings his lay!
The scent of flowers and shining dreams
Drift through rosy realms of space
Towards some golden far-away!
Blessed, heavenly far-away,
Where iridescent rainbow gleams,
Flower petals hang in veils like lace.
O childish heart, so full of love,
You long to be like turtle dove,
To bill and coo and peck and patter
Where no one sees and 'tis no matter.
All this is in the singer's lay.
He sings the blissful far-away,
And drifts with his dreams through heavenly space
Where starlight knits its golden lace.
Eternal longing fills his breast,
He sings his song at love's behest.
The flames of love that blaze within
Set his poor, heated brain a-spin.
Out of the world and out of time
He puts his burning thoughts in rhyme
And . . .'

Daucus Carota, who had shrunk to a tiny little carrot, uttered a loud screech, slipped down from Ännchen's lap and into the earth, so that in a moment he had completely disappeared. Thereupon the grey toadstool that seemed to have grown up during the night beside the grassy bank, shot up into the air; but the toadstool was in fact Herr Dapsul von Zabelthau's grey felt cap, and he himself was underneath it and flung himself upon Herr Amandus von

Nebelstern's chest and cried ecstatically: 'O my dearest, best beloved Herr Amandus von Nebelstern! With your powerful poem of conjuration you have outdone all my Cabbalistic wisdom. What the most profound magic art, what the reckless courage of the despairing philosopher was unable to achieve, your verses have done, entering into the body of the treacherous Daucus Carota like the strongest poison, so that despite his gnomic nature he would have perished miserably of the colic if he had not escaped fast enough into his own kingdom! My daughter Anna is set free, and I am set free from the terrible spell that held me here in the shape of an obnoxious toadstool, in danger of being slain by the hands of my own daughter! For the good girl mercilessly removes all toadstools from garden and field with a sharp spade, if they do not at once prove their noble character like mushrooms. Thanks, my warmest and most heartfelt thanks and—is it not so, most esteemed Herr Amandus von Nebelstern, everything will remain as it was with regard to my daughter? It is true, woe is me, that she has been cheated of her pretty appearance by the villainy of the malignant gnome, but you are far too much of a philosopher to . . .'

'O Papa, my best Papa,' exulted Fräulein Ännchen, 'just look there, just look there, the silken palace has disappeared. He has gone, the ugly monster, along with his train of lettuce princes and pumpkin ministers and all the rest!'

With these words, Fräulein Ännchen raced off to the vegetable garden. Herr Dapsul von Zabelthau ran after his daughter as fast as he could go, and Herr Amandus von Nebelstern followed, grumbling into his beard: 'I really don't know what to make of all this, but I can say for sure that the horrid little carrot fellow is an impudent prosaic clown and no poetic king, otherwise he would not have got the colic and crawled into the ground on hearing my sublimest song!'

As Fräulein Ännchen stood in the vegetable garden, where there was not a blade of green to be seen, she felt an atrocious pain in the finger on which she was wearing the fatal ring. At the same time a heart-rending cry rose from the depths and the tip of a carrot peeped forth. Correctly guided by her intuition, Fräulein Ännchen quickly and easily slipped off the ring, which hitherto she had been unable to remove from her finger, and set it on the carrot; the latter vanished and the lament ceased. But, oh wonder, Fräulein Ännchen was all at once as pretty as before, well proportioned, and as white as can be expected of any country maid. Both Fräulein Ännchen and Herr Dapsul von Zabeltthau rejoiced vociferously, while Herr Amandus von Nebelstern stood there utterly bewildered and still not knowing what to make of it all.

Fräulein Ännchen took the spade from the hand of the maid, who had come running up, and swung it in the air with a jubilant cry of 'Now let us work'; but as bad luck would have it she struck Herr Amandus von Nebelstern hard on the head (just on the spot where the 'bump of common sense' is said to be located), so that he fell down as though dead. Fräulein Ännchen flung the murderous instrument far from her, threw herself down beside her beloved, and burst into desperate wails of anguish, while the maid poured a whole jug of water over him and Herr Dapsul von Zabeltthau quickly ascended his astronomic tower, to inquire of the stars as fast as he could whether Herr Amandus von Nebelstern was really dead. It was not long before the latter reopened his eyes, jumped up, wet as he was, took Fräulein Ännchen in his arms, and cried with all the rapture of love: 'O my best, my dearest Ännchen! Now we have each other again!'

The very remarkable, almost incredible effect of this incident on the lovers was soon apparent. The minds of both were curiously changed.

Fräulein Ännchen had acquired an aversion to handling the spade and really ruled like a true queen over the vegetable kingdom, which she cared for lovingly, making sure that her subjects were properly hoed and weeded, but without taking any part herself in the work, which she left to faithful maids. Herr Amandus von Nebelstern, on the other hand, came to regard everything he had written and his whole ambition to be a poet as extremely silly and pretentious, and instead devoted himself to studying the works of the great, true poets of the past and present; in this way his whole inner being was filled with a beneficial enthusiasm that left no place for thoughts of his own ego. He became convinced that a poem must be something other than the muddled jumble of words produced by a sober delirium, and after he had thrown into the fire all the versifyings with which he had previously given himself airs in a spirit of boastful self-approval, he became once more a sensible young man, lucid in mind and heart, as he had been before.

One morning Herr Dapsul von Zabelthau really did come down from his astronomic tower and escort Fräulein Ännchen and Herr Amandus von Nebelstern to the church to be married.

Thereafter they lived a happy and contented married life; but as to whether anything finally came of Herr Dapsul's wedlock with the sylph Nehahilah, the Chronicle of Dapsulheim is silent.

GAMBLER'S LUCK

I N THE summer of 18—, Pyrmont had more visitors than ever. The influx of wealthy and aristocratic foreigners increased from day to day and gave a spur to the avidity of every kind of speculator. Thus, too, the proprietors of faro banks heaped up greater quantities than usual of their glittering gold, so that the bait should effectively lure even the noblest game which, skilled hunters as they were, they hoped to entrap.

Who does not know that the magical attraction of gambling can become irresistible, especially during the season in watering places, where everyone has stepped out of his normal surroundings and is deliberately devoting himself to the enjoyment of leisure and freedom. One sees people who, in the ordinary way, would never touch a card, among the most ardent gamblers at the bank, and moreover good tone demands, at least in more genteel circles, that one should repair to the bank every evening and gamble away some money.

One man alone, a young German baron—we will call him Siegfried—seemed unmoved by this irresistible magic, this rule of good tone. When everyone else hurried to the gaming-table, when he was deprived of every opportunity, every prospect of the intelligent conversation he loved, he preferred to abandon himself to the play of his imagination on lonely walks, or to pick up some book or other in his room, or even to try his own hand at composing poetry or writing.

Siegfried was young, independent, rich, of noble appearance and charming nature, thus he could not fail to be highly esteemed and loved and fortunate with women. But it also seemed that in everything he embarked upon, everything he undertook a lucky star ruled over him. People spoke of all sorts of sensational love affairs which were forced upon him and which, harmful as they would surely have been to anyone else, were in an incredible manner happily and easily resolved. In particular, however, when the Baron's luck came to be discussed, the old gentlemen of his acquaintance liked to tell a story concerning a watch that had occurred to him in his early youth. It happened that Siegfried, while still a minor, quite unexpectedly found himself so short of money while travelling that, in order to continue his journey, he was compelled to sell his gold watch richly inlaid with brilliants. He was prepared to let the watch go for a pittance; but since it so happened that a young prince staying in the same hotel was just looking for such a trinket, he received more than the watch was really worth. Over a year had passed, Siegfried had become his own master, when in another town he read in the public newspaper that a watch was to be the prize in a lottery. He bought a ticket for little or nothing and—won the gold watch inlaid with brilliants that he had sold. Not long afterwards he exchanged this watch for a valuable ring. He entered for a short time into the service of the Prince of —, and on the termination of his employment the Prince, as a token of his goodwill, sent him—the same gold watch inlaid with brilliants on an expensive chain!

From this story, talk would move to Siegfried's eccentric refusal ever to touch playing-cards, to which his striking luck would have been an added incentive, and everyone agreed that, in spite of all his other wonderful qualities, the Baron was a niggard, far too timid, far too pusillanimous, to risk the slightest loss. That the Baron's behaviour decisively contradicted all suspicion of meanness passed unnoticed; the majority of people are always desperately anxious to attach a dubious 'but' to the reputation of any highly gifted man and always manage to find this 'but' somewhere, even if it only exists in their imagination; so everyone was highly satisfied with this interpretation of Siegfried's aversion to gambling.

Siegfried soon learnt what was being said about him, and since, generous and liberal as he was, he hated, loathed nothing more than niggardliness, he resolved to crush his detractors by buying himself free from the evil suspicion with a few hundred *louis d'or* and even more, much as he was revolted by gambling.

He went to the bank with the firm intention of losing the considerable sum which he staked; but even in gambling, the luck which stood by him in everything he undertook remained true to him. Every card he chose won. The cabbalistic calculations of old, practised players came to grief on the Baron's game. He could change cards, he could carry on with the same ones, it made no difference, he always won. The Baron displayed the rare spectacle of a punter who is beside himself because the cards come out favourably to him, and obvious as the explanation for this behaviour was, people nevertheless looked at one another thoughtfully and made it quite clear that they believed the Baron, swept away by his tendency to strangeness, might finally fall victim to some madness; for the gambler who was horrified by his luck must undoubtedly be mad.

The very fact that he had won a large sum compelled the Baron to go on playing and thus, since according to the laws of probability his considerable win was bound to be followed by an even more considerable loss, achieve what he had set out to do. But the expected entirely failed to occur, for the Baron's decisive luck remained quite unchanged.

Without his being aware of it himself, pleasure in the game of faro, which in its simplicity is the most fateful of all, grew more and more intense within the Baron.

He was no longer dissatisfied with his luck, the game gripped his interest and held him fast for whole nights on end, so that, since it was not the gain but very definitely the game that drew him, he was forced to believe in the special magic of which his friends spoke and which he had by no means wished to confirm.

One night when he raised his eyes, after the banker had just finished a turn, he espied an elderly man who had taken up a position facing him and was gazing at him steadily with melancholy, earnest eyes. And every time the Baron looked up during the game his eyes met the sombre eyes of the stranger, so that he could not escape an oppressive, uncanny feeling. Not till the game was over did the stranger leave the room. The following night he once more stood facing the Baron and stared at him unwaveringly with sombre, spectral eyes. The Baron still controlled himself; but when the stranger returned yet again on the third night and stared at the Baron with a consuming fire in his eyes, the latter burst out: 'Sir, I must ask you to find another place to stand. You are interfering with my game.'

The stranger bowed with a painful smile, and without a word left the gaming-table and the room.

The following night the stranger stood facing the Baron yet again, piercing him with his sombrely burning gaze.

This time the Baron burst out even more angrily than on the previous night: 'Sir, if you enjoy gaping at me please choose a different time and a different place to do so, but for the moment will you please . . .'

A movement of the hand towards the door served instead of the harsh word which the Baron had been about to utter.

And as on the previous night, bowing slightly with the same painful smile, the stranger left the room.

Excited by the gambling, excited by the wine he had drunk, indeed even by the scene with the stranger, Siegfried could not sleep. Dawn was already breaking when the stranger's whole figure appeared before his eyes. He saw the distinguished, sharply drawn, embittered face, the deep-set, sombre eyes that stared at him, he observed that in spite of the poor clothes the noble bearing bespoke a man of breeding. And then he recalled the way in which the stranger accepted his harsh words with painful resignation and left the room, forcibly suppressing his bitter feelings.

'No,' cried Siegfried. 'I did him an injustice, a grave injustice. Is it then in my nature to flare out in vulgar abuse like any rough fellow, and utter insults without the slightest excuse?'

The Baron became convinced that the man had stared at him like that as the result of an oppressive awareness of the glaring contrast brought home to him by the way in which the Baron was piling up gold upon gold in reckless gambling, at a moment when he was perhaps struggling with the direst poverty. He resolved the very next morning to seek out the stranger and settle the matter.

Chance willed that the very first person whom the Baron met strolling in the avenue was precisely the stranger.

The Baron addressed him, emphatically apologized for his behaviour the previous night and concluded by formally begging the stranger's pardon. The stranger commented that he had nothing to forgive, since much must be forgiven a gambler involved in a thrilling game, and that in any case he had brought the harsh words upon himself by obstinately remaining in a place where he was bound to be an annoyance to the Baron.

The Baron walked on; he spoke of the fact that there were often moments of temporary embarrassment in life which most painfully oppressed the man of breeding, and gave the stranger clearly to understand that he was prepared to give him the money he had won, and even more, if it might be of assistance to him.

'Sir,' replied the stranger, 'you believe me to be in want, but I am not, for although I am poor rather than rich I yet have all my simple way of life demands. Moreover you will see for yourself that if you believe you have offended me and wish to make retribution by a large sum of money, I, as a man of honour, could not possibly accept it, even if I were not a nobleman.'

'I believe,' replied the Baron, crestfallen, 'I believe that I understand you and am ready to give you satisfaction as you demand.'

'Oh heaven,' continued the stranger, 'how uneven a duel between the two of us would be. I am convinced that like myself you do not regard a duel as a childish tantrum and do not believe that a few drops of blood, flowing perhaps from a scratched finger, can wash clean stained honour. There are many cases in which it becomes impossible for two people to exist side by side on this earth, even if one of them lives in the Caucasus and the other by the Tiber, there is no separation so long as thought encompasses the other's existence. Here the duel, which decides which one shall make room for the other on this earth, becomes necessary. Between us two, as I have said, a duel would be unequal, since my life can on no account be placed on a par with yours. If I were to bring you low, I should be killing a whole world of the finest hopes, if I were the one to fall, you would have put an end to a wretched existence ruined by the bitterest, most agonizing memories. But the chief thing is that I do not consider myself in the least insulted. You told me to go and I went.'

The stranger uttered these last words in a tone that betrayed his inward mortification. Reason enough for the Baron once more to excuse himself politely by saying that, though he himself did not know why, the stranger's gaze had penetrated the depths of his soul, so that in the end he simply could not bear it.

'I wish my gaze would really penetrate the depths of your soul,' said the stranger, 'for if it did it would render you conscious of the danger that threatens you. With a gay heart, with youthful insouciance, you are standing on the edge of an abyss; one push and you will fall beyond rescue. In a word—you are in the process of becoming an impassioned gambler and ruining yourself.'

The Baron assured the stranger that he was entirely mistaken. He recounted at length the manner in which he had come to the gaming-table and asserted that he was entirely devoid of any real interest in gambling, that he merely wished to lose a few hundred *louis d'or* and that when he had achieved this he would give up punting. But up to now he had had the most striking luck.

'Oh,' cried the stranger, 'this very luck is the most terrible, most insidious enticement of the hostile power. This very luck with which you gamble, Baron, the whole way in which you have come to gambling, indeed your whole manner while gambling, which betrays only too clearly how your interest in it grows ever greater— everything—everything reminds me only too vividly of the horrible fate of an unhappy man who, similar to you in many respects, began just as you did. For this reason I could not take my eyes off you, could scarcely restrain myself from telling you in words what my gaze was meant to convey to you. "Oh, see the demons stretching out their claws towards you to drag you down into Hades!" That was what I should have liked to cry out to you. I wished to make your acquaintance, at least I have succeeded in that. Let me tell you the story of the unhappy man whom I mentioned; perhaps you will then be convinced that it is no empty figment of my imagination if I regard you as being in the most imminent danger and warn you.'

The two of them, the stranger and the Baron, sat down on a solitary bench; then the stranger began as follows.

'The same brilliant qualities that distinguish you, Baron, gained the Chevalier Menars the esteem and admiration of men and made him the darling of women. Only in respect of wealth, Fortune had not favoured him so greatly as you. He was almost indigent, and only by means of the most regulated way of life was he able to keep up the appearances appropriate to his position as the scion of an eminent family. For that reason alone, since the slightest loss would have made itself painfully felt and upset his whole way of life, he could never take part in any gambling; at the same time, he had absolutely no feeling for it, and it was no sacrifice for him to eschew gambling. Apart from this, he succeeded in everything he undertook, to such a degree that the Chevalier Menars's luck became proverbial.

'One night, contrary to his habit, he had allowed himself to be persuaded to visit a gambling-house. The friends who had come with him were soon involved in the game.

'Taking no interest in what was going on around him, deep in quite different thoughts, the Chevalier now strode up and down the room, now stared at the gaming-table, where more and more gold was flowing towards the banker from every side. Then suddenly an old colonel caught sight of the Chevalier and called out loudly: "Devil take it! The Chevalier is among us and his luck, and we cannot win anything, because he has not declared himself either for the banker or for the punters, but that shall not remain so any longer, he shall immediately punt for me."

'The Chevalier tried to excuse himself on the grounds of his lack of skill, his want of all experience; say what he would, the colonel insisted and the Chevalier had to go to the gaming-table.

'Things went with the Chevalier exactly as they did with you, Baron; every card won for him, so that he had soon amassed a considerable sum for the colonel, who could not rejoice enough at his splendid idea of making use of the Chevalier Menars's well-tried luck.

'His luck, which amazed everyone else, made not the least impression upon the Chevalier; indeed, though he himself did not know why, his aversion to gambling grew even greater, so that next morning, when he felt the consequences of a strenuous and sleepless night in the shape of mental and physical exhaustion, he resolved most earnestly never again under any circumstances to visit a gambling-house.

'This resolve was further strengthened by the behaviour of the old colonel, who, as soon as he took a single card in his hand, had the most striking bad luck, and with strange stupidity blamed this bad luck on the Chevalier. He demanded in the most importunate manner that the Chevalier should punt for him, or at least stand beside him while he played, in order by his presence to exorcize the evil demon who thrust into his hand the cards that never won. (Everyone knows that preposterous superstition is nowhere more prevalent than among gamblers.) It was only by speaking with the greatest gravity, indeed by declaring that he would rather fight with him than gamble for him, that the Chevalier was able to keep the colonel, who was no lover of duelling, at arm's length. The Chevalier cursed himself for having yielded to the old fool in the first place.

'Moreover, as was only to be expected, the story of the Chevalier's miraculously lucky play ran from mouth to mouth and all sorts of enigmatic and mysterious fictitious incidents were added to it, making him out to be in league with the higher powers. But the fact that the Chevalier, disregarding his luck, never touched a card was bound to create the highest impression of his force of character and greatly increase the esteem in which he stood.

'Something like a year may have passed when the unexpected non-arrival of the small sum upon which he lived placed the Chevalier in the most depressing and painful embarrassment. He was forced to confide in his most faithful friend, who without more ado lent him the sum he needed, but at the same time upbraided him with being the most eccentric fellow who ever lived.

' "Fate," he said, "drops hints to us as to the path

along which we should seek and find our salvation, it is only the fault of our indolence if we do not heed, do not understand these hints. The higher power that rules over us has whispered very distinctly in your ear: If you wish to acquire money and goods, go and gamble, otherwise you will remain forever poor, indigent, dependent."

'Only now did the thought of how miraculously fortune had favoured him at the faro bank come vividly into his mind, and in a waking dream he saw cards, heard the banker's monotonous *"gagne—perd"*, the clinking of the gold pieces.

' "It is true," he said to himself, "one night like that will raise me out of want, save me from the oppressive embarrassment of being a burden on my friends; it is my duty to follow Fate's hint."

'The selfsame friend who had advised him to gamble accompanied him to the gambling-house and gave him another twenty *louis d'or,* so that he could start to play without worry.

'If the Chevalier had played brilliantly on the occasion when he punted for the old colonel, he now played twice as brilliantly. Blindly, without choosing, he drew the cards which he staked; not he, however, but the invisible hand of the higher power which is familiar with chance, or rather is itself that which we call chance, seemed to guide his play. When the game was over he had won a thousand *louis d'or.*

'He awoke next morning in a kind of stupefaction. The gold pieces he had won lay scattered over the table beside him. He thought for the first instant that he was dreaming, he rubbed his eyes, he took hold of the table and pulled it closer to him. But when he remembered what had happened, when he ran his hands through the gold pieces, when he complacently counted them and re-counted them, delight in filthy lucre passed for the first time through his whole being like a noxious, poisonous breath; it was all up with the purity of mind he had so long preserved.

'He could scarcely wait for night in order to get to the gaming-table. His luck remained the same, so that in a few weeks, during which he played almost every night, he had won a considerable sum of money.

'There are two kinds of gambler. For many the game itself as a game, irrespective of gain, affords an indescribable, mysterious pleasure. The singular effects of chance work themselves out in the strangest concatenations, the rule of the higher power emerges more clearly, and it is just this that stimulates our spirit to stir its wings and try whether it cannot soar into the dark kingdom, into the fateful workshop of that higher power, and eavesdrop on its workings. I knew a man who for days and nights on end, alone in his room, made a bank and punted against himself; in my opinion, he was a true gambler. Others have only gain in mind and regard the game as a means of quick enrichment. The Chevalier fell into this latter class, thereby confirming the dictum that the real, profound feeling for gambling must be contained in the individual nature, must be inborn.

'For this very reason, the sphere in which the punter moves was soon too narrow for him. With the considerable sum which he won he established a bank, and here too luck so favoured him that in a short time his bank was the wealthiest in all Paris. As lies in the nature of the matter, the majority of gamblers came streaming to him, the wealthiest, the luckiest banker.

'The wild, dissolute life of the gambler soon destroyed all the mental and physical assets that had previously gained the Chevalier love and respect. He ceased to be a faithful friend, a relaxed, gay companion, a chivalrous, gallant squire of dames. Extinguished was his feeling for science and art, gone all his striving to advance in useful knowledge. On his deathly pale face, in his eyes blazing with a sombre, dark fire, lay the full expression of the ruinous passion that held him in its toils. It was not the gambling mania, no, it was the most hateful greed for money that Satan himself ignited in his inmost soul. In a word, he was the most perfect banker there can possibly be.

'One night, although the Chevalier did not actually lose a large sum, luck nevertheless proved less favourable to him than usual. Then a dried-up little old man, poorly dressed, of almost loathsome appearance came to the gaming-table, took a card with a trembling hand and staked a gold piece on it. Several of the gamblers looked at the old man at first with astonishment, but then treated him with withering contempt, without the old man batting an eyelid, much less uttering a single word of complaint.

'The old man lost—lost one stake after another, but the higher his losses rose, the more the other gamblers rejoiced. Yes, when the old man, who kept on doubling his stakes, staked five hundred *louis d'or* on one card and this failed to come up, someone cried with a loud laugh: "Good luck, Signor Vertua, good luck, do not lose heart, keep staking; you look to me like a man who will eventually break the bank with his enormous winnings."

'The old man cast a basilisk's glance at the mocker and ran quickly from the room, but only to return in half an hour with his pockets stuffed with gold. During the last turn, however, the old man had to stop, because he had once more lost all the gold he had brought with him.

'The Chevalier, who, in spite of all the villainy of his deeds, still insisted on a certain decency being maintained at his bank, had been greatly displeased by the contempt with which the old man had been treated. Reason enough, when the game was over and the old man had left, to speak very seriously to the scoffer and a few other gamblers whose contemptuous behaviour towards the old man had struck him most and whom he had asked to stay behind.

' "Oh," exclaimed one of them, "you do not know old Francesco Vertua, Chevalier, otherwise you would

224

not complain about us and our behaviour but rather wholeheartedly approve of it. Learn that this Vertua, a Neapolitan by birth, for fifteen years resident in Paris, is the basest, most abominable, most malevolent miser and usurer there could be. All human emotion is alien to him, he could see his own brother writhing in the death throes at his feet and one would try in vain to extract a single *louis d'or* from him, even if it would save his brother's life. The curses and execrations of many people, indeed of whole families, who have been cast into utter ruin by his Satanic speculations, weigh heavily upon him. He is bitterly hated by all those who know him; everyone wishes that the vengeance for all the evil he has done should descend upon him and end his guilt-stained life. He has never gambled, at least not since he has been in Paris, and after all this you should not be surprised at the profound amazement that came over us when the miser came to the table. Similarly, we could not help rejoicing at his considerable losses, for it would have been wicked, very wicked if luck had favoured the scoundrel. It is only too certain that the wealth of your bank, Chevalier, has dazzled the old fool. He thought he could fleece you and lost his own wool. Yet I still cannot understand how Vertua, contrary to the true character of a miser, could have made up his mind to play for such high stakes. Well—he will not come back, we are rid of him."

'This assumption was by no means correct, however, because the very next night Vertua returned to the Chevalier's bank and staked and lost even more money than the day before. As he did so he remained calm, indeed he smiled at times with a bitter irony, as though he foresaw with certainty that things would very soon change. But like an avalanche, the old man's losses grew more and more rapid on each of the following nights, so that in the end people calculated that he must have paid close on thirty thousand *louis d'or* to the bank. Then one day he came to the room long after the game had started, deathly pale and with a distraught expression, and took up a position far from the gaming-table, his eyes rigidly fixed upon the cards turned up by the Chevalier. Finally, when the Chevalier had shuffled the cards, cut them and was about to begin dealing, the old man cried out in a screeching voice: "Stop," so that everyone looked round, almost horrified. Then the old man forced his way to the Chevalier's side and said in a hollow voice, speaking into his ear: "Chevalier, my house in the Rue Saint-Honoré together with all its furnishings and the gold and silver and jewels I possess is estimated at eighty thousand francs, will you hold the stake?" "Very well," replied the Chevalier coldly, without looking round at the old man, and began to deal the cards.

'"The queen," said the old man, and at the next turn the queen had lost! The old man staggered back and leaned against the wall motionless, as rigid as the pillar. No one took any further notice of him.

'The game was over, the gamblers were disappearing, the Chevalier aided by his croupiers was packing away the money he had won in the cash-box, when old Vertua reeled forward like a ghost from out of his corner to the Chevalier and said in a dull, hollow voice: "One more word, Chevalier, one single word."

'"Well, what is it?" the Chevalier replied, drawing the key out of the cash-box and measuring the old man contemptuously from head to foot.

'"I have lost my whole fortune to your bank, Chevalier," the old man continued. "Nothing, nothing is left to me, I do not know where tomorrow I shall lay my head, with what I shall still my hunger. I turn to you, Chevalier, I turn to you for succour. Lend me the tenth part of the sum you have won from me, so that I can start my business over again and rise from the abysmal depths of poverty."

'"What are you thinking of?" replied the Chevalier. "What are you thinking of, Signor Vertua? Do you not know that a banker may never lend money from his winnings? That would be contrary to the old rule, from which I never deviate."

' "You are right," Vertua went on. "You are right, Chevalier. My request was senseless—excessive—the tenth part indeed! No, lend me the twentieth."

' "I have told you," the Chevalier answered with annoyance, "that I never lend any of my winnings."

' "It is true," said Vertua, his face growing paler and paler, his eyes more and more fixed and staring, "it is true, you must not lend anything—I used not to do so either. But one gives alms to the beggar—give him a hundred *louis d'or* from the wealth which blind luck threw to you today."

' "In truth," the Chevalier burst out angrily, "you know how to torment people, Signor Vertua. I tell you, not a hundred, not fifty, not twenty, not a single *louis d'or* will you get from me. I should have to be mad to make you the slightest loan so that you could start your shameful trade all over again from the beginning. Fate has trodden you down into the dust like a poisonous worm, and it would be wicked to lift you up again. Go away and perish as you deserve."

'Pressing both hands to his face, Signor Vertua collapsed with a hollow sigh. The Chevalier ordered his servants to take the cash-box into the carriage and then cried in a loud voice: "When will you hand over to me your house and your effects, Signor Vertua?"

'At this, Vertua picked himself up from the floor and said in a firm voice: "Now, at once, this very moment, Chevalier. Come with me."

' "Very well," replied the Chevalier, "you can ride with me to your house which in the morning you shall leave forever."

'On the whole journey no one, neither Vertua nor the Chevalier, utttered a single word. When they came to the house in the Rue Saint-Honoré Vertua rang the bell. A little old woman opened the door and, on seeing

Vertua, exclaimed: "O Christ our saviour, it is you at last, Signor Vertua. Angela has worried herself half to death over you."

' "Silence," replied Vertua. "May heaven grant that Angela did not hear the unhappy bell. She must not know that I have come."

'And with that the old man took the candelabra with the burning candles from the hand of the old woman, who seemed quite turned to stone, and lit the way for the Chevalier into the room.

' "I am prepared for anything," said Vertua. "You hate, you despise me, Chevalier. You are ruining me for your own and others' pleasure, but you do not know me. Learn then, that I was formerly a gambler like you, that capricious Fortune was as favourable to me as it is to you, that I travelled through half Europe, staying everywhere where high stakes, the hope of great gain enticed me, that I ceaselessly amassed gold in my bank as you do in yours. I had a beautiful, true wife, whom I neglected, who was miserable in the midst of all my shining wealth. Then it came about that one night when I had opened my bank in Genoa, a young Roman gambled away his rich inheritance to it. As I did with you today, he begged me to lend him money so that at least he could travel back to Rome. I refused with scornful laughter, and in the mad rage of despair he stabbed me deep in the breast with the stiletto he carried on him. With difficulty the doctors saved my life, but my illness was protracted and painful. My wife nursed me, comforted me, kept me going when I felt like succumbing to the agony, and with my recovery a feeling dawned in me, and grew stronger and stronger, that I had never known before. All human emotions become foreign to the gambler; thus it was that I did not know the meaning of love, the faithful attachment of a woman. Realization of what my ungrateful heart owed to my wife, and to what a dissolute activity I had sacrificed her, burned deep into my soul. All those whose happiness, whose whole existence I had murdered with vile indifference appeared before me like tormenting spirits of vengeance, and I heard their cavernous, hoarse, tomb-like voices reproaching me with all the guilt, all the crimes whose seeds I had planted. Only my wife could exorcize the nameless distress, the horror, that had taken possession of me."

' "I took an oath never again to touch a card. I withdrew, I tore myself free from the bands that held me fast, I resisted the enticements of my croupiers, who did not wish to do without me and my luck. When I had completely recovered I bought a little country-house near Rome and took refuge there with my wife. Alas, only for one year was I vouchsafed a peace, a happiness, a contentment which I had never known before. My wife gave birth to a daughter and died a few weeks later. I was in despair, I inveighed against heaven and then again accused myself, my atrocious life, for which the eternal power was wreaking revenge by taking away my wife, who had saved me from perdition, the only being who gave me consolation and hope. Like the criminal who fears the terrors of solitude, I felt driven from my country-house hither to Paris. Angela blossomed, the lovely image of her mother, my whole heart hung on her, for her sake I set about acquiring and multiplying a great fortune. It is true that I lent money at high rates of interest, but it is a shameful slander to accuse me of deceitful usury. And who are these accusers? Profligates who torment me unendingly until I lend them money, which they then squander like a thing of no value, only to be outraged when I collect with relentless sternness the money which belongs not to me, no, which I am merely holding in trust for my daughter. Not long ago I saved a young man from shame, from ruin, by lending him a considerable sum. Knowing him to be as poor as a church mouse, I said not a word about repayment until he had come into a very rich inheritance. Then I claimed the debt. Would you believe it, Chevalier, the dissipated rascal, who owed me his life, sought to deny the debt and called me a base miser when, compelled by the court, he had to repay the money. I could tell you more such cases, which have made me hard and unfeeling when I meet profligacy and wickedness. More than that. I could tell you that I have dried many bitter tears, that I have sent many a prayer for myself and my Angela up to heaven, but you would regard it merely as false vapouring and in any case attach no importance to it, since you are a gambler. I believed that I had expiated my crimes in the eyes of the eternal power—it was but a delusion. For Satan was given leave to trick me more horribly than ever."

' "I heard of your luck, Chevalier. Every day reports reached me that such and such a man had punted himself to beggary at your bank. Then the thought came to me that I was destined to pit my gambler's luck, which had never deserted me, against yours, that it lay in my hands to put an end to your activities; and this thought, which only a strange madness could have engendered, henceforth left me no peace, no rest. So I appeared at your bank, and my terrible besottedness did not leave me until my possessions—my Angela's possessions—were yours. Now it is all over. Will you at least allow my daughter to take her clothes with her?"

' "Your daughter's wardrobe," replied the Chevalier, "is no concern of mine. You may also take your beds and the necessary household utensils. What use is that rubbish to me? But see to it that nothing of value that is due to me is withheld."

'Old Vertua stared at the Chevalier for a few seconds, speechless; then a torrent of tears poured from his eyes; overcome by distress and despair, he sank to his knees before the Chevalier and cried with raised hands: "Chevalier, if you have any human feeling left in your breast, be merciful, merciful. It is not I, it is my daughter, my Angela, the innocent, angelic child, whom you are casting into perdition. Oh, have mercy on her, lend *her, her,* my Angela, the twentieth part of the fortune of which you have robbed her. Oh, I know you will listen to my pleading—oh, Angela, my daughter!"

'At this point the old man began to sob, to whimper, to groan, and cried out his daughter's name in a heart-rending tone.

' "This preposterous, theatrical scene is beginning to bore me," said the Chevalier indifferently and irritably; but the same moment the door flew open, and a girl in a white nightdress, with her hair loose and a look of death on her face, burst into the room, rushed up to old Vertua, took him in her arms and cried: "Oh, my father, my father, I heard—I know all. Have you lost everything? Everything? Have you not your Angela? What need have you of money and possessions, will not Angela feed and care for you? Oh, father, do not abase yourself any longer before this contemptible monster. It is not we, but he, who remains poor and wretched amidst all his filthy riches, for he stands there abandoned to dreadful, hopeless loneliness, there is no loving heart in the whole wide world that presses itself to his breast, that opens itself to him when he feels like despairing of life and of himself. Come, father, leave the house with me, come, let us hurry away, so that this abominable man may not revel in your misery."

'Vertua sank half swooning into an armchair, Angela knelt before him, took his hands, kissed and stroked them, enumerated with childish loquacity all the talents, all the knowledge which was at her command and with which she could earn a comfortable living for her father, besought him with hot tears not to distress himself, since now that she could embroider, sew, sing and play the guitar not for pleasure, but for her father, life would really be of value to her for the first time.

'Who, what stubborn sinner could have remained indifferent to the sight of Angela, radiant in all her heavenly beauty, as she comforted her old father in a sweet and lovely voice, as the purest love and the most

231

childlike virtue flowed from the depths of her heart?

'Something very different happened to the Chevalier. A whole hell of anguish and pangs of conscience awoke within him. Angela appeared to him as the avenging angel of God, before whose radiance the mist-veils of foul delusion vanished, so that with horror he saw his miserable ego in repulsive nakedness.

'And through the very centre of this hell, whose flames were raging in the Chevalier's soul, there darted a divine, pure ray whose refulgence was the sweetest bliss and heavenly beatitude; but in the light of this ray his nameless anguish only grew more terrible.

'The Chevalier had never yet loved. The moment he saw Angela he was seized by the most violent passion and at the same time by the annihilating pain of utter hopelessness. For no man could hope who appeared to the pure child of heaven, to Angela, as the Chevalier did.

'The Chevalier tried to speak but could not, it was as though a cramp were paralysing his tongue. Finally, he forcibly pulled himself together and stammered in a trembling voice: "Signor Vertua, hear me, I have won nothing from you, nothing at all. . . . Here is my cash-box—it is yours—no! I must pay you even more —I am your debtor. Take, take. . . ."

' "Oh, my daughter," cried Vertua, but Angela rose, stepped forward to the Chevalier, gazed at him with proud and radiant eyes and speaking gravely and with composure said: "Chevalier, learn that there is something higher than money and property, sentiments which are strange to you, which, by filling our souls with the consolation of heaven, enable us to reject your mercy with contempt. Keep the filthy lucre upon which there lies a curse that pursues you, the heartless, dissolute gambler!"

' "Yes," cried the Chevalier, wild-eyed and beside himself, in a terrible voice, "yes, accursed—let me be accursed, flung down into the deepest hell, if this hand ever again touches a card. And if you thrust me away from you, Angela, it will be you who brings irretrievable disaster upon me. Oh, you do not know—you do not understand—you are bound to call me mad—but you will feel it, you will know everything, when I lie before you with shattered brains—Angela. My life and death are at stake. Goodbye."

'So saying, the Chevalier rushed out in utter despair. Vertua saw through him completely, he knew what was going on within him and sought to make it clear to the lovely Angela that circumstances might arise which would render it imperative to accept the Chevalier's gift. Angela refused to understand her father. It was incomprehensible to her that she should ever regard the Chevalier with anything but contempt. Destiny, which often moulds itself from out of the deepest depths of the human heart, unknown to the person himself, caused the unthought of, the undreamt of to happen.

'The Chevalier felt as though he had suddenly woken from a frightful dream; he now saw himself on the edge of the abyss of hell and stretched out his arms in vain towards the shining figure of light that appeared to him, not to save him—no!—to warn him of his damnation.

'To the amazement of all Paris, the Chevalier Menars's bank disappeared from the gambling-house, he himself was no longer seen, and so the most various, most sensational rumours were put about, each of them more mendacious than the other. The Chevalier avoided all society, his love expressed itself in the deepest, most insurmountable dejection. Then one day he chanced upon old Vertua and his daughter in the lonely, gloomy paths of the garden of Malmaison.

'Angela, who believed she could not look upon the Chevalier in any other way than with aversion and contempt, felt strangely moved when she saw him before her, deathly pale, utterly stricken, so shyly overawed that he scarcely dared raise his eyes. She knew very well that since that fateful night the Chevalier had entirely given up gambling, that he had changed his whole way of life. She, she alone had brought all this about, she had saved the Chevalier from perdition— could anything be more flattering to a woman's vanity?

'Thus it came about that, while Vertua was exchanging the usual polite phrases with the Chevalier, Angela asked in a tone of gentle, beneficent compassion: "What has happened to you, Chevalier Menars? You look ill, distraught. In truth, you should consult a doctor."

'It is easy to imagine that Angela's words sent a ray of comforting hope through the Chevalier. At that moment he was no longer the same man. He raised his head, he was able to speak that language welling up from the depths of his soul which had once opened all hearts to him. Vertua reminded him to take possession of the house he had won.

' "Yes," cried the Chevalier enthusiastically, "yes, Signor Vertua, I certainly will. I shall come to you tomorrow, but let us discuss the conditions with great care, even if it should take months."

' "Let it be so, Chevalier," Vertua replied, smiling. "I have an idea that in time all sorts of things may come to be discussed of which at the moment we may have no inkling."

'As was inevitable after the Chevalier had been thus inwardly comforted, all the charm he had possessed before the mad, pernicious passion overwhelmed him was revived. His visits to old Vertua became increasingly frequent, Angela grew increasingly well-disposed towards the man whose saving guardian spirit she had been; until finally she believed that she loved him with all her heart and promised to give him her hand, to the great joy of old Vertua, who only now regarded the matter of the property which he had lost to the Chevalier as being entirely settled.

'Angela, the Chevalier Menars's happy bride, was sitting one day by the window deep in all kinds of thoughts of amorous bliss and beatitude, such as brides

234

are wont to have. To the accompaniment of merry trumpet calls a regiment of riflemen passed, no doubt on their way to the Spanish campaign. Angela was looking with sympathy at these men dedicated to death in wicked war, when a very young man, quickly turning his horse aside, looked up at Angela and she fell back swooning in her chair.

'The rifleman on his way to meet a bloody death was none other than young Duvernet, the neighbour's son, with whom she had grown up, who had been in the house almost daily and whose visits had only ceased since the arrival of the Chevalier.

'From the youth's reproachful look—in which lay death itself—Angela realized for the first time, not only how inexpressibly he loved her, but also how boundlessly she herself loved him, without having been aware of it, stupefied and dazzled as she was by the refulgence which the Chevalier increasingly spread around him. Only now did she understand the youth's timid sighs, his silent, undemanding wooing, only now did she understand her own constrained heart, did she know what moved her restless breast when Duvernet came, when she heard his voice.

' "It is too late, he is lost to me," said an inner voice to Angela. She had the courage to fight against the feeling of hopelessness that threatened to tear her soul apart, and because of her courage she succeeded in crushing it.

'Nevertheless, the Chevalier's eyes were too sharp for him to fail to see that something disturbing must have happened; however, he was gentle enough not to try to uncover a secret which Angela felt she must hide from him; in order to take away all power from any threatening enemy, he contented himself with hastening the wedding, the celebration of which he succeeded in arranging with such fine tact and deep feeling for the situation and mood of his lovely bride that she once more recognized her future husband's charm.

'The Chevalier behaved towards Angela with attentiveness to her slightest wish, with the unfeigned esteem that springs from the purest love, and so the memory of Duvernet was bound to fade completely from her mind. The first cloud to cast a shadow over her bright life was the sickness and death of old Vertua.

'Since the night on which he had lost all his possessions to the Chevalier he had never again touched a card, but during the last moments of his life gambling seemed to fill his soul completely. While the priest, who had come to give him the consolation of the Church as he passed away, was speaking to him of spiritual things, he lay with closed eyes muttering between his teeth, *"perd . . . gagne"*, and with hands trembling in the death struggle he made the movements of cutting and dealing the cards. In vain did Angela and the Chevalier bend over him and address him by affectionate names; he seemed no longer to know, no longer to perceive either of them. With an inner sigh of *"gagne"* he gave up the ghost.

'In her deepest anguish Angela could not avoid an eerie shudder at the manner of the old man's death. The picture of that horrible night on which she first saw the Chevalier as the most hardened, vicious gambler, returned vividly to her mind's eye and the dreadful thought entered her soul that the Chevalier might cast off the angel's mask and, mocking her in his original devilish shape, might begin his old life all over again.

'Angela's terrible premonition was soon to prove all too true.

'Great as was the Chevalier's horror to see how, at his end, old Francesco Vertua, scorning the comfort of the Church in his last death agony, could not cease thinking of his earlier sinful life, this sight, he knew not why, brought gambling so vividly back into his mind that every night in his dreams he sat at the bank and amassed fresh wealth.

'To the degree to which Angela, gripped by the memory of how the Chevalier had formerly appeared to her, grew more constrained, as it became impossible for her to maintain the loving, confident demeanour with which she had previously confronted him, to this same degree the Chevalier's soul became filled with suspicion of Angela, whose constraint he attributed to that secret which had once disturbed her calm and which remained undisclosed to him. This suspicion engendered uneasiness and dejection, which he expressed in all sorts of utterances that wounded Angela. In a curious mental reaction, the memory of the unhappy Duvernet revived in Angela's heart and with it the hopeless feeling of a love that had blossomed like the loveliest flower in youthful hearts. Ill feeling between husband and wife rose higher and higher, till a point was reached when the Chevalier found his whole simple life tedious and insipid and longed with all his might to go out into the world.

'The Chevalier's evil star began to rule. What inner discomfort and profound dejection had begun was completed by an abominable man who had once been the Chevalier's croupier and who succeeded, by all sorts of cunning talk, in making the Chevalier look upon his conversion as childish and absurd. He could not understand how, for the sake of a woman, he could have left a world that alone seemed to him worth living in.

'It was not long before the Chevalier Menars's bank, well stocked with gold, shone more radiantly than ever. Luck had not deserted him, victim after victim fell to him and he accumulated more and more wealth. But Angela's happiness was destroyed, horribly destroyed, like a brief but lovely dream. The Chevalier treated her with indifference, indeed with contempt. Often she did not see him for weeks and months on end, an old house-steward looked after the domestic affairs, the servants changed according to the caprice of the Chevalier, so that Angela, a stranger even in her own house, found no consolation anywhere. Often when, during sleepless nights, she heard the Chevalier's coach draw up outside the house, the heavy cash-box being dragged up the stairs, the Chevalier spitting out rough, monosyllabic words and then slamming the door of the distant room with a rattle, a stream of bitter tears burst from her eyes; in the deepest, most heart-rending misery she cried out a hundred times the name of Duvernet, begged the eternal power to end her wretched, afflicted life.

'It happened that a youth of good family, after losing his whole fortune to the Chevalier's bank, put a bullet through his head in the gambling-house in the self-same room in which the Chevalier's bank was established, so that blood and brains spattered the gamblers, who jumped apart in horror. Only the Chevalier remained unmoved and asked, when everyone was about to leave, whether it was the rule and custom to leave the bank before the appointed time on account of a fool who did not know how to conduct himself while gambling.

'The incident attracted great attention. The most inveterate, hardened gamblers were indignant over the Chevalier's unexampled behaviour. Everyone turned against him. The police closed down his bank. Moreover he was accused of cheating and his unparalleled luck lent credibility to the accusation. He was unable to clear himself and the fine he was obliged to pay robbed him of a significant part of his wealth. He found himself execrated and despised—then he returned into the arms of his wife, whom he had maltreated and who willingly took back the penitent, since the memory of her father, who had also turned away from the dissolute life of a gambler, caused a glimmer of hope to dawn in her that the Chevalier's change of heart, now that he had grown older, might really prove lasting.

'The Chevalier left Paris with his wife and went to Genoa, Angela's birthplace.

'Here he lived at first a somewhat retiring life. But he sought in vain to restore the conditions of peaceful domesticity with Angela that his evil demon had destroyed. It was not long before his inner despondency drove him out of the house in restless instability. His evil reputation had followed him from Paris to Genoa, he could not venture to open a bank, even though he was impelled to do so by an irresistible force.

'At that time the wealthiest bank in Genoa was kept by a French colonel rendered incapable of military service by severe wounds. With envy and deep hate in his heart, the Chevalier made his way to this bank, thinking that his usual luck would soon enable him to ruin his rival. The Colonel called out to the Chevalier, with a gay humour not normally characteristic of him, that the game would now become worth while for the first time, since the Chevalier with his luck had come to take part, for now there would take place the struggle that alone makes gambling interesting.

'In truth, at the first few turns the Chevalier's cards came up as usual. But when, trusting to his unshakeable luck, he finally called *"Va banque"*, he had at one blow lost a considerable sum.

'The Colonel, normally unmoved by either good luck or bad, raked in the money with every sign of extreme delight. From that moment on, luck turned completely and utterly against the Chevalier.

'He gambled every night, lost every night, until his possessions had shrunk to the sum of a few thousand ducats, which he still kept in paper.

'The Chevalier had been out and about all day, had changed his paper money into coin and did not come home till late in the evening. At nightfall he was about to go out, with his last pieces of gold in his pocket, when Angela, who must have suspected what was going on, stepped in his path, threw herself at his feet, a stream of tears pouring from her eyes, and besought him by the Holy Virgin and all the saints not to pursue his evil purpose, not to cast her into want and misery.

'The Chevalier raised her up, pressed her to his bosom with anguished passion and said in a hollow voice:

"Angela, my dear sweet Angela, it is so, I must do what I cannot leave undone. But tomorrow—tomorrow all your worries will be over, for I swear by everlasting Destiny which rules over us that I shall gamble today for the last time. Be calm, sweet child, sleep, dream of blissful days, of a better life that lies before you; that will bring me luck."

'So saying, the Chevalier kissed his wife and ran off without stopping.

'Two turns and the Chevalier had lost everything, everything!

'He stood motionless beside the colonel, staring in dull stupefaction at the gaming-table.

' "Are you not punting any more, Chevalier?" asked the colonel, as he shuffled the cards for a new turn. "I have lost everything," replied the Chevalier with forced calm.

' "Have you nothing left at all?" asked the Colonel at the next turn.

' "I am a beggar," cried the Chevalier in a voice trembling with rage and anguish, continuing to stare at the table and not observing that the gamblers were gaining more and more advantage over the banker.

'The Colonel calmly played on.

' "But you have a beautiful wife," said the Colonel in a low voice, without looking at the Chevalier, shuffling the cards for the next turn.

' "What do you mean by that?" the Chevalier burst out angrily. The Colonel turned up the cards without answering.

' "Ten thousand ducats or—Angela," said the Colonel, turning half round as he cut the cards.

' "You are mad!" cried the Chevalier, who however, now that he had recovered somewhat, began to notice that the Colonel was continually losing.

' "Twenty thousand ducats against Angela," said the Colonel in a low voice, stopping for a moment in the middle of shuffling the cards.

'The Chevalier remained silent, the Colonel played on, and almost all the cards came out in favour of the punters.

' "Done," the Chevalier said into the Colonel's ear as the new round began, and pushed the queen onto the table.

'At the next turn-up the queen had lost.

'Grinding his teeth, the Chevalier withdrew and stood leaning against the window, despair and death in his pale face.

'The game was over; with a scornful "Well, what now?" the Colonel came up to the Chevalier.

' "Ha," cried the Chevalier, quite beside himself, "you have made a beggar of me, but you must be mad to imagine that you could win my wife. Are we on the islands, is my wife a slave, the helpless victim of her atrocious husband's disdainful caprice so that he can sell or gamble her away? But it is true, you would have had to pay me twenty thousand ducats if the queen had won, and so I have gambled away every right to object if my wife wishes to desert me and follow you. Come with me and despair, when my wife repudiates with revulsion the man she is supposed to follow as a dishonoured mistress."

' "Despair yourself," retorted the Colonel with a mocking laugh, "despair yourself, Chevalier, when Angela repudiates you, you the vile sinner who made her wretched, and throws herself with bliss and delight into my arms—despair yourself when you learn that the blessing of the Church will bind us and fortune crown our dearest wishes. You call me mad. Oho, all I desired to win from you was the right to object, I was certain of your wife. Oho, Chevalier, learn that your wife, as I know, loves me beyond words; learn that I am that Duvernet, the neighbour's son, who was brought up with Angela, bound to her by ardent love, whom you drove away with your devilish arts. It was not until I had to go away to war that Angela realized what I meant to her;

I know all. It was too late. The dark spirit revealed to me that in gambling I could ruin you, therefore I devoted myself to gambling, followed you to Genoa—and succeeded. Away now to your wife!"

'The Chevalier stood annihilated, struck by a thousand red-hot flashes of lightning. The fateful secret lay open before him, now he saw for the first time the full measure of the unhappiness which he had brought upon poor Angela.

' "Let Angela, my wife, decide," he said in a hollow voice and followed the Colonel as he rushed out.

'When they had entered the house and the Colonel had the latch of Angela's door in his hand, the Chevalier thrust him back and said: "My wife is asleep; will you disturb her in her sweet sleep?"

' "H'm," replied the Colonel, "has Angela ever lain in sweet sleep since you brought nameless misery upon her?"

The Colonel was about to enter the room, when the Chevalier threw himself at his feet and cried in utter desperation: "Be merciful! Leave me, whom you have made into a beggar, leave me my wife."

' "That was how old Vertua lay before you, unfeeling scoundrel that you are, but he could not soften your stony heart; therefore the vengeance of heaven descended upon you."

'Thus spoke the Colonel and took another step towards Angela's room.

'The Chevalier sprang to the door, tore it open, rushed to the bed in which his wife was lying, drew the curtains, cried "Angela, Angela!"—bent down over her, took her hand—quivered as though seized by the throes of death, then cried out in a terrible voice: "Look! You have won my wife's corpse!"

'The horrified Colonel stepped up to the bed—not a sign of life. Angela was dead, dead.

'Then the Colonel raised his clenched fist to heaven,

uttered a hollow cry and rushed out. He was never heard of again.'

Thus the stranger ended his story and quickly left the bank, before the deeply shaken Baron could utter a word.

A few days later the stranger was found in his room, struck down by nervous apoplexy. He remained speechless till his death, which occurred a few hours later; his papers showed that he, who had called himself simply Baudasson, had been none other than the unhappy Chevalier Menars.

The Baron recognized the warning of heaven, which had led the Chevalier Menars into his path to save him just as he was approaching the abyss, and he vowed to resist all the enticements of the illusory gambler's luck.

Up to now he has faithfully kept his word.

POSTSCRIPT

Ernst Theodor Wilhelm Hoffmann (the name Wilhelm he himself later replaced by Amadeus in homage to Mozart) was born on 24 January 1776, in Königsberg, East Prussia, the third son of Christopher Ludwig Hoffmann, a councillor of the High Court of Justice, and his wife and cousin Luise Albertine Doerffler. His parents' marriage was an unhappy one, and they parted when E. T. A. Hoffmann was only two years old. Thereafter he was brought up by his ailing mother and her family, his one surviving brother remaining with his father. His maternal grandfather and uncle were also lawyers, and in fact the whole of his mother's family were typical civil servants whose lives were dominated by a narrow and conventional outlook. Hoffmann's father, by contrast, was something of a rebel and a man of intellectual interests and considerable poetic gifts. This dual heritage soon became apparent in Hoffmann's life. After leaving school he studied law at Königsberg, but simultaneously devoted much of his time to music; throughout his life he displayed, on the one hand, a marked capacity for closely reasoned thinking and consistency of action, and on the other, a highly artistic temperament, great powers of imagination, and all the uninhibited vitality of the true artist.

His achievements in the field of music were noteworthy. His opera *Undine* (1816), to a libretto by Fouqué, was perhaps his major musical success; prior to this he had written an opera entitled *Love and Jealousy*, based on a drama by Calderon, and incidental music for two other theatrical works. He also wrote some excellent musical criticism under the name of 'Johannes Kreisler, Kapellmeister'. Kreisler also appears as a character in some of Hoffmann's stories, where he represents the romantic musician and composer brought into contact with the real world, the first adumbration of a type-character drawn from life who was to acquire considerable importance in Romantic literature and exemplifies Hoffmann's whole profoundly sympathetic view of the artist and his problems. Hoffmann's Kreisler was also the inspiration for Schumann's *Kreisleriana* (1838), in which the composer uses him as a vehicle for the expression through music of his own personal experiences. Hoffmann was for a time musical director of a theatre at Bamberg, and then at Dresden. However, he is probably best known to musicians through having provided the inspiration and the book for Offenbach's *Tales of Hoffmann*, based on three of his fantastic stories, one of which, 'The Sandman', is included in the present selection. (The film of Offenbach's opera has perhaps contributed even further to making Hoffmann's name known to the English-speaking world.) In addition to his talent as a musician Hoffmann was also a skilful draughts-man with a special gift for caricature. He always succeeded in combining his duties as a lawyer with his artistic aspira-tions; for example, while working as a lawyer in Warsaw he founded a Music Society which grew at such a rate that he received a subsidy from the King of Prussia and was able to acquire larger premises, the interior of which he designed himself, decorating the walls with his own murals.

Hoffmann completed his legal studies at Königsberg, and in 1795 began to practise in that town. From there he re-moved first to Glogau and then to Berlin, and in 1800 he received an official legal appointment at Posen. This post he subsequently lost through having offended the authorities by his caricatures, as a result of which he was transferred to the little country town of Plozk in virtual banishment. In 1802 Hoffmann married Micheline Rorer, the daughter of a former magistrate. The marriage appears on the whole to have been a happy one and produced one child, a daughter, who died at an early age—a tragedy by which Hoffmann was deeply distressed. In 1804 he received an appointment in Warsaw, then part of Prussia, where his friend Zacharias Werner introduced him to the work of the German Roman-tics and where he wrote his three earlier operas. The French invasion of 1806 interrupted his peaceful and creative existence in Warsaw and forced him to leave the city, which then became the capital of an independent duchy of the same name. There followed a hazardous and unsettled period of his life spent between Dresden, Bamberg, and Leipzig, in which he supported himself and his wife by various musical and literary enterprises.

A change for the better took place in 1814, when he resumed his legal profession in Berlin, and a further improvement followed in 1816, when he was appointed councillor of the Court of Appeal. This latter post left him leisure in which to develop his literary interests and ushered in his most productive period in this field. It was in Berlin that he wrote the majority of the grotesque and strange tales upon which his reputation chiefly rests, and during this final phase of his life he enjoyed high esteem as an excellent jurist and a conscientious official, a composer of merit and popular acclaim, and a story-teller of outstanding brilliance and imaginative power. His life, now so full of promise and achievement, was cut short by locomotor ataxy brought on by the excessive drinking that had already cast a shadow over his earlier years and was now intensified. He died on 24 July 1822, to the very last dictating to his friends the stories which paralysis of the hands prevented him from writing down for himself.

Hoffmann was a perfect example of the Romantic conception of the artist in whom life and art are inextricably interwoven. He created, and above all wrote, to resolve his inner conflicts and preserve his emotional balance, and there is little in his stories that does not refer directly, though in a highly fantastic and grotesque disguise, to actual events, situations, and relationships in his own life. Hoffmann himself was fully aware of this, and he gives an ironic comment on the way in which an artist transfers his problems from the realm of life to that of art—where they are more easily solved!—in his delineation of the poet Amandus von Nebelstern in 'The King's Bride'. The strong element of humour in his work ranging from pure wit through Romantic irony to savage satire, clearly has the function of reducing to manageable proportions the hidden fears and wishes that might otherwise have overwhelmed him and actually threatened his sanity—fears and wishes stemming directly from an unhappy and insecure childhood in an unsympathetic and uncongenial environment. The extent to which Hoffmann succeeded in maintaining his inner, psychic equilibrium through artistic creation is evident from the great competence with which this highly emotional and imaginative man was able to carry out his humdrum but exacting duties as a lawyer and an official.

Without a doubt, E. T. A. Hoffmann is one of the major

figures of the Romantic Movement in German literature, and the range of his talents perhaps greater than that of any of its other exponents. His imaginative powers, in particular, were unsurpassed by any of his contemporaries, and his vivid and convincing handling of the grotesque and even gruesome gives him an almost unique place in world literature. The key to Hoffmann's considerable influence on his contemporaries and successors, which was as great in France and Britain as in his own country, is perhaps to be found in the core of reality that informs even his most fantastic stories. Everything he describes seems to have been real and living to him, and indeed it was—either because it was a disguised reference to actual events or because it expressed an inner psychological reality of intense importance to the author.

Perhaps Hoffmann's most striking characteristic from the point of view of the contemporary reader is his modernity. In the free play which he allows to his imagination he is in complete harmony with current trends in all fields of art, while his intuitive psychological insights prefigure many of those subsequently reached analytically by Freud. Thus the stories contained in this present selection, and chosen to represent various facets of his talent, from sheer drama through fantasy to ironic humour, demonstrate the concepts of a mother fixation ('Datura Fastuosa'), the mechanism of the projection of fantasies on to the outer world, where they appear real ('The Sandman'), a split personality, and a psychological compulsion resulting from an early—in this case, pre-natal—experience ('Mademoiselle de Scudéry') and the symbolic value of objects ('The King's Bride'). By contrast, 'Gambler's Luck' is a more or less naturalistic tale with a moral—a warning against the perennial dangers of gambling, which is perhaps as apposite today as at the time it was written.

MICHAEL BULLOCK